Praise for

BEYOND BEAUPORT

"Masciarelli's *Beyond Beauport* is a fast-moving read that keeps you on edge page after page! Sailing through Shannon Clarke's adventures and lucid dreams returned me to Irving Johnson's brigantine *Yankee* voyages! This tale of sea rovers, treasure, and adventure pulls you into this epic narrative."

—Ron Gilson, author of *An Island No More*

"Full of deeply researched nautical tradition and seafaring lore, *Beyond Beauport* is about one woman's quest to catch a second wind in life by letting her dreams fill her sails. If you like adventure, Caribbean seas and family intrigue, you'll surely enjoy this tale."

—Katherine A. Sherbrooke, author of *Fill the Sky*

"James Masciarelli's mastery of plot, suspense, pacing, dialogue and story belies any sense that *Beyond Beauport* is his first novel. The history that frames this gripping narrative is impeccable. Embarking on this adventure with such appealing characters offers a pleasure that only the most well-crafted novels can provide."

—Peter Anastas, author of *At the Cut*

"Loaded to the scuppers with history and intrigue, *Beyond Beauport* fastens a shackle to the heartstrings of the pirate in all of us, then pulls us along in its powerful riptide of adventure! Bravo!"

—**Jim Tarantino**, Gloucester doryman

"When our intrepid heroes, Shannon Clarke and her uncle Paddy, sail off in search of pirate treasure in the mangrove islets off southwest Florida, they fall prey to a vicious syndicate of international smugglers. James Masciarelli has written a riveting and irresistible novel of adventure and intrigue on the high seas. *Beyond Beauport* will remind you of why you started reading stories in the first place: to be carried away to a world more vivid and, in this case, more frightening than the one you're living in. Paddy and Shannon have room for one more mate on the *Second Wind*, and you have permission to board. You might want to keep that life jacket close by—the waters are a little rough ahead."

—**John Dufresne**, author of *I Don't Like Where This Is Going*

"James Masciarelli has crafted a unique contribution to American letters, an adventure saga that is sweeping in scope yet intensely personal. *Beyond Beauport* resonates intrigue from its first pages, and it does not disappoint in the delivery of a narrative that moves quickly through crests and valleys creating curiosity, suspense and fulfillment. But just as compelling is the personal journey of its main persona. Shannon Clarke may well emerge as one of the more memorable, fully formed and complex characters in modern literature. Her progressive levels of self-awareness and identity wed a compelling adventure to the universal processes of self-discovery. Masciarelli writes of time, place and history, and in the process has woven a lasting work that speaks to discovery that is both epic in scope and deeply personal."

—**Greg Fields**, author of *Arc of the Comet*

"From the working waterfront to the high seas, *Beyond Beauport* captures the nautical adventures of a Gloucester woman looking to catch a second wind. Shannon has salt in her veins and ancestors in her head as she sails the eastern seaboard, searching for the treasure of the fearless 18th-century pirate Anne Bonny, and hoping to find herself in the process. Full of history, geography, maritime life, storms, and recipes, Masciarelli has created an exciting tale of today's woman at one with the sea."

—JoeAnn Hart, author of *Float*

Beyond Beauport

by James Masciarelli

© Copyright 2018 James Masciarelli

ISBN 978-1-63393-655-3

Published by

köehlerbooks™

210 60th Street
Virginia Beach, VA 23451
800-435-4811
www.koehlerbooks.com

BEYOND BEAUPORT

AN ADVENTURE NOVEL

James Masciarelli

VIRGINIA BEACH
CAPE CHARLES

For Judi,
Fortress of my heart

INTRODUCTION

Beauport is a real place, named by French explorer Samuel de Champlain. He was a man of incalculable talent—navigator, cartographer, ethnologist, soldier, diplomat, artist, and writer. Born to a non-noble family of sea captains, Champlain was a robust man with good sea legs and insatiable appetite for adventure.

During his 1606 voyage to the Atlantic shores of North America, he was thirty-two and had returned to an irresistible island cape with high granite bluffs, rugged coastline, inlets, deep forest, and sandy beaches. He entered a southwest-facing harbor with good navigable waters and protected anchorage, populated with friendly native tribes in summer garb. Champlain noted the surrounding landscapes of diverse hardwood trees and cultivated vegetables, and drew a detailed chart of the beautiful port, giving it the memorable name *Le Beau Port.*

Champlain's cartography and descriptions inspired the arrival of English settlers in North America. An expedition by the Dorchester Company, chartered by King James I in 1623, established a settlement of the beautiful port. That special place, located north of Boston on Cape Ann, is Gloucester, Massachusetts—America's oldest seaport.

Beyond Beauport takes place between the Labor Day weekend Gloucester schooner festivals of 2012 and 2013 but harkens back to the Golden Age of Piracy, when a woman set out to sea.

GLOUCESTER SCHOONER FESTIVAL

S hannon Clarke sniffed the cool briny air and winced. Another Cape Ann summer gone forever. She was in a stealthy blue mood and decided to fight back with a bit of mischief.

It was Labor Day weekend, and summer's last hurrah in Gloucester was marked by its annual Schooner Festival. Shannon giggled like a schoolgirl at her planned hijinks, even though she, at forty-six, was old enough to have two children in their twenties. No matter. She felt youthful and daring again, and recruited her three best friends as accomplices.

Marcy and Gael joined her to drag sea kayaks across a small cove on Rocky Neck to the water's edge. Standing with their paddles set in wet sand like tall spears, they gazed beyond tiny Ten Pound Island and its lighthouse in mid-harbor, to the horizon where the massive granite Dog Bar Breakwater guarded Gloucester's deepwater port. The sleek local schooner *Vega* sat in strategic position to welcome arriving historic vessels. By nightfall, visiting sailors would gather in taverns and bars as they had for more than 300 years.

Shannon drew strength from her troupe of women friends, who rowed competitively for years in pilot gig boats and kayaks. Her brawny Sicilian pal, Marcy, was a no-nonsense registered nurse who never spared criticism when deserved. Shannon and Marcy shared teenage years as single moms in the same tough neighborhood. Their friend, Gael, a laugh-at-life Irish comrade, was a dockmaster and winter marine mechanic at her father's boat basin. Shannon worked there to ready and store boats in spring and fall.

Shannon bumped Gael with her elbow. "Where is Allegra?"

"On her way from the gym."

Marcy shrugged.

"We don't do late," Shannon said, and marched back to fetch Allegra's red kayak from the jumble of skiffs, paddleboards, and rowing shells tethered to iron rings on a granite wall that framed the narrow path to the street. She set Allegra's kayak next to her green one and nudged it with her foot to space it with the rest at the waterline.

Shannon had been like a big sister to Allegra when the girl got sideways with parents, teachers, and a married cop. At thirty-six, Allegra worked days at a garden center—by night, as a sassy bartender with uncanny ability to attract males.

Shannon's attention returned to the *Vega* as she pulled her red mane back with a blue-green stretchy neck scarf that matched her eyes. She respected the local boat captains who still made a life in Gloucester. The reserved but gracious Captain Bill Davis of the *Vega* was no exception. These were family men who loved the sea, men you could count on.

"What's up?" asked Allegra, bounding toward them in vibrant blue sports tights, with her blond hair swinging in a ponytail.

Shannon waited to answer, and cleared her throat. "We race around the red buoy by the paint factory, then out to Ten Pound Island."

"Not much of a contest," Allegra said.

Shannon raised her hand. "I propose a biathlon."

"What?" Allegra asked.

"After we paddle to Ten Pound, we swim to the *Vega*. First one to climb up the anchor chain and stand on deck wins."

"That's dicey," Gael said. "Never done it."

"None of us have," Shannon said.

Marcy adjusted her black thermal riptide top. "Should we?"

Allegra rubbed her hands together. "I like it. What are the stakes?"

Shannon stretched out her arms, rolled her wrists, and yawned. "Ten bucks each for the kitty. First place takes the cash."

Gael gave a sardonic glare. "You took all the prizes on my boat during July 4th weekend. You won 'First-fish,' 'Most-fish,' and 'Biggest-fish.'"

Shannon bit her lip with a half-smile. "Nice keepers."

"You rubbed it in all summer," Allegra said.

Shannon opened her palms. "Hey, if I don't win today, I make us dinner."

They agreed.

The friendly rivals paddled in a convoy of brightly-colored kayaks around lobster pot markers and rocking vessels at their moorings. Allegra stroked fast to take the lead, with Gael flanking her. Ten minutes into the race, Allegra and Gael were first and second to make the turn at the big red buoy near the old paint factory slouching on its rotted pilings.

Youth was winning—Allegra and Gael kept a frantic, splashy pace. Shannon and Marcy stroked long, smooth and steady, with tight turns around the buoy. Onshore headwinds bashed them all with spray over choppy waves as they punched their way toward the stout lighthouse on Ten Pound.

Marcy's strength and Shannon's paddling technique got them within three kayak lengths of Gael and Allegra. The hundred-foot schooner *American Eagle* crossed their way, forcing them to navigate left through its wake. Allegra was first to the island but miscalculated and shoved out of her kayak too soon. Knocked over by a wave, she scrambled in hip-high water to pull her drifting kayak up on the gravelly beach. Gael had beached hard, sprinted to the far side of the island and dove ahead for the *Vega*. The rest followed suit.

Boisterous currents made for an arduous 200-yard swim to the *Vega*. Shannon and Marcy stroked ten yards behind Allegra. Shannon, only five feet tall and the shortest of the bunch, swam like a trophy fish. With her indifference to water temperatures and preference for green bathing suits, some still called her by her childhood nickname, "Mermaid."

Male friends on the working waterfront affectionately called the four women "Sea-Tramps." Third-generation-plus daughters of fishing families commanded respect in Gloucester, especially from boat captains. Without a nickname, you were a nobody.

All four approached within thirty yards of the *Vega*. Shannon kicked into a sprint, and Marcy used her power and reach in steady strokes like a large, dark sea creature with braids of jet-black hair. Shannon and Marcy closed in to make a churning pack on the port side of the *Vega*, whose bow bobbed on the waves. Cheers rose from the far, starboard side of the vessel, and cannon salutes thundered.

A young boy, alone on *Vega's* deck, watched the women fight for holds on the vessel's undulating anchor chain. The boy swung his arms and shouted, but the wind stole his words.

Gael was first to scramble up a few feet on the thick, slick, mossy chain. To climb aboard a tall, sleek schooner from under its flared bow was no trivial pursuit. Gael's hands were strong and the race now hers to lose.

At the waterline, Allegra timed her climb as the *Vega* dipped in the waves. With the upswing boost of the bow, she made three fast pulls up the anchor chain, grabbed Gael's ankle and clambered over her. Allegra's foot landed on Gael's wrist. Gael shrieked and fell into the water. Shannon muscled up the chain and swung over to grab the rigging under the bow. She looked down. Thankfully, Gael was okay, and Marcy had dropped back into the water to help.

The sole witness, Boy-on-deck, cheered.

Allegra reached for a trailing rope but slipped several links down the anchor chain. Shannon swung her leg up from the head rig, without success, to reach the deck of the vessel.

The boy yelled, "Over here. Swimmers are boarding." Passengers turned their attention to the improbable event with mouths agape. A woman reached for the boy. In a motherly tone, she said, "Stand back, Robert. Give them some room."

Fueled with adrenaline, Shannon pulled herself up the rigging with Allegra by her side, using knots as steps. Shannon swung her leg up with enough force to maneuver over the gunwale. Both women flopped onto the deck. Allegra was first to spring to her feet and raise her hands in victory. Shannon straightened up beside her, expressionless.

Allegra shifted in her stance.

Shannon reached out to shake Allegra's hand. "Congrats, I make dinner."

"I'll bring champagne," Allegra said.

The boy stepped forward. "Wow—better than WrestleMania." He glanced back to his mother, and then looked up to Shannon. "Hi, I'm Bobby." With his face beginning to redden, he added, "I'm from Lexington, here for my birthday. I'm ten."

"Happy birthday, young man. I'm Shannon. This is my friend, Allegra. Let's see, a good Glosta nickname for an able seaman like you would be 'Wobby.'"

"Wobby, definitely," said Allegra.

"I like that," he said, throwing his shoulders back. He stared at the playful dolphin tattoos on Shannon's arms. "I love dolphins, Miss Shannon. They're really smart."

"Wicked smart, Wobby."

He smiled with a major overbite.

A crewmember tossed flotation devices down to Marcy and Gael. He motioned for the boy to help lower a rope ladder. Gael scaled up the anchor chain without a slip. Marcy gave a hearty laugh and climbed up the rope ladder instead.

In a few moments, the four swimmers stood on deck wrapped in large towels, surrounded by crew and guests chatting about the dare.

The boy basked in their attentions. *Vega*'s guests, including a *Gloucester Daily Times* photographer, took photos of smiling Wobby amid the tattooed Sea-Tramps. He held a round flotation device marked *Vega* tight to his chest and stood proud as a soldier in front of Marcy with her big hands on his shoulders.

Shannon stood to the boy's side with a Cheshire Cat smile.

Flinty-eyed Captain Bill Davis was not amused. "What now, Shannon?"

"We swim back to Ten Pound."

"Nobody dives off this vessel," Captain Davis said. "We finish our sail and take you women to the harbormaster's office. Do you have a clue, the freakin' paperwork for unauthorized boarding, Shannon?"

"Sorry, Bill . . . won't happen again."

Gael congratulated Allegra on the win with a slow crushing handshake. Allegra groaned.

Marcy snugged her hand behind Allegra's neck with faces close, and sneered. "That was foul. Be glad nobody got hurt."

Allegra shrugged. "Let's not get all swamp-ass."

Captain Davis stroked his beard, covered a smile, and called to a crewmember, "Get these invaders some hot tea."

The *Vega* headed back into port. The passengers waved to the harbormaster, who motored past them in festival tradition to welcome each inbound schooner and sailing vessel with pineapples and fresh baked loaves of semolina bread from the local Italian bakery.

Captain Davis used marine radio to contact the harbormaster to meet later. After his guests disembarked, Davis detained the swimmers with a bit of scolding and spiced rum.

Later, Jack, the harbormaster, silently reviewed the details of the incident while the infamous four sat in suspense. With large forearms folded over his barrel chest, he said, "I've known your families for years. This stunt in the middle of a field of vessels and coasties showed little respect or concern for safety. Swimming one hundred feet or more offshore in a non-scheduled, unregulated swim event is a finable offense. Considering today's activity in the harbor, it should be double. Captain Davis can take the illegal, unannounced boarding further."

The women apologized—and flirted. Gael teased out her long black hair and summed it up: "You have the whole world out here to worry about, Jack, and the world needs good men like you."

He blushed, rocked back and scratched his neck.

Shannon cleared her throat. "Would you consider a day of public service from us?"

Jack weighed that. With a bemused smile, he said, "This building and equipment could use a good straightening up."

The women nodded.

He looked each of the four beauties in the eye and tilted his head to Gael with a raised brow. "And a tune-up for the launch boat."

All agreed.

After he wrote out a warning and waived the fines, he said, "Let's schedule that service day for late September. I'll take you all to Ten Pound to get your kayaks." With a grin, he added, "You women sure know how to put the 'fest' in a festival."

✌

That evening, Shannon made dinner at her rustic shingle-style cottage. Allegra popped open bottles of brut champagne for starters. Gael set out ingredients for Irish Car Bombs—each with three-quarters of a pint of Guinness stout, a half shot of Bailey's Irish Cream and a half shot of Jameson whiskey. Shannon made her signature lobster bisque. Marcy held back a rebuke for Allegra's aggressive surge to win the race. They all savored the bubbly before imbibing rounds of Gael's mixology.

Gael made a trip to the kitchen to refresh everyone's drinks and noticed a marked-up script on the table. "Eh, Shan, who's Rachel Wall? You got a new part at Gloucester Stage?"

"Yeah, October," Shannon said as she took the script back from Gael. On her way out the kitchen, she added, "Bring a pitcher of water and cups."

Back in the living room Shannon shook out her wavy red hair and looked over her friends as if a large audience. Using her best gravelly pirate voice she said, "You fish-bait know I'm always cast as a witch, a pirate, or a prostitute."

Her friends chuckled and leaned in to hear more. "What's it about?" asked Allegra.

"Pirate Rachel Wall, a thief who ran away from her strict religious family in Pennsylvania at sixteen and married fisherman George Wall. They came to Boston. She worked as a servant on Beacon Hill, but George had a get-rich-quick scheme. They moved up this way to Essex to become pirates."

"Never heard of her," said Marcy.

"Rachel Wall was the only American-born female pirate, and the last woman hanged at Boston Common." Shannon plopped on the sofa and downed another shot. "John Hancock placed his seal upon Rachel's death warrant in 1789." Shannon held her friends in rapt attention.

"Here's the thing," she continued. "Rachel was a seductress and thief. George was a murderous thug. He'd borrow a schooner and head north for the Isles of Shoals as a storm passed. George and his men would hide below deck while Rachel pretended to be alone and adrift, calling out for help with a torn blouse. When another vessel came to her rescue, George and his men would ascend on deck to plunder the other vessel, scuttle it, and drown the crew."

"Bastards," Marcy said.

"Ah-ha," said Gael. "No suspicion when ships didn't return from storms back then. Give us more of Rachel's lines."

"Get me another drink, and I'll give you her words from Boston court records."

Shannon stood with one hand holding the script and the other placed over her heart. She took a deep breath and spoke in a nasal voice, "Your Honor, I swear to acknowledge myself to have been guilty of a great many crimes, such as Sabbath-breaking, stealing from sailors as they slept, lying, disobedience to parents, and almost every other sin a person could commit."

She paused for their chuckles to settle and took a sip of her drink. "I have not lived in the fear of God, nor regarded the kind admonitions and counsels of man."

Gael said, "Bad girls have all the fun."

Shannon stood sullen, bowed her head, slowly raised her eyes, and leaned forward. "In truth, Judge, I was there when each of twelve ships were pirated and sunk, but I never murdered anyone."

Shaking her finger at an empty chair, she added a raucous tone. "And I certainly did not meet or attack that Boston woman, Margaret Bendar, or take her bonnet."

Her friends tittered.

"That's the charge of a petty crime they dragged her into court for, and connected her to the piracy," said Shannon.

"More," said Marcy.

"Okay, Rachel's last words." Shannon felt her neck as if to test the hangman's noose, and put her hands behind her back. With her chin high, she said, "Into the hands of Almighty God I commit my soul, relying on his mercy . . . and die an unworthy member of the Presbyterian Church, in the twenty-ninth year of my age.'"

Shannon downed a full glass of water. "I'm wasted. Time for me to hit the sack."

Gael made the final toast of the night. "Gloucester got the tall ship *Bounty* for the festival, but we were the entertainment out there today."

"Can't wait to tour the *Bounty* tomorrow," Shannon said. "Saw that ship in the Marlon Brando film *Mutiny on the Bounty*, and the more recent pirate movie, *Dead Man's Chest*. She's an aging star with a history."

"We all got a little hard-won experience here," Gael said, slurring her words.

"From what I hear, Allegra, you are quite experienced," Marcy said.

Allegra flipped Marcy the bird.

Marcy stood. "I'm driving you drunks home."

"Joy go with thee, sisters," Shannon said. "Our wakes will cross again."

SEPTEMBER BREEZE

The next morning, Shannon awoke with a dry mouth and a mild hangover. The clock on her nightstand glowed 3:35. She was not a marathon sleeper. *At least no tossing with bad dreams,* she thought. Slugging down a glass of water, Shannon got to work.

By sunrise, she had pecked through emails, checked coastal weather radar, fixed a stew in a slow cooker, and organized her fishing gear. She grabbed a windbreaker and took her mobile from the charger. Two voice mails from yesterday.

"Shannon, this is Paddy. Been too long, Godchild. I'll try later."

"Arrgh," she said aloud. "Where in the world is my uncle now?"

She listened to his modulated voice on a second message. "Shannon, I'll call back Monday. We need to talk in private about your great seafaring ancestry . . . and inheritance . . . a legacy beyond earth, wind, fire and water. I can visit you in early November. You're the best, sweetie. Life is about changes. Goodnight."

Shannon blew out a long breath. Soon she would be marking the days to see her mysterious Uncle Paddy. He had joined the Navy after graduating from Gloucester High School and only returned for occasional visits. He told stories but never talked about himself. Her first memory of Paddy was when her father, John, brought him to her fourth-grade classroom. That was Paddy's grand entrance into Shannon's life. He talked about Navy ships protecting America, put up large posters of aircraft carriers and destroyers on the walls, and gave the kids souvenirs. He treated Shannon like a child goddess, and her father was overjoyed when his brother visited every five or so years. Paddy sent postcards of coastal cities from around the world, and always included money with Shannon's birthday card.

A brisk walk along the deepwater harbor helped Shannon center her thoughts as she surveyed the waterfront. She took pride in knowing everything that moved in the small port city and its salty economy. On a social level, her friends absorbed and spread every morsel of gossip.

Local rhythms shifted in cool September breezes. Few recreational boats lingered, and beach crowds had vanished. The skies would soon take on a gray cast. Shannon walked to Buddy's, a cozy breakfast spot named after the proprietor's best friend in doggie heaven. The place was a hangout for boat captains and locals. She always enjoyed the way the old-timers bantered with her.

As she approached the restaurant, bits of lively debate wafted out along with the aroma of bacon, diced potatoes and onions. Warm air mixed with strong-brewed coffee wrapped around her in welcome embrace as she entered.

Family friend Brooks Washburn motioned for Shannon to join his table with three retired fish-boat captains she knew. The men stood to greet her. At eighty-two, Washburn was sharp as ever and holding court as usual. He gestured to the adjacent table.

"Shannon, we're talking the birth of the first schooners, and this English couple from across the pond has joined in."

She acknowledged the men and the smart-casual dressed British couple in baggy trousers and knitwear. The man was pitched forward, hyperalert in his chair. His intense eyes sparkled behind round eyeglasses. His spouse, with a lovely don't-care mop of silver gray hair and benevolent ruddy face, sat back in comfort.

Shannon shrugged out of her slicker, sat and ordered coffee. The debate about origins of the schooner resumed.

Fred, a lanky old Gloucester salt wearing a ball cap, said, "I looked it up in Wicked-pee-dee-yah." He pointed out the window. "Right there in Smith's Cove three hundred years ago, Captain Andrew Robinson built and launched the very first vessel called a *schooner*."

The British man said, "Called a *schooner* only because a bystander said 'see how she *scoons*' when it first launched." He went on to say the Dutch had similar riggings decades earlier, as well as the English with their ketch designs.

Shannon spent her life around paddle-craft and powerboats. Her sailing experience was limited as an occasional guest on well-to-do friends' yachts.

While the British man challenged Gloucester's claim of inventing schooners, the man's wife nudged him in the side. He conceded that Yankee schooners evolved with superior shipbuilding and marketing.

"What made the schooner so unique?" asked Shannon.

Brooks answered. "Unlike full square-rigged ships, the schooner design was swift, sturdy, and agile for shifting coastal winds in deep and shallow waters."

"What was so different about the Gloucester captain's design?"

Barry, a former teacher and charter boat captain, eyed Shannon and the British man. "He rigged his finished ketch in a new way. He eliminated the square mainsail, put fore and aft sails on the two masts and a jib sail at the bow. With sails running the length of the deck, his schooner caught the wind at a close angle to sail fast to the wind."

Barry's tutorial seemed to quiet the Brit.

Washburn, a self-styled local historian, weighed in. "By the 1800s, the schooner was the most important ship in North America for coastal trade and fishing. Our schooners served decisively among America's first navy as armed privateers that outflanked British vessels in the Revolutionary War."

The Brit shrank in his seat. "There's the rub, for sure. Let's all enjoy watching the race on Sunday."

"I understand there'll be fewer vessels venturing here this weekend, with remnants of Hurricane Isaac still in the Gulf and southeast," Shannon said.

Fred piped up, "Speaking of hurricanes, I've heard modern women are like hurricanes, arriving wet and wild and leaving with your house and car."

The men roared, but Shannon had a different take. In a husky voice she said, "Aha, but a Glosta girl takes sweet revenge. She lets you keep your stuff, steals your heart, your soul, and leaves you wanting more."

"Indeed," murmured one man.

"Happened to me . . . twice," said another. "We gotta go."

"Good to see you, Shannon," Fred said as he paid the bill and walked out with his friends.

Brooks Washburn and Shannon stood outside the restaurant. "How you doing?" he asked.

Her mouth turned down. "I'm good, just moody. I always get that way in September."

Washburn peered over his glasses.

She studied his kind eyes and rugged face. He was always close with her dad's family, and had consoled her through some tough patches when she was a young single mom, and later when her father lost his battle with cancer.

Washburn's attentive silence hinted concern.

Shannon's chin trembled. "I never thought my kids would grow up so fast and move so far away. I miss Grandbaby Paula."

He took her hand. "I understand, Shannon. I've outlived my whole family."

She hugged him. "I won't bullshit you," she said. "I've got major abandonment issues. Eric and I are on the outs too."

"I'm here for you, Shannon. Let's talk whenever you want."

She nodded, looked away and wiped her eyes.

As they parted, Washburn turned back to her. "As hard as things can get, being in the midst of change can be invigorating."

୨

Shannon walked into town for the first tour of the spectacular HMS *Bounty* as it sat at Gloucester Marine Terminal. An early morning web search of the vessel's history primed her curiosity.

At the dock, she was first in line, shifting her feet behind a roped-off area. Her eyes swept the eighteenth-century replica *Bounty*'s 10,000 square feet of sail on three masts, 120-foot-long deck, and 32-foot beam—180 feet overall with its spars. Sunlight danced on its lashed sails and curves.

Shannon discerned a strange mix of wonder, magic, and dread that overcame her as she observed the captain, first mate, and busy crew of mostly ages fifteen to thirty. She began to sweat. The vessel seemed to age before her as she spied worn boards, ropes, cleats, and cracked layers of paint. *A time warp,* she thought. She was sobered by an empathetic feeling of how difficult life was on historic vessels like the *Bounty*. No one seemed to have a care, but Shannon sensed danger.

When the tour began, Shannon stepped onto the vessel and was greeted by *Bounty*'s longtime captain, Robin Walbridge. She stayed at his side to hear details of the hundred-foot main mast and the names of the sails: coarse, topsails, topgallants, and royals on both the main and the foremast.

Surrounded by people shuffling by, Shannon strained to hear of the *Bounty*'s 500 tons of displacement, the 2,300-pound bow anchor, 400,000 board feet of timber, 12 tons of screw bolts, 14 tons of bar iron, and 2.5 tons of spikes. Her neck muscles relaxed as Walbridge spoke. She broke from the group to stand amidships. Her worries of seaworthiness melted to a pleasant bond of invincibility with the massive wooden ship.

"Rock solid," she muttered as she paced to the ship's bow to examine the array of spars, rigging, and great forged iron chain plates. *Easy to imagine heroic days of courageous captains,* she thought.

A handsome sailor in his early forties approached her with a folded copy of the *Gloucester Daily Times* in one hand and a clipboard in the other. He wore a crinkled tan sun hat snapped up on one side.

"Hi there, I'm Rod, first mate of the *Bounty*. You must be Shannon." He held up the newspaper. "It's not every day I meet women making front page headlines as pirates. We'd like you and your three friends to join us for dinner tonight. Can you pick a place with some atmosphere for us?"

Shannon squinted at the newsprint and winced. "Crap. I'll be razzed for years . . . but dinner with *Bounty*'s crew . . . fantastic." She had worked at most of the bars and restaurants along the Gloucester waterfront. "I know just the place."

The wind picked up as she walked home along the harbor. Her thoughts drifted to her kids and the sour uncertainty of any year-end holiday plans as a family.

Stopping at a small park by the narrow head of the working harbor, Shannon sat on a bench to calm her mind. She surveyed the piers and working boats idled for the long holiday weekend.

By Tuesday, lobstermen would head for deeper waters before sunrise to return after sunset with hauls of hard-shelled bounty, hoping for higher prices. Her local rock, blues, and jazz musician friends would start to claim their winter perches in Gloucester's cozy bars and restaurants.

Shannon closed her eyes and sighed. Her cherished Uncle Paddy would visit with new information about her ancestry and some kind of inheritance. She became nostalgic. Ten years had passed since he came for her father's funeral. She knew so little of him other than his good character, and was determined to get his life story. As to his news, she could not possibly know what was in store for her.

DRIFTING ON
THE ROCKS

By the end of September, Shannon and Gael were working ten-hour days at the boat basin. Each day, vessels were encased in shrink wrap and put up for winter storage. Gael's dad paid well for the work and had asked Shannon to do repair work on some vessels. Staying busy kept her from constant overthinking. On off-days she did home repairs and yard work. Two nights a week she helped out at the local theater for upcoming productions. Setting daily goals and reading helped to deal with the waves of depression that seemed worse in the evenings. She obsessed about Paddy's upcoming arrival and whether to raise or lower her expectations for the visit. Paddy had made it clear he would only reveal important matters in person, and she had some news to share with her uncle, too—like the meltdown of her marriage.

Shannon took a day off to go fishing. That was her most reliable joy and antidote for stress. Her inshore, open fishing skiff, with a 25 hp hand tiller outboard, rested at the ready at a half-tide dock in East Gloucester. She walked the short distance from her cottage to the dock carrying two fishing rods and a small cooler for bait—one rod for trolling a tube lure with a sea worm, another for catching bait mackerel on a tree rig and using a bait runner reel to let fish run.

As a patient sole caster, Shannon knew that fifty-pound striped bass lingered into October. There would also be less boat traffic and fewer clueless anglers in the harbor. Local fishermen have a word for them—*googans*.

She thought how her husband, Eric, liked to fish and entertain friends offshore in his well outfitted Grady White 26, but his job as a commercial construction supervisor on sites up and down the East Coast left him few days to use it.

Fishing quietly in the harbor with Marcy or Gael was a pleasure because they focused on the hunt and appreciated the ever-changing skies, shorebirds, and seascapes. Shannon would indulge in soul-searching chats with Marcy, particularly when the fish were not biting.

She remembered the way her teenaged daughter and son would open up to her when angling from her small skiff in Gloucester Harbor or along the Annisquam River. It lulled them into sharing their problems. Or maybe she was just a better listener out on the water.

Midmorning, Shannon positioned her boat at one of her favorite fish holes where a large flat granite and quartz rock sloped below the water line. Sunlight reflected swift movements of baitfish, mackerel, and larger species feeding. She set anchor, selected a bait rig, and brought up some energetic mackerel.

Two seals dunked a few yards away. She considered them friends, good luck, and had nicknames for them—Randy and Sparkle. Something caught her attention—a boat drifting close with a man bent over its transom, pulling something. She shook her head. The *googan* had fouled his fishing line on the propeller, left his engine idling, and had not set his anchor.

"Watch out for the rocks," Shannon shouted. "Turn your motor off. I'll tow you away." She tossed her bowline to him and recognized the fool—a local self-impressed attorney. She scowled. Her face reddened and her heart pounded.

Shannon began to sweat, breathing heavily. She balled her fists and spoke under her breath. "Crap!" She directed him to secure the line to his bow cleat and then gunned her small engine in reverse for several yards.

It did the trick, and she reset her anchor. After pulling the boats together, she lashed them and jumped onto his boat. Shannon pulled her fishing knife from the sheath on her belt, bent down over the stern, and worked the line from around the propeller. The two boats rocked as she stretched to free the tangle. She knew too well that this situation could easily ruin a good boat and was a very good way to get hurt.

Shannon steadied back up—the boats had drifted dangerously toward the rocks. It did not occur to the googan to set his anchor, and she realized hers had popped off the sea bottom. Lowering her stance to steady, she tossed an oar to him. "Push away from the rocks."

She plopped back into her skiff, pulled the starter cord, and backed them from danger. She set both anchors. Disaster averted.

A perfect fishing day ruined, she thought.

The man made a slim apology. "Please don't tell anyone about this."

She glared at him with bared teeth. This was the second time she rescued the pompous lawyer. Last season, he ran out of gas near her on a borrowed client's boat.

"Don't *ever* stalk me or my fishin' spots again," said Shannon.

The man shrugged.

"Give me your eels, let me fish in peace, and get out of my face."

This was no big deal, she thought. *Why can't I just calm down?*

When he was gone, Shannon caught and released two fish, used up the bait and headed home. She had planned to meet her friends at the Gloucester Main Street Block Party that night where shops stayed open and restaurants offered outdoor dining with live music. Instead, she went home to drink. Alone.

After a hot bath, Shannon put on sweatpants and devoured a tub of chocolate almond ice cream. Moments later, she returned to the kitchen for a bottle of pinot grigio and ice.

Shannon turned on a blues radio station and wandered about the house with the bottle in one hand and wineglass in the other. She studied family pictures, her own paintings, and folk art she had fashioned from small objects and shells from local beaches.

With a critical eye, she assessed two of her early paintings in the living room. The lack of restraint screamed pain and confusion. Her later work showed more sophistication, with a happier palette.

A favorite photograph of her husband as a fresh Gloucester High graduate caught her eye. *I was so crazy for you,* she thought. *We got me pregnant at sixteen. Your parents sent you out of state to live with relatives. Your mother wanted you to stay away from me, the 'wharf rat girlie.' I was not the type you take home to the folks.*

Nobody wanted me to have the baby, but I did it, Shannon mused. *Two and a half years later, you came back, held our daughter, Delphina, and wanted a family.*

Setting Eric's photograph down, she looked at a picture of their daughter as a first-grader and then spoke aloud. "I chose your pretty Portuguese name for 'dolphin.' You won Eric's family over. Being a good mother is what I am most proud of. Eric is a good father. Was I too overbearing, Delphina?"

Their daughter, now twenty-nine, had moved to the Blue Ridge Mountains with four-year-old Grandbaby Paula. Shannon kept asking herself, *Why would anyone leave Cape Ann to go to such a landlocked place?* For Shannon, having to spend an entire day doing "land stuff" was a drag. At least her son, Alex, at twenty-four, moved to the California coast to pursue his passion for surfing, and had steady work as an emergency medical technician near the docks.

Given her own rebellious childhood, Shannon thought it ironic that she had become a clinging mother of grown kids trying to find their way in the world—getting sappy about the weight of an empty nest. She would have to deal with the breakdown of her marriage, and her part in it, but not yet.

Padding over to a bookcase stuffed with papers, maps, books, scripts, CDs, and mementos, she hesitated and then pulled out a letterbox containing photos, legal papers, and documents for safekeeping.

She set out obituaries of her father, John, deranged mother, Regina, and criminal older brother, Mike. As an adult, Shannon was the caregiver for her dad when he suffered with cancer; then her mother with cirrhosis of the liver; and then her brother, who became terminally ill after serving time in jail and using hard drugs. Her heavy-drinking big sister, Janet, had moved away years ago.

Shannon held up her father's obituary, which showed him as a young smiling boat captain. She thought of his kindness, how he never complained and he did what he could to support his family through great difficulties.

She located another picture of her dad with Patrick, his younger brother by four years.

Shannon tried not to think about her mother's cruelty, finding it difficult to forgive and impossible to forget.

A senior prom photo of Delphina sat on a prominent shelf over her computer. "I wanted to be nothing like my mother. But why did you move so far away?"

With a refill of her wine glass on the coffee table, she rested on the sofa and looked at the wall clock: 8:30. Laying her head back, she gazed up as if there were a list of her life's blessings and hurts on the ceiling. She wondered if she should raise or lower her expectations for Paddy's visit in six weeks.

Shannon fell into a deep sleep and dreamed. She was a child in pajamas, drumming two wooden spoons on a table in the parlor of her parents' house. Hard hands clapped her ears. Sharp pain. A hard slap to the face, then shoved onto the floor. Curled up with her hands over her ears, she was kicked and dragged and locked in a closet. She pounded on the door. Her mother growled, "I never wanted you. I tried to kill you before you were born." The dream shifted. Suddenly outside, Shannon ran past closed storefronts and dim city light posts and into an alleyway where she crouched in the shadows.

Awakened, upright in bed, Shannon shook in a cold sweat; her clothes were damp and the bedsheets were tightly pulled over her shoulders. Her breath calmed. She moaned and her voice croaked, "No, not this again."

STORMY MONDAY

The New England coast was in for trouble, but no one knew how much. Hurricane Sandy tore through the Caribbean in late October, throttled up the East Coast, dumped snow in West Virginia, and cut a violent path of tropical winds 800 miles wide through New York, New Jersey, and Pennsylvania. Now, it was headed their way.

Tensions had grown between Shannon and Eric. They had separated informally, but neither knew what came next. Now he wanted to talk. Assuming he could drive safely ahead of the storm from New York, he would be at their Massachusetts home by lunchtime Tuesday.

Shannon spent Sunday preparing for the storm. She moved her pickup truck to higher ground. She dragged two kayaks from the marsh grass at the edge of the yard to the back of the house. She loaded up on provisions and secured Eric's boat at Smith Cove Marina. He made a reservation for her at a nearby motel on a high ledge overlooking Good Harbor Beach—she thought it unnecessary.

With most items secure in the yard, Shannon put on work gloves and grabbed a length of chain attached to their weary pop-up camper trailer. The bald tires reminded her of family hikes and fishing trips with the kids and their friends. Shannon huffed and pulled the chain back with her legs, back and arms to work the stubborn camper to a tree several feet away. The camper wheels stuck in soft stony ground near her raised garden of two dozen fish totes brimming with dead summer plants, composted soil, and seaweed cover.

Winds dried her sweaty face as she panted. She dropped the chain, straightened up and stretched her back. Deep tracks across the ruddy yard marked her halfway progress to the tree. The camper sat frozen in defiance.

Not to be defeated, Shannon retrieved a cable puller from the toolshed, hooked the long cable end around the tree, and connected the come-along tool to the camper. She ratcheted the lever to haul the stubborn camper close to the tree and secured it. After twenty-six years in the cottage, storm preparations were routine.

The small house and outbuildings for tools, work and art spaces had window boxes, painted shutters, roof extensions and tiny porches that surrounded a central fire pit with a medley of small gardens. An array of narrow pathways with stepping-stones meandered through salt marsh meadow grass to the beach and neighboring homes. Inside the cottage, a raised hearth fireplace centered the open living space.

Shannon rested on her living room couch watching the six o'clock news for weather updates and then called Marcy, Gael, and Allegra to share drinks at the Harbor Grille. Shannon walked nearly a mile in windy gusts to get there. Extreme weather made her feel alive.

The Harbor Grille was busy and her pals guarded a corner seat for her at the bar. They faced a bank of TVs with news and sports. Large tobacco-leaf-style ceiling fans moved lazily above the noisy diners. For several minutes, she gazed out the sliders to the two factory fishing boats snuggled with security lights on. After twenty-five years working along the Gloucester waterfront, she knew the working boats, the captains, and many of the crewmembers. She understood the deprivations they faced with the drastic decline of the fishing industry.

Allegra spotted Shannon. "Hey, fish whore, what's doing?"

"What are you trolling for?

"Something new," Allegra retorted.

"Any update on the storm?"

"It's nasty and will reach us with rising tides through the night—

might flood your cottage again," Gael said.

"Stay at my place," Marcy said.

"Thanks, no."

"Well at least keep your phone on. If it gets bad, I'll get you."

Shannon sat quiet for a while, and after finishing a second drink said, "I'm going home," and abruptly left. Marcy followed. Allegra and Gael stayed at the bar where two attractive guys had beckoned them to join.

Marcy drove Shannon home in her old Chevy. The defroster was not keeping up with ice forming on the windshield. Marcy pulled over, wiped the inside of the windshield, and offered Shannon a piece of her mind.

"Stubborn as usual," Marcy said.

"That defines me sometimes."

"More than that, Shannon."

"Don't be concerned."

"You aren't yourself."

"I am."

"But I'm concerned about you."

"You're not my mother, and she wasn't."

"You're aloof, edgy, drinking too much—"

"Maybe I don't give a shit."

"Now we're getting somewhere."

"Yeah, taking me home."

"You're in denial."

"I don't know what I want anymore."

Early Monday morning, Shannon kept watch of wind chop on the marsh and beach. When a nor'easter hit this side of Cape Ann, she knew that easterly winds could push water into her cottage. Fortunately, winds flowed more from the north, so she judged the storm less trouble and relaxed a bit. She continued her interior preparations during the day and kept tuned to the Weather Channel, listening to CDs to pass the time.

Shannon sang along with the Allman Brothers' version of "Call it Stormy Monday." Storms held strange excitement for her, and she embraced the turmoil. Shannon pressed her face to the window overlooking the windy marsh and wondered, *If I surrender to an emotional abyss, will that blow over? Maybe I'm not so tough.*

Gloucester was hundreds of miles from the core of the superstorm but took a pounding with gusts up to eighty-five miles per hour through midday Tuesday, downing trees and power lines. The storm punished the coastline with menacing gray surf while cutting electricity to more than 3,000 homes and businesses. The damage on Cape Ann was nothing compared with the dire situation in the Mid-Atlantic.

For local fishermen, the storm was more than inconvenient. Transportation systems along the eastern seaboard shut down, and fisheries could not move product to the markets. Most of the fish catch went to auction frozen. Just before the storm, the catch was strong and most boats were secured. The natural shape of Gloucester's harbor and breakwater protected its fleet.

At noon on Tuesday, Shannon stood outside her cottage in a soiled gray sweatshirt, blue jeans, red rubber muck boots and a large bandanna tied around her braided red hair. Soggy household contents sat in the ruddy yard.

It had been much worse over the past twenty-five years when tides were high with a full lunar cycle and the house took on water. Twenty-one years ago to the day, surf had rolled through the house during the infamous Perfect Storm.

She now watched the receding tide with her mobile phone pressed to her ear. "Marcy, I'm fine; done here. Don't bother coming over, just a splash of green seawater on the floor. All squeegeed out. Have to go. Eric will be home for lunch."

Shannon pocketed her mobile. She thought how her wimpy neighbors were whining because they got a little puddle in their basements. Her morning included taking furniture down from sawhorses and hanging wet clothes on plastic lines strung in the living room.

She closed her windows with a measure of satisfaction. Balmy sea breezes had dried most of the clothes, furnishings, and flooring. She heard Eric's car pull up in the gravel driveway, and watched through the kitchen window as he walked to the house sporting a fresh crew cut, plaid flannel shirt, black garrison belt, blue jeans and low-cut work boots. They had happier times when he had local jobs, came home for lunch, and they were busy with the kids. Now he spent weeks at distant sites for his construction management job. After they exchanged wary greetings, Shannon turned red when he walked across the kitchen floor with muddy shoes.

Boiling over, she threw a wet towel at Eric's feet. He shifted as it glanced by and landed next to a curio cabinet. She caught a glimpse of her wildcat face in the mirror-back of the curio and welled up.

He reversed his steps. "Sorry."

"Sorry?" She tossed another wet towel. His muddy shoes were a minor infraction, but straying with other women was not. He removed the towel from his shoulder and brushed over the water stain on his shirt. His impassive look riled her more. She turned away and ripped down the plastic clothesline still strung on hooks through the house. Eric leaned against the kitchen table as she cursed.

"Don't you feel anything?" Shannon said, charging back and pushing the bundle of clothesline into his chest. They both slipped and toppled onto the floor.

He worked his jaw. "What now?"

Moments later, they sat at the kitchen table, staring at their sandwiches in silence.

"So?" Eric asked.

"You need to figure what you're going to do. This marriage is toast," she said.

Eric opened his hands slowly, as if to defuse a bomb. "We've been depressed about the kids moving away. We didn't recognize it, talk about it, or comfort each other."

"I haven't exactly been a peach."

Eric stared into her eyes. "I have been lonely too long, Shannon."

Shannon lowered her head and tried to speak, but no words would come.

"We should have been talking about our feelings," he said. "You know I'm not good at it. I'm not in love with anyone else. I came to you weeks ago. Told you everything but how I feel."

"Right about that," she said, staring at her untouched sandwich.

Shannon leaned back in her chair and blew out her cheeks. "I've made mistakes, but not the same one."

They sat without words for a while.

"Infidelity begins at home but changes everything," she said.

Eric let that sit. "Can we agree to keep talking and not make decisions right now?"

Shannon folded her hands and took a deep breath. "We will always be friends, Eric, but we can't trust each other's hearts anymore."

After he left, Shannon walked the path to Good Harbor Beach where shorebirds and seabirds fed on easy meals amid seaweed and driftwood.

It was calming to watch gulls, terns, ducks, and storm petrels on patrol. She identified red-throated loons and Atlantic puffins blown off course, strutting along the shoreline. She expanded her walk to nearby Long Beach, and followed the coastline to the craggy shore of the neighboring town of Rockport. A good walkabout with fresh sea air might ensure a decent night's sleep.

Shannon returned home to a shocking news story. The HMS *Bounty* sunk off North Carolina in the throes of Hurricane Sandy. The ship keeled over in eighteen-foot waves. The Coast Guard airlifted fourteen of sixteen crewmembers in life rafts and reported them in good condition. One was dead and Captain Robin Walbridge was lost at sea.

The faces of the *Bounty's* captain and young crew flashed in her mind. *What happened out there? Did Captain Walbridge make a terrible mistake?* She curled up on the sofa as news cycles repeated the grim details.

PIRATE BLOOD

Uncle Paddy boarded a Miami flight to arrive at Boston Logan Airport. Shannon had been up most of the night, reading or tossing in bed. She obsessed about seeing her uncle and what he knew about their ancestry. Her family experience was mostly damaged and filled with broken dreams, except when it came to her father and his brother.

Shannon needed a task to occupy her, and spent the morning helping a friend, Captain Steve, fix a rotted pier by his father's house in Smith Cove. The modest dwelling was the last fishing family home on the waterfront in East Gloucester.

"Thanks for pitching in," Steve said.

Shannon moved a heavy piece of lumber. "Small payback for all the lobsters you give me from your boat. Besides, this is fun."

They worked from a crude, dilapidated barge with a pile driver. The clanging sounds added percussion to the weekday cacophony of the working harbor. The hardest part of the job was jockeying new, treated wooden piles by winch and by hand into position next to the rotted ones in the water.

Shannon and Steve struggled to seat the last pole. She ran the pile driver for fifteen more minutes before shutting the raucous contraption down.

She removed her earmuffs. "We did it."

"Nice job, Shannon," said Steve. "It's hard to drive every pile six full feet into the seabed. The new dock will be awesome."

A car had stopped in the road nearby, with two older women observing them. Shannon recognized the women, removed a glove, and wiped her hand across her brow. She chuckled and nudged Steve with her elbow. "Those gasbags will start rumors about us."

"Maybe we should have lunch in town sometime, and really get them talking."

"I value our friendship, Steve. Lunch would be nice." Shannon smiled. "They'll say you're too young for me and be right. Anyway, I have to get moving and pick up my uncle at the airport at one."

Shannon gathered up her tools and tossed them in the cab of her dimpled and dented green truck. Steve smiled. "I have an extra tool lockbox that would fit the bed of your pickup, if you want."

"You're a sweet man. Thanks, but I need the hauling space." Shannon fired up her truck, filled with its usual clutter of protein candy bar wrappers, thermos, fishing tackle, and tools in the cab. She had swept out the truck's rusty bed earlier, ignoring the expired inspection sticker, cracked windshield and loose muffler.

Driving off the island was not her favorite thing to do. As usual, US Route 1 to Boston became a slog. She sat in traffic with the engine in a rough idle and muffler throbbing. The smashed radio in the dash reminded her of a party gone wrong.

At Logan Airport, it was easy to spot her bearded, lean, and windburned uncle. He stood outside the baggage claim with a pipe clenched in his teeth. Paddy left home long ago but was still a Gloucester man at heart, with a denim jacket, jeans, Redwing boots, black wool fishing cap, and a green duffel bag slung over his shoulder. She cleared the hand tools off the passenger side of the bench seat.

He tossed his bag into the truck bed and sat in the cab. With a big hug he said, "You still got the green monsta. Great to see you, Shan; been ten years."

"You look wonderful, Uncle Paddy. Awesome to have you here." Shannon looked out the window and wiped her wet eyes with her sleeve.

Like a commuter rail conductor, Paddy announced, "Next stop, Glosta." Shannon liked the way he still pronounced Gloucester like the locals. She accelerated away from the airport, double-clutched into third gear, eased into fourth and ramped north. She squeezed Paddy's hand on the bench seat. "I'm making lobster bisque, with a seafood mac and cheese casserole for dinner."

"Excellent. I'll stay over at Brooks Washburn's place while I'm in town. You and I have a lot to talk about in the morning."

"Stay at my place. Plenty of room, and we can talk right away."

"Brooks said you and Eric are in a tough patch."

"So, you keep tabs on me with Brooks?"

"Don't blame him," Paddy said. "He looks out for you."

"He's like family. I totally trust him."

"Let's swing by his place right now to touch base and pick up a trunk I kept there. You and I talk tonight."

"Wait, what trunk?" Shannon asked.

"Be patient. I'll tell you all about it after dinner."

Paddy settled in at Shannon's place as she rummaged through the kitchen gathering the supplies to make lobster bisque. "A mariner earns his keep," he said. "I'll help with dinner, and maybe learn to make your lobster bisque."

"Okay," she said, "I'll talk you through the prep while I catch up on a few things."

Shannon brought out a heavy nonstick skillet and said, "This is much better than using a stew pot." She set out the ingredients: olive oil, Irish butter, shallots, frozen lobster base, cheap brandy, cooked lobster meat, heavy cream, white pepper, thyme, two bay leaves, a bottle of hot sauce and a shaker of black pepper.

"Thaw two tablespoons of lobster base and finely chop two shallots. When the shallots turn clear in the oil and butter, add the lobster base." She continued her instructions from the next room as she did some light cleaning and responded to text messages and emails on her mobile phone.

Paddy slipped Shannon's prepared seafood mac and cheese casserole into the preheated oven and started the shallots.

"Splash some brandy in it," she said.

Paddy was already chopping up the lobster meat.

"Chop it fine, no big chunks," she said, cradling her phone tight to her ear in the next room.

Paddy said, "Small bits. Roger that."

"Don't put the cream in till the alcohol cooks out; don't want to curdle it."

"Yes, dear," he said, adding in the cream, thyme, and bay leaves. He glanced at the wall clock and rummaged the kitchen to whip up something to go with the dinner. He put butter, white pepper, and garlic in a saucepan, finely chopped some artichokes and simmered the mix. He hollowed out two pieces of crusty French bread with a fork and mixed the fluffy bread in a bowl with the artichokes, cheddar cheese, butter, and sour cream. The French crusts were quickly stuffed with the bread mixture, wrapped in foil and placed in the oven.

Paddy stirred the bisque to a rolling boil, shut the burner off, took Shannon's mac and cheese casserole out of the oven, and set the table. She finished her last phone call and returned to the kitchen.

"Dinner is served," he announced.

"Oh my God, lost track of time." She pocketed her mobile.

They did not speak until the last slurp of lobster bisque was gone.

Paddy smiled at his niece. "You could make a fortune as a chef."

"I learned a few things working the bars, kitchens, and restaurants in town. My fortune was raising my kids as a young mom, and the free time I have now." She wiped her mouth and bunched up the napkin. "What about this story of yours?"

Paddy motioned for her to join him in the easy chairs. He fetched a bottle of single malt scotch from his duffel. Shannon smiled when she recognized the expensive brand. She brought over two tumblers with one ice cube in each. Paddy grinned wide and poured the dark amber, eighteen-year-aged whiskey.

His expression turned serious. "What I have to say may change your life. No one can know about it, or things can get complicated and miserable."

"I'm the expert in keeping secrets," she said. "Go ahead."

They raised tumblers together with a swish-clink of ice and glass. Shannon took a draw of the scotch.

"You grew up with no idea of your fabulous and infamous seafaring ancestry," said Paddy.

Shannon raised her eyebrows and leaned in.

"You come from a long line of early European settlers and famous sea captains here, and have pirate ancestry."

She laughed. "There's the infamous part. You joked about that, and called me a pirate on my tenth birthday. Remember? You took me to the park at Lynn Woods. We climbed down into the pirate cavern at Dungeon Rock."

"What do you remember?"

"The ice cream on the way home, and the old story of a pirate and his crew in Lynn Harbor unloading a steel and wooden chest from a black ship with no flag. They rowed up the Saugus River and made camp."

Paddy nodded. "The pirate captain left an anonymous note on the door of the Saugus Iron Works by the river—an order for shackles, hatchets, shovels, and tools to be made in exchange for silver left at a secret drop point."

"I returned several times to hike those woods and looked into the history of it," she said. "He hid treasure in that natural cave at Dungeon Rock, built a shed at the entrance, and made it his home for years. He paid local merchants with silver doubloons, and repaired shoes for the locals who thought him batty. He was crushed in the cave years later by a natural earthquake."

"Served him right," Paddy said. "The scoundrel had made off with the booty from their pirate camp, leaving his mates to be captured and hanged by the British."

Shannon held her glass to the lamp and swirled the scotch. "As a kid,

I loved *Treasure Island* and movies like *Captain Blood*."

"Real piracy is not so romantic, Shannon, and hunting for treasure can drive people nuts. The treasure at Dungeon Rock was a curse. People spent over 200 years looking for it. The townspeople spent a fortune blasting the site to find it."

She gave Paddy a wistful look. "I remember your stories and you saying I had pirate blood back then. As a kid I imagined that life with a swashbuckling crew. I even have lifelike dreams about it."

Paddy set his tumbler sharply on the table between them. "You are a descendant of Anne Bonny, the wild, fearless, redheaded pirate of the Caribbean from the 1720s. I couldn't tell anyone until now."

She laughed, "Paddy, I'm not a kid anymore. Maybe I got a recessive gene for red hair and another for a pirate's heart."

"Listen. We had a family legend no one believed. Now I have evidence beyond doubt. You are the bona fide eleventh-generation descendant of Anne Bonny, and Jack Rackham's family."

"You're serious."

He nodded.

Shannon stared at him. "I only know snippets of Anne Bonny and Jack Rackham. I read that the child Anne conceived with Jack was left to be brought up by his retired pirate friends in Cuba. But nobody knows for sure if that child survived or what really happened to Anne."

"There is much more. We have the chance to solve a legend."

Shannon offered him her glass. "Refill, please. Do you have piratical blood too?"

He chuckled. "My side descended from the Rackham family."

"Tell me more."

Paddy shook an open palm. "Anne Bonny and Jack Rackham's bloodlines took generations to meet when your father married Regina."

Shannon reeled back in her chair. "My mother?"

"She didn't know her lineage. Think about nature *and* nurture; heredity *and* environment. As a young bride, your mother was fun-loving, beautiful, energetic, and yes, swore like a sailor. Regina never learned to read and was berated by her father, Donato Silva, growing up. He was crude and uneducated." Paddy frowned. "He beat Regina's mother, Maryanne O'Connor."

Shannon shuddered. "My grandmother was a nice lady. I heard he kept other women in a boardinghouse."

Paddy continued. "It was unusual then for a woman of Irish and English background to marry a Portuguese man. Hard times had come to the O'Connor family and Silva was a fishing boat captain with some means. It was during those hard times when the family history was lost."

Shannon shifted in her chair. "I really don't know much about my grandparents."

Paddy swished his drink. "Donato was respected here as a boat captain among local Gloucester men for his skill with the harpoon. They said he could stand on a bowsprit in choppy seas and spear a tiny mackerel in the water. I don't think people in town knew his dark side."

"Did my dad ever say much about my mother?" asked Shannon.

"He stayed with Regina for you kids. Her crazy moods blossomed when she became a parent."

"Ya think?" said Shannon. "She beat me senseless and locked me in a closet so she didn't have to deal with me. She beat all of us kids but had a special hate for me. Sometimes, she shoved me in the closet to take her lovers, while dad worked eighteen hours a day."

Paddy frowned and wiped his eyes with a handkerchief. "John never told me about her emotional and physical abuse of you kids."

"Maybe he didn't know, or didn't want to." Shannon took a long slow sip and stared down at her sneakers. "My dad was the shining light—kind, loving, and cheerful. He let me ride with him in his truck sometimes. He taught me how to use tools. Said I was the son he always wanted." She shook her head and shrugged. "As you know, my brother was in and out of jail for robbery. He was also a drug addict. Thirty-five is too young to die. I still have friggin' nightmares over this stuff, sleepwalk, and wake up terrified of what I may be capable of."

Paddy's voice softened. "I'm so sorry you went through all that. If that wasn't bad enough, it was tough when John lost his uninsured boat in a nor'easter. Your father was a good man, and a terrific older brother for me. He's the one that told Brooks to look out for you." Paddy sipped the scotch. "It was years later when I found out you moved in with a neighborhood kid's family."

"I ran away from home and school in seventh grade. Regina didn't come looking for me. The people that took me in weren't better off, but they had each other." Shannon took a long stare at her drink. "Early on, my mother didn't want me to go to kindergarten because she wanted me to do the housework. I was her maid. She withheld food. She popped painkillers and black beauties, hardly left the house, and never worked. At fourteen, I worked jobs under the table sorting, cutting, and packing fish. I also sold marijuana and pills that I got from my brother."

Paddy buried his head in his hands. "I didn't know that."

"The time limit on that secret has expired."

Shannon went to the kitchen and returned with a pitcher of water and two glasses. Her eyes were wet. "You're the only family I can talk to." She let out a long sigh. "Other than you and my dad, I'm from the World Cup of dysfunctional families—thieves, drug addicts, child beaters, smugglers and outlaws. Why not pirates?" She lowered her head and rubbed her palms together. Her bottom lip turned up. "The kids are gone. I'm separated, and I was a mess before you came."

Paddy held her until she sobbed out.

After Shannon composed herself, Paddy spoke low. "Want to talk about it?"

She wiped her eyes. "Yeah, but not now. Tell me more about my connection to Anne Bonny."

"Okay. Let me get that trunk that I know you've been dying to peek in." Paddy dragged his green storage chest from the corner, unlocked it, and pulled out a tattered leather mail carrier sealed in a large plastic bag and something wrapped in a purple cloth. He folded back the cloth and presented Shannon with a beautifully jeweled sword sheathed in an ornate scabbard.

"This was Anne Bonny's short sword."

Shannon froze and held her breath.

"It's yours now," Paddy said. "It was meant to be."

She weighed the magnificent sword in her hands to admire the emeralds and rubies set in bezels on scrolled goldwork over the scabbard, guard and pommel. She stood, unsheathed it, and ran her index finger over its curved twenty-inch blade.

With her free hand back, she made a few light parries, and darted forward with three practice thrusts. "Light and deadly," she said. "So, this is what an Irish girl who came to America in the early 1700s used to board vessels and slay men alongside her pirate lover, 'Calico Jack' Rackham."

"Indeed."

"Where did you get this sword?"

"After your sister was born, your father got concerned about your mom's wild mood swings. Regina stole a small chest containing the sword and other items from her grandmother Elizabeth before she left home. It was a family curiosity trotted out on holidays, but the letters and documents were difficult to decipher. Regina bragged to your father that she made the theft look like a break-in with other things missing."

"Sounds like her," Shannon said as she slid the sword back in the scabbard.

"Your dad took it away from her when he came home and saw her drunk and cavorting around with it. Your older brother and sister were in the house and you were still a toddler. John gave the sword and other items to me for safekeeping, and I in turn trusted Brooks Washburn to watch over it while I was at sea."

"Now I believe it. Let me get something."

With the sword tucked under her arm, Shannon retrieved a book from the den. "This is about female seafarers. Got it when I prepared for my first play as a lady pirate. There's a short piece on Anne Bonny, and how unusual it was, since life on those ships was brutal and unfriendly to women."

Paddy took the book in his hands and flipped through it. "Imagine their daring, to be so accepted and revered. What did you like best in this book?"

"There is only a little about Anne Bonny, so I'd say Grace O'Malley, born a hundred fifty years earlier in Ireland. Grace became chieftain of her father's clan and shipping business. She harassed and took tribute from English vessels passing along the northwest and central coast of Ireland. She battled Irish warlords. Queen Elizabeth I negotiated for Grace to focus on England's enemies, with a promise for Grace to keep her lands."

"I'd love to read it," he said.

"Grace ran armies of ships and men, was widowed and imprisoned twice," Shannon said. "There is a lot about her life, family, and heroics."

Paddy cleared his throat. "I've pieced together some of Anne's untold story along with your ancestry. The artifacts your mother stole from her grandmother spurred my early research. Two safe deposit boxes at Cape Ann Savings Bank hold more for you to see. A lot happens in eleven generations over three hundred years."

"Why do you think this is so important?" Shannon asked.

"Our heritage and priceless historical information. Possibly treasure."

"Whoa, that's what you meant by a sort of inheritance."

"The sword you hold was a bequest from Anne Bonny, to be passed down to the oldest or ablest daughters of her descent. Now, that's you. There could be artifacts, even authentic pirate gold, but we have to find it."

Shannon kept turning the sword in her hands to catch the light. "You and me?"

"Yes. It won't be easy."

"Whatever it takes, Paddy. I'm all in."

"There are no friends of treasure, Shannon. Whether we find any or not, even friends turn enemies. We have information about what happened to Anne Bonny after she disappeared from jail after her sentence of execution at the Pirate Trial of Jamaica, November 1720."

Paddy rummaged in his storage chest and set a worn leather document folder on the side table. "The fascination with Anne Bonny and Mary Read's unusual story as pirates, dressing as men, persists in literature, plays, legends, and movies. Their conquests and skills with weapons were extraordinary in those times."

Shannon grinned. "One should never underestimate a woman."

Paddy laughed. "Only young or foolish men make that mistake."

He held the leather document folder in his hands. "Many have tried to unravel the mystery of Anne's life after prison without success, and I fear some will do anything to find out."

"Now I get the risk."

"Tomorrow, I'll tell you about your rich ancestry of sea captains, patriots and privateers."

"I want to know more about Anne now."

"Okay. A leading pirate historian says that family records and accounts from Jamaica show that Anne Bonny's father, William Cormac, bribed Jamaican officials for her prison release, and she returned to his Charleston plantation that was known for tobacco and indigo. Anne later married a merchant named James Burleigh, but there's no information on him."

He tapped the leather folio. "The three letters Anne wrote to her granddaughter helped me prove this story. Anne prospered in Charleston, and had eight children. Her youthful identity as pirate Anne Bonny scrubbed. She left clues about her life, including where some of her fortune may be."

Shannon pushed her drink away. "Now I have a mission."

BLOODLINES

addy and Shannon enjoyed coffee the next morning from Adirondack chairs in her patio garden. Briny breezes flowed over the beach dunes and through marsh grasses. Shannon had prepared two plates of locally smoked salmon with sliced avocados and tomatoes with olive oil, apple cider vinegar, dried seaweed seasoning and sea salt.

"That was delish," Paddy said. "We have some time before the bank opens up."

Shannon adjusted her threadbare gray Red Sox hat. "Let's kick off our sandals and walk the beach first. I want to hear more about our roots."

"Great, let's go."

They followed a winding sandy path through the marsh grass.

Paddy shared how his genealogical research began with reviewing historical records and family letters from Anne Bonny's time. He then worked back from contemporary birth, death, and marriage records, wills, deeds, military and census records, journals, and news events.

"Tracking ancestral lines back to 1650 is rare, but we have a complete eleven-generation chart from Anne's father to you," said Paddy.

"That's a long way back," said Shannon, picking up pieces of driftwood as they walked Good Harbor Beach, a local landmark frequently ranked in the top ten beaches of New England for soft sand, steady breakers, and views of Thacher Island's twin lighthouses.

"Yeah, eight to twelve generations from the present, based on the ages of the parents when various ancestors were born."

"How did you connect Jack Rackham's family to ours?" Shannon asked.

Paddy pulled up a long narrow stick from the sand to use as a hiking staff. "Trouble is, pirates didn't keep good records, and Jack didn't live that long. I kept at it, and traced the Rackham family from Suffolk, England to the New World. The family split in separate crossings—Jack Rackham went to the Caribbean to seek his fortune, and his older brother, James, went to Prince Edward Island in Canada."

Shannon hooked Paddy's arm to walk the shallows along the beach. "Tell me more."

"James's great-granddaughter, Sarah, came to Gloucester and married our ancestor John Clarke, an Irishman. One of his descendants, Harry Clarke, married my grandmother, Shannon Connell, from Limerick, Ireland."

"So, the Rackham bloodline in our family comes from Calico Jack's brother."

"You got it."

"How old was Jack when he reached the Caribbean?"

"Thirty-two. In three years there, he established a wily reputation and met twenty-year-old Anne Bonny."

Shannon imagined bodacious young Anne Bonny romancing and pirating with fanciful Calico Jack in his prime. Her thoughts ran to wild adventure and earthly delights.

"How did you figure my lineage to Anne?"

"First I researched Anne's early life from available records. Anne's father, William Cormac, was an attorney. She was born in Kinsale, in County Cork in 1698; her teenage years were spent on her father's American plantation in Charleston. After that was her short marriage to James Bonny, her pirating days with Jack Rackham, an apparent bribed release from prison, and her return to Charleston as Anne Burleigh."

"How do we know about her husband, James Burleigh?"

"From a few torn pages from Anne's diary and some letters that survived in the box that was handed down with that sword and eventually sat in your grandmother's attic. Anne returned to her father in Charleston, had an arranged marriage to James Burleigh, and lived to be a wealthy respectable mother of eight."

"Paddy, you can't make this stuff up."

He put his hands over his eyes, slid them down his face and tugged his beard. "I had a devil of a time connecting Anne Bonny to New England families, but I did it. Joseph Burleigh was born only a few miles from here, in Ipswich, where his ancestors from England first settled."

"Ah-hah."

Paddy freed a broken boogie board partly buried on the beach. "Your dad saved my life here. We got to catch the waves with air mattresses on this beach with some rich kids here on vacation. I got too far out on a riptide, and the damned thing deflated. Your dad was four years older, and a strong swimmer. You know, he never said a word about it."

"Neither did you, until now." Shannon tossed driftwood aside and wiped her hands on her jeans.

Paddy continued. "Seven years ago, I gave up this family history project—too many dead ends. Then, I tried internet ancestry sites to fill the gaps. I found out that Burley is an early English family name with over twenty coats-of-arms for branches of the name. In record-keeping over the centuries, family members and clerks often spelled things phonetically."

"So, we could be related to people with the same pronunciation of a name but spelled differently?"

"Right," he said. "Giles Burleigh came from England to Ipswich, Massachusetts, around 1648, became a commoner in the town in 1664, and then was a planter for eight years on Great Hill on Hogg Island. His name was also spelled Burley in the Ipswich records. His wife Elizabeth's name was given to many daughters of their descent."

"What do we know about them?"

"Giles and Elizabeth had several prosperous sons that married into prominent early families of Cape Ann. Their grandson, Joseph James

Burleigh, born in 1705, became Anne Bonny's husband."

"That's a lot of investigating."

Paddy nodded. "This is where it gets interesting. Burleigh used James as his first name when he to moved to Charleston, South Carolina, as a young merchant with wealthy ties in New England. He met Anne's father, William Cormac, for a business transaction. With financial incentives, Cormac encouraged James to court and marry his daughter, the former pirate Anne Bonny, who was seven years his senior. They were married in 1724."

Shannon laughed, "She was an eighteenth-century cougar. And Hollywood thought they were on to something."

"After her pirate career, it appears that Anne ran a colonial smuggling enterprise in Charleston with her husband and their sons and daughters. Trade connections between the colonies were as important as the triangle trades they had going with other countries. Family relationships and personal networks between landowners, merchants, and governors were valuable and Anne knew how to capitalize on it."

"Way ahead of her time," Shannon said.

"Even more, she became a shrewd trader, merchant, and financially supported the American Revolution. She anticipated changes to come, urged her adult children to take their families north to rejoin relatives in Ipswich, Essex, Gloucester, and New Hampshire towns. She wanted them safe and to play a stealthy role in resistance to British rule."

"A rebel to the end. Tell me more."

"The Burleigh line intermarried with many prominent wealthy families up and down the East Coast, the most important being the Haraden family of Gloucester."

Paddy signaled for Shannon to go ahead of him on the path from the beach to her yard. "Soon you'll know about your Haraden family ancestors who were great sea captains and historymakers. Sadly, their legacy has been forgotten in Gloucester. They packed even more salt in your veins."

He looked at his watch. "Time to go. Need to head over to the bank."

ぺ

Paddy and Shannon walked Gloucester's iconic Main Street. The downtown was a daily celebration of life, its harbor lined with small family restaurants and businesses defying the large chain stores.

The Cape Ann Savings Bank had served local merchants, the fishing industry, and families since the mid-1800s. Its stately granite headquarters continued to grace Gloucester's Main Street. A senior bank officer recognized Shannon and Paddy and greeted them warmly.

"I want to transfer my two ten-by-ten safe deposit boxes to Shannon," said Paddy. "The account balance should cover the next five years. She will take it from there." The paperwork was quickly finished and the banker ushered them to a private room to review the contents.

One safe deposit box contained old letters and documents pressed in sealed plastic. The other box held an item wrapped in a purple satin cloth, and a bulging white business envelope.

Paddy handed the cloth-covered item to Shannon.

She ran her hand over the satin and untied a gold, corded rope. The satin fell back to reveal a double-edged dagger.

"Anne Bonny's dagger," he said.

She weighed it in her hand, speechless.

"This dirk was made from hand-forged carbon steel," Paddy said. "It has a sturdy cross-guard and black walnut handle."

"It's brutal," Shannon said.

The business end was about six and a half inches long. Shannon envisioned Anne using a brace of pistols, a boarding ax, the jeweled short sword, and this dagger to attack or defend herself.

"Grab the cross-guard in one hand and the steel ball at the end of the handle with the other," said Paddy. "Keep the blade away from you. Pull hard."

Shannon struggled with it twice. On the third try, it popped apart, revealing a rolled piece of vellum inside the handle.

He took a pair of exam gloves from the white envelope. "Put these on;

we don't want to contaminate anything. Be careful handling the vellum. It's durable but should be gently held by its edges."

She flattened and spread the three-by-five-inch vellum, and puzzled over the lettering.

"It seems no one discovered that hidden compartment," Paddy said. "Ten years ago, I put the knife under X-ray at a friend's veterinarian's office. The tang of the blade has a split under the wooden handle, allowing for a metal tube and press fit for the steel knob."

Shannon tried to decipher the inscription on the vellum. "Says something about *Isla de San Marco . . . Casimba . . .* on top high *Iflan . . . Eaft . . . Three chests . . .* Dated and signed by Anne Bonny. Holy mackerel!"

"I believe that there could be treasure in those chests near Caxambas Pass by Marco Island, along the Southwest Florida Gulf Coast. Bonny and Rackham took a reprieve there from pirating. Marco Island is the largest of the Ten Thousand Islands. You and I are going to follow Anne's journey, find her memoirs, and hunt for treasure."

Shannon was speechless. Paddy reassembled and wrapped the dagger, and placed it as before with the documents, mail carrier, and a new digital thumb drive in the safe deposit boxes.

"We're done here," he said. "I made digital scans of the documents and my research and they're stored on three memory sticks. One is now in this box. Here is one for you, and one for me. Let's go. We have a lot to do."

SEA ROVERS

Shannon spent the next day reviewing Paddy's research while he visited Brooks Washburn. The digital files had a nifty indexing system, and Shannon drilled into the history of their seafaring ancestors. It was clear that her uncle was hunting for more than artifacts or treasure: The quest to follow the trail of Anne Bonny and Jack Rackham's life and legend was also his keen interest.

Paddy returned at five o'clock with two bags of takeout food. Shannon was bursting with questions.

"I figured we'd talk right away," he said.

Shannon smiled. "You figured right."

She peeled open the bags of Thai food.

"You're a mind reader. Do you read hearts, too?"

Paddy smiled. "If only I could. Where do you want to start?"

"Where and when are we going?"

"The general plan is to start in South Florida, spend most of our time in the Caribbean, and learn about Anne Bonny's life in Charleston, South Carolina, and Yorktown, Virginia, where she may be buried. We can leave in three days and may be gone for three to five months."

"Awesome, but how do I pay for all this?" asked Shannon.

Paddy had a wide grin. "You don't. I want to do this with you. There's a long shot we could be splitting a fortune. But don't count on it—we don't have a treasure map and, as I mentioned, there's a lot of area to cover by Marco Island."

Shannon sat stupefied.

Paddy leaned back with the inscrutable look of a monk from a teaching order. "What do you hope for?"

"To explore places I've never been, buy my own working vessel, and live aboard."

Paddy's face beamed.

"I've got nothing to lose," she said. "More than anything, I'll learn a lot from you."

"You may not know it, but your name means 'wise.' It's from *Sionann*, the goddess of the river Shannon in Ireland, which courses through Limerick where my grandmother, Shannon Connell, lived."

Shannon smiled. "Huh, I'm more street-smart than wise. I read Anne's letters that you deciphered. She wrote them, long after her pirating days, to her granddaughter, Elizabeth."

Paddy nodded. "Anne's father was a lawyer and made sure she got educated."

"I can't wait to explore the bay near Marco Island where she and Calico Jack Rackham buried something on a Calusa Indian mound. You think it is Pirate Charles Vane's gold that Rackham confiscated?"

"Yes. What else grabbed you?"

Shannon looked at her notes and recounted what she learned.

"Nassau in the Bahamas was called New Providence when it became a pirate haven after a returning Spanish treasure fleet was shipwrecked in a hurricane. Most of the wrecks were along eighty miles of the Florida coast. The Spanish set up a salvage operation there, with a base camp in New Providence." She glanced up at Paddy, who nodded as he ate.

"News of the treasure wrecks brought British seamen who raided the camp and took a galleon ship loaded with recovered treasure. The Spanish took back the whole operation and finished the salvage job, but British still sifted the shallows off Florida." Shannon stopped and checked her notes.

"New Providence was the perfect spot for pirates; plenty of food, fresh water and protected harbors. It was a British colony without a governor and close to Florida wreck sites and the shipping lanes between our colonies and the Caribbean."

Shannon spoke faster, her enthusiasm bubbling. She spoke of how more than 500 pirates were there by the summer of 1717, including Blackbeard, Sam Bellamy, Charles Vane and "Calico" Jack Rackham. The British had appointed Captain Woodes Rogers to implement an anti-piracy campaign. Rogers had been their most successful privateer against the Spanish. The strategy was to offer a royal pardon to pirates because so many of them had been enticed into that life by their government as privateers and then their privateer contracts were canceled.

Paddy sat back. "What do you know about privateers?"

Shannon cleared her throat. "Like legal piracy. In those days, many governments issued letters of marque to license individuals to attack and capture vessels of a declared enemy."

"And haul them before admiralty courts for censure and sale."

She pushed her hair back. "When Charles Vane's letter of marque expired, he kept plundering Spanish treasure ships and French merchant ships. He became the pirate leader at New Providence with others that refused the pardon. Blackbeard was smart to leave the area."

Shannon stood. "Rogers's ships amassed for an attack on the harbor. Vane and his pirates took to his brigantine ship, the *Ranger*, in the night, along with a stolen vessel that they made into a fire ship. They aimed the burning ship at Rogers's manned vessels and fired broadsides. Vane and his pirates escaped unscathed."

"Bravo," said Paddy. "And then?"

Shannon picked at the remaining bits of Thai food with her fingers. "I can't believe the irony in the next part." She told of how Vane headed for the Carolinas outside of Charleston and seized inbound cargoes along the coast as far north as Long Island. Jack Rackham became his quartermaster, and when they encountered a formidable French warship, Vane refused to attack. Rackham called him a coward and the crew voted Jack the new captain of the *Ranger*. Rackham allowed Vane and sixteen of his loyal men to leave on a small sloop previously taken as a prize.

Paddy began cleaning up the kitchen as Shannon continued. Vane shipwrecked on an island, was rescued, and then was recognized and hanged, his body put on display in an iron cage in Port Royal, Jamaica, in March of 1721. Rackham faced his execution four months earlier.

"It was Anne Bonny who called Rackham a coward." Shannon slipped into the gravelly pirate's voice she often used on stage. "If you had fought like a man, Jack, you need not be hang'd like a dog."

"Anne Bonny will always be remembered for that line," Paddy said.

Shannon cleared her throat. "Here is the irony. Rackham was hanged in Port Royal and his body displayed in a gibbet in the very same spot as his old boss, Vane."

She sat down on the couch and folded her hands. "You figure from Anne's letters that Rackham secretly took Vane's personal chests of Spanish gold and silver?"

"Yes, and it makes sense, because Rackham was not a big-league pirate taking treasure ships. Without a large vessel, he was known more for fast attacks on smaller trade and fishing vessels for provisions, food, wine, rum and valuables. He left crews on their own boats."

With her eyes closed, she murmured softly, "I learned a lot today."

"Let's get some sleep, and a good start in the morning."

Shannon lay in bed with Anne Bonny's sheathed short sword next to her. She envisioned the two months after Vane's demise when Rackham returned to Jamaica, took the pardon in April 1719, and met Anne. Soon, Captain Jack would be pirating again, but this time with Anne Bonny.

Shannon dreamed about Anne Bonny with handsome Captain Jack Rackham. As the movie in her mind unfolded, the fuzziness of a dream became more vivid, and she felt transported back in time. Shannon wasn't merely dreaming about her distant relative—she was Anne, living her life, feeling her excitement, joy and anticipation, walking in her body.

It was early evening, luminous with a nearly full moon. The ship's crew drank rum aboard their vessel and worked up courage for the hard work ahead: returning to the Windward Passage to the Bahamas to plunder and evade capture.

Anne stood by Captain Jack as he spoke to the first mate. "Bonn and I are taking the jollyboat ashore to fetch fresh water for our sail at dawn." The suspense of deception heated Anne's passion.

She bluffed the resolute first mate. "I suspect tainted water sits in the large water storage casks on the ship. We must inspect."

Anne stepped down to the ship's dim hold with the first mate in tow. They tipped open the covers of four huge oak casks. "Smell this one. Turning rank," she said with authority. "Pump it out or add some spirits to freshen it before we return with fresh water. You don't want to face an angry crew with foul water on a long sail."

"Tell Jack I'll pump it," he said and hurried off.

Anne was giddy with the ploy, and entered the galley to distract imbibing crewmembers with inquiries and stories. She started a drinking game and made sure the first mate joined in the clamor.

Anne returned topside. "Have you secured the booty, Jack?"

He pointed to the bulging canvas in the rowboat.

She chuckled. "That *is* a jollyboat."

Anne passed small rope-handled wooden buckets down to Rackham on the jollyboat. The first mate returned topside to help.

"We're all set here," Anne said, handing the last bucket down to Jack, who stood between two rowing stations of the small boat.

Jack called up to the first mate, "We'll need your assistance later. Take some grog with the men."

With a glance at Anne, the first mate said, "Aye, Captain. Ring the bell on deck twice and I'll be up to help."

Jack and Anne rowed away from the main vessel to the freshwater spring in a coastal island's small inlet. Well out of sight, they evaluated where to hide the treasure.

Anne gave Jack a triumphant kiss. "Vane's treasure is ours. It won't even be missed."

"We hide the sea chests near the spring and complete our watering task," Jack said. "By then, our men will take full measure of the drink while we find the proper place to bury the booty."

Anne put her back into each row from the bow position to match Jack's strokes from the stern seat. She adjusted her oar strokes to keep them on the heading. After they crisscrossed the stretch of flat water from the spring to the ship the second time, the first mate didn't respond to the ship's bell. Jack and Anne set full water buckets onto the deck.

Jack peered down to the galley. Dim lantern light spread over the first mate fast asleep at the table along with a slumbering drunk crew.

This time they took only two empty wooden buckets to the freshwater spring and reloaded the booty on the jollyboat. Anne pointed up a narrow channel alight with moonbeams through the mangroves. They rowed a considerable distance until entering a shallow bay behind Marco Island overlooking lesser island keys. The steep mound of Marco was tall as the mainmast of a warship. Anne and Jack scrambled in a race to the top. Each step crunched on rotting leaves, twigs, and damp dirt. When they reached a flat spot, Jack sat and rolled on his back to rest. Anne straddled him and bent down to give him a kiss.

"Your kisses are extraordinary, Anne."

"So I'm told. Let's get to work."

They walked along the top of the moonlit knoll. They spied an abandoned hut and fire pit with blackened soil and ash, most likely a spot for summer fishing and oyster harvesting by migratory Indians.

Jack winced. "No good. This place is too well traveled."

Anne pointed to a nearby island and they headed back down to the water. After a short row, they hiked the rising slope of the island. They bushwhacked through thick red mangroves and buttonwood. Thorny bushes sliced Anne's hands as she hacked away at the brush with a machete. Jack was also cut as he yanked away branches by hand. They lugged each of the three sea chests to the edge of a small natural clearing at the top of the bluff.

Jack removed a jeweled short sword from one of the chests and gave it to Anne. She held it in the moonlight, quite pleased. With a small shovel, Jack buried the sea chests in the decaying shell mound. They both looked back to where they had stood on the larger Indian hill on Marco and committed to memory the orientation of the two island peaks.

"I have noted this location," Anne said. "Now we can go back to the springs for a good soak."

They splashed, hugged, and kissed under the moonlight, in agreeable warm water. Anne sniffed the mild garlic scent of the red mangroves. "I am with child, Jack."

He reached down to touch her belly and pulled her close. "We will go to Cuba where you and the baby will be safe with my friends. The hoard will secure our future."

"When the baby is strong enough," Anne said, "I will be back on the seas with you." She jumped up to wrap her legs around him in the water. They kissed and rocked with joy.

Still dreaming, Shannon left Anne's body and floated above the ecstatic lovers, feeling the sensations of the delightful coupling. She jolted awake as Anne's face morphed into that of her mother, Regina.

Shannon felt wetness between her thighs, a cut on her hand, and confusion with the image of her mother. *Too strange and real,* she thought. *Hellcats have a long reach.*

SEA CAPTAIN
LEGACY

When Shannon arose the next morning, Paddy was well on his way to Boston on the commuter rail. He left a note with an old book by the coffeemaker. She sniffed the fresh brew and smiled to see a fresh carrot cake muffin from a local bakery.

> *Godchild,*
>
> *I have business up the line. Be back for dinner. Please read the marked section of this book. You will want to visit the Peabody Essex Museum library to view the ship logs of your ancestor, Captain Jonathan Haraden, of the Massachusetts Colony armed vessel Tyrannicide in 1777, and privateer captain of the large Salem merchant ship General Pickering in 1778. The reference librarian is available before 3 p.m.*
>
> > *Paddy*

Shannon shook her head. *My uncle is here for less than two days and my life has completely changed.* She removed the protective cover from Paddy's first edition book, *The Ships and Sailors of Old Salem* by Ralph D. Paine, published in 1908. It was in surprisingly good condition, and engagingly written with firsthand sources that drew her deep into the history of local privateers during the American Revolution.

It was one thing to learn of her pirate ancestry, and quite another to learn of her family lineage of famous sea captains, privateers and patriots. With the old text in hand and some fact-checking on internet sites, she read of the massive insurgency at sea by American privateers with armed sloops and schooners. George Washington had issued letters of marque.

Privateering was a risky, honorable, patriotic and profitable enterprise to cruise for prizes of enemy merchant vessels and warships. The formidable force of American privateers weakened the British fleet's trade routes and thus its economy and resolve. The biggest concentration of Colonial privateers came from the shores of Essex County, Massachusetts, and only Massachusetts had more craft designed for deep water than for inshore work.

It was news to Shannon that while the Continental navy had fewer than a dozen ships at command in the naval battles, there were over a thousand privately owned American ships taking British prizes. Nearly 3,000 Colonial privateer vessels, carrying more than 70,000 men, were active over the course of the war compared with the Continental navy's 53 ships and 3,400 men.

She learned how the privateers of 1776 faded into history with little credit for their critical role in America's independence, yet Gloucester-born Captain Jonathan Haraden's legacy lived on with two destroyers of the United States Navy named USS *Haraden*, one in the First World War, and the other in the Second.

She searched the Peabody Essex Museum library's online archives, which confirmed Paddy's findings about the seafaring and adventurous Haraden family. Jonathan Haraden's great-grandfather, Edward, came to Ipswich, Massachusetts, from Sussex, England, and in 1657 built the first house of the period, on Planter's Neck by the Annisquam River.

Shannon's heart jumped. *My ancestors were the first European residents of the Annisquam.* Jonathan's grandfather was a ship's captain, as was his uncle, Andrew Haraden, also from Annisquam, who killed the wicked

English pirate John Phillips. Phillips had ravaged thirty-four vessels off the New England coast—four of them from Gloucester.

Shannon thought she knew Gloucester history and was stunned to read a naval tribute to a Nathaniel Haraden. *In Honor of an Intrepid Son of Gloucester, Nathaniel Haraden, Sailing Master of the U.S. Frigate Constitution, Commended for Gallantry in Action at the Siege of Tripoli, August 3, 1804.* Nathaniel was Captain Jonathan Haraden's cousin. She lingered on the word *intrepid.*

Web links led her to naval narratives about the meticulous logbooks Nathaniel kept while serving on the storied frigate *Constitution.* The logbooks provided the only firsthand accounts of what happened in the ship's important sea battles and movements. Known as "Jumping Billy" Haraden for his intense command, Nathaniel pounced about the vessel like one of the firing cannons, which were called Jumping Billys on decks. When possible, Nathaniel made adjustments in her riggings and ballast to improve speed and agility. In later years when Old Ironsides lay rotting in a navy yard, Jumping Billy Haraden restored her. He knew the ship better than any captain who sailed her, and his seamanship earned the ship's favor on the high seas. Shannon wondered how the historic contributions of Gloucester's sea captains to America were forgotten by locals, and left behind by the national consciousness.

Shannon returned to follow her ancestral descent from Captain Jonathan Haraden, to Elizabeth Burleigh, down to Shannon's grandmother, Mary Burleigh O'Connor, who had the Anne Bonny artifacts until her daughter Regina stole them. Shannon shook her head to think how her mother could do that.

Shannon notified friends and family members of her planned Caribbean sail with Uncle Paddy. She would somehow stay in touch but not in constant contact.

She paid bills, listed household instructions for Eric, changed outbound messages, stowed her boat, and secured the outdoor furniture, garden tools, and other items for winter. Once everything was in order, Shannon called her friends to invite them for a potluck dinner on Thursday night. Shannon needed a farewell with friends. She had a feeling it would be a long time before she saw them again.

At the Peabody Essex Museum library, Shannon passed through security to the reading room. She knew a bit of Salem history from volunteer work at a child development program for kids at risk and from tours she chaperoned.

The East India Marine Society, an organization of Salem captains who had sailed beyond either the Cape of Good Hope or Cape Horn, gathered natural and manmade curiosities from around the globe, and founded the museum over 200 years ago.

The reference librarian pulled material relevant to Captain Jonathan Haraden and his family. One document had a portrait of Jonathan's ruddy but serene face, with the intense eyes of a hawk. From every angle that Shannon viewed Jonathan's image, his eyes followed.

Her purse fell on the floor, smashing her reverie. She continued reading narratives by people in Haraden's time from both sides of the Atlantic. They knew him in war and peacetime, gave tributes at his burial, and wrote remembrances in letters and articles. *Captain Jonathan Haraden was an extraordinary leader with a cool temperament,* she thought as she read their tributes:

> *A most daring and skillful navigator.*
>
> *A hero among heroes.*
>
> *A most intrepid commander.*
>
> *He never rashly sought danger, nor did he shrink from duty.*
>
> *As he was intrepid, so was he modest as he was brave.*
>
> *The more imminent the peril, the more perfect was his self-command.*
>
> *He not only knew no fear himself, but he made everyone around him equally fearless.*

A chill of wonder stiffened Shannon's back. She was awestruck by the monstrous talent and achievements of Jonathan Haraden on the seas. *There is that word intrepid again*, she thought—a form of detachment she could identify with.

Shannon was keen to the approving gaze of the two library staff as she gingerly handled the materials. She sat back to reflect—no need to ask them another time if they had located the eighteenth-century ship's logs.

Moments later, the head reference librarian came through a double door from the archives holding, with special care, the large logbook kept by Captain Jonathan Haraden. She set the pages, bound with covers of tightly woven burlap, on the library table next to Shannon.

The handwritten title read *General Pickering*. Each parchment was eighteen inches tall by twelve inches wide with neat lines and well-constructed letters of India ink.

Jonathan Haraden wrote with a strong hand and fine control in short, eloquent phrases. The pages were two-sided without error or smudge. *How can a captain in times of battle take such vivid notes with such composure?*

She closed her eyes as she held the logbook. *When I hold Anne Bonny's sword, I am fierce, reckless, and bold. I am alive. Captain Jonathan Haraden's logbook turns me cool, and in control. These are not mere legends. For once, I am proud of my heritage and my crazy battling temperaments.*

At the Peabody Essex Museum store, she learned that Jonathan Haraden's grave was only a few blocks away at Broad Street Cemetery. With a Salem visitor's map, Shannon walked out to a sunny, pleasant afternoon and hustled to the old graveyard.

She pushed open a spiked iron gate to a grassy dome of thin slate and granite monuments. Stillness embraced her. The din of the city center vanished. Her breath and heart slowed to easy calm.

Jonathan's grave stood in the southeast corner of the iron-gated square of old flat tombstones with humped heads and shoulders aligned in straight rows at their bases. Shannon noticed how they leaned back, forward and to the sides in odd ways, like a pantomime of a laughing crowd.

She also thought it a humble place for a great hero. She ran her fingers over the worn lettering, *Jonathan Haraden B. November 11, 1744, D. November 23, 1803 age 59. 'A distinguished naval commander in the war with Great Britain.'*

Shannon sat by the stone with closed eyes, with flowing supernal energy. *You are part of me, Jonathan. Your memory and honor will carry on.*

A GOLDEN DRAGON

Thursday was Shannon and Paddy's last day in Gloucester and a visit with Brooks Washburn was in order. Washburn's house in East Gloucester eyed a fabulous view of crashing surf on Bass Rocks along the backshore, and the twin lighthouses of Thacher Island. Washburn greeted Shannon with a gentle bear hug. The spry senior of eighty-two kept a strict regimen. The shelves in his library were neatly stacked with maritime and Gloucester history books. Shannon noted his desk was the only station of disorder, for he was a writer who chronicled stories of the Gloucester fishing industry and its harvest of the sea.

Washburn brewed jasmine tea for himself and Shannon. Paddy took a cup of black coffee. Settling into his wingback chair, Washburn looked at his guests, who took seats on the couch.

"So, what's this Caribbean sail all about?"

Paddy took the lead. "Shannon always wanted a sailing adventure, and this is a good time for us to follow the trade winds. She's the one who took care of my brother and everyone else I left behind. As her godfather, I owe her." He shrugged. "Besides, we both have time on our hands. She will find out what it takes to be an able seaman."

"I never thought you owed me anything," said Shannon. "But I'll be grateful for the experience and your training."

Paddy nodded to Washburn, who pressed a question to Shannon. "What do you think it takes to be a good captain beyond coastal waters? Not just a skipper of a fishing boat. I am talking blue water, deep water, without sight of land for days."

Shannon stared at Washburn, the ex-Marine, and then at her uncle, the decorated ex-Navy Vietnam veteran and sailor who circumnavigated the globe. They were stone-faced. *This is a test.*

She recalled an acronym for teaching life skills to disadvantaged kids in an after-school program. Ideas flowed into a structure of knowledge, attitudes, skills, and habits—KASH. Shannon brightened.

"First, a captain must know how to navigate, read the weather; know the vessel, its condition and its systems, to calculate loads, stress and capacity—safety measures."

Paddy and Washburn leaned in.

Shannon took a deep breath and continued. "The captain needs to ensure proper provisioning, repairs, and troubleshoot problems. And have skills in electronics and the medical training of an EMT." Feeling more confident, her thoughts rolled out. "They need to stay on top of local and international laws—"

"That is all very important, Shannon, but that's it?" Washburn asked.

Shannon sat mum.

He waited before speaking. "Shannon, the captain of a ship has the rare kind of total authority that still exists in the world where life-and-death decisions must be made in seconds. How does a captain meet that responsibility?" Washburn sat back.

Shannon looked at Paddy, who wore a poker face. A pothole of self-doubt welled up inside her, spiced with regret for her lack of formal education. She let her thoughts run . . . *met plenty of people with fancy degrees, big houses, piles of debt, and miserable lives. I got common sense, and no one killed my desire to learn.* She looked up to face Washburn. "Please clarify."

Washburn asked, "What about leadership?"

Is this a rope or a noose? Shannon wondered, as her heart pounded and palms sweated onto the wooden arms of her chair. The commanding image of Captain Jonathan Haraden came to mind and then answers came freely as if he were speaking to her.

Shannon folded her hands on her lap and sat back. "Leadership and know-how are different things. Leadership demands respect both ways. A captain must set the example, be willing to do whatever he asks of the crew, and empower them to do their best; a captain must demonstrate courage, stay cool under pressure and take calculated risks."

"What else?" Washburn pressed.

"A captain maintains discipline, resolves conflict, keeps accurate logbooks and records."

"How exactly does a captain select a crew? Do you think he or she should hire their buddies?"

"I'll have to think more on that."

"Do you have what it takes? And will you do what it takes?"

Shannon surveyed their serious faces. "I have the fortitude, but only experience will test what I'm capable of."

Washburn exchanged a smile with Paddy, and they peered back at her.

Shannon cocked her head. "Do you think a sense of humor could be a good asset?"

Paddy and Washburn both laughed and stood. Paddy shook her hand vigorously and patted her on the back. "We're totally busted. You're not just going on a vacation; I'll show you the ropes to get your captain's license." He turned to his friend with a smile. "Thanks, Washburn."

"I'll have better answers next time," she muttered.

"You did well, Shannon, with top-of-the-class answers. I needed to understand your thinking and just how much you want it."

Washburn added, "You have to stay a little afraid out in the deep and never ever get complacent."

"I will always remember that," Shannon replied.

That evening, Shannon made a large haddock stew for the farewell potluck dinner with Paddy and friends. Marcy, Gael, and Allegra arrived just after six with their savory contributions: calamari ready to bake, fishcakes ready to heat, a fruit and cheese platter with dates and olives ready to nibble, a gorgonzola salad with mixed greens and roasted pecans, and a freshly baked carrot cake. It seemed everyone brought white wine. In minutes, they had set up a buffet, put on some music and set a long table. Paddy sat at one end and Shannon the other.

She held up her glass, toasted everyone and announced that on their trip Paddy would help her qualify for her captain's six-pack license with a sailing endorsement to operate and charter power or sail craft and later upgrade to a 100-ton license.

"Maybe I'll finally make some real money, doing something I love. Got a lot to learn, and my uncle will be a tough taskmaster. More wine, please."

Gael held up a green gift-wrapped box. "Not yet. We have something for you."

Inside was a set of large Galway Irish crystal friendship wine goblets. Shannon set them out with a big smile and Gael filled them to the brim with white wine.

Shannon considered her words as they all held the crystal orbs. "You all know damned well that the hardest part for me on this voyage will be to take direction." They all nodded, guffawed, and drank.

Allegra said, "Good luck on that, Paddy."

Gael asked, "What kind of vessel do you have?"

"A motor-sailer of sorts," Paddy said. "Seaworthy enough to get me around for the past few years. I hope Shannon won't be disappointed."

After dinner, Paddy suggested they play poker. Shannon excused herself and insisted on cleaning up. After a few rounds with poker chips and plenty of wine, Paddy put forth a challenge to Allegra, Gael, and Marcy.

"You ladies like cards. I propose we play blackjack. I will put up a hundred dollars a round."

They hesitated.

"You decide; we don't have to play for money," Paddy said.

"I have an idea," said Gael, who summoned Allegra and Marcy to another room. They returned after some hushed debate.

Allegra spoke for them. "We're all grownups here. Marcy, Gael and I will play blackjack with you for bucks and skins."

"Never heard of it," said Paddy, "and I've played a lot of cards."

"We just made it up. Think of it as a classy version of strip poker," said Gael. "You put up the bucks and if we lose, we show our upper body art."

Allegra continued. "For a hundred of your dollars a round, we're in."

Paddy hesitated and glanced over to Shannon.

Allegra stuck both of her arms out wide, pranced and spun slowly, articulating the artistry of ink images from her hands to short sleeves.

Paddy asked Shannon, "You okay with this?"

From the kitchen, Shannon answered. "Yeah, and I'll put a fire on to get the temperature up in here a bit. Someone may need it."

Allegra snapped back to Shannon, "Don't give us the 'Now that he has our price, he knows what we are' speech."

Gael snorted. "Everyone is a whore. I would have done it for less. Way to go, Allegra. I'll go first."

Marcy spoke up. "I breast-fed my kids in restaurants. I would have done it for fifty, and have lap danced for less. Who cares? I plan on winning."

"You lap danced down there in Saugus?" asked Allegra.

"I had a life and a figure before I was a mother."

Paddy held up his wine glass. "For the sake of art, let's play. To art and discretion." He pushed away the dinner plates and poker chips, shuffled the card deck and laid out three crisp hundred-dollar bills.

"I'll play the house against each of you individually and be the dealer, with the deck shuffled at the beginning of each round. The hands will go quickly." He looked at each woman and cemented the game rules. "When any of you win, you may elect to stay in and double down for an extra round on your next turn until the pot is exhausted. We will settle it all when the rounds are completed."

"At the end of the game," said Allegra.

"Yes, ladies. I wouldn't want any of you to feel a chill for too long while we play."

Shannon finished stacking paper, fatwood, and split wood in the raised hearth and struck a long match. She sat on a stool by the fireplace. "I think you should all follow our house tradition for playing cards and select a hat from the trunk in my room."

They went, and a few moments later, Marcy, Gael, and Allegra came out of Shannon's bedroom wearing a jester's cap, a top hat, and a fedora, respectively. Gael had a red boa and two scarves over her arm and with the other placed a brown Stetson hat with a black band on Paddy's head. She draped the boa over her own shoulders, did a shimmy, and then handed a purple scarf to Allegra and a green one to Marcy.

Shannon brought out two more boas for Allegra and Marcy.

The fire began to crackle as the players watched Paddy shuffle the deck. Shannon pulled up a chair behind the players. Paddy dealt out the rounds. Marcy had blackjack on the third round but Paddy won the last hand with a pair of kings.

"It's time for an art show," he said.

Gael, Marcy, and Allegra went to Shannon's bedroom and reappeared with Gael in the lead and their hats tipped forward. Draped over necks and upper bodies, their large colored scarves and boas flowed as the women sauntered around Paddy at the table.

Paddy donned his glasses and rose to pace with his hands behind his back like a captain of an old sailing ship. He inspected the dark Celtic and colorful Irish designs on Gael's neck, upper arms and down to the tramp stamp on the small of her back.

"Finely crafted," he said. "I like the rising claddagh and the ropework designs. Ahh . . . a highlander's cross, the butterfly of renewal, and the wings of freedom on your shoulders—a tribute to all good things Irish."

Marcy and Allegra had listened intently as they followed Paddy's tour around Gael's lovely torso. The conga line shifted as Marcy struck a pose.

"None of you have seen my body art," Marcy said.

Paddy faced Marcy and considered the powerful large-boned woman with radiant skin. Above the left and right of her full breasts were roses, wildflowers and songbirds. A triangle design on her right upper arm sported the words *Mind, Body, and Spirit* with lightning bolts emanating from the center. On her left upper arm was the Trinacria, the ancient symbol of Sicily with three bent human legs and a Medusa head in the center. She slipped off the green scarf that covered her upper back and the room went silent.

"You always cover with baggy clothes, even on the beach," said Allegra. "Why hide such a beautiful bod?"

Paddy circled Marcy. "My goodness, you are the living Artemis, Apollo's twin sister, Diana, goddess of the hunt with her bow, a wilderness with wild animals—the symbol of female fertility and the moon. This is classy and represents your power, Marcella."

Marcy basked in his approval. "But, unlike Diana, I'm no longer a sworn virgin or fierce protector of young girls since I bore only sons."

"You brought up your boys to be fine young men," said Gael.

Everyone now focused on Allegra, who flipped off her boa and purple scarf, revealing the body of a lean Olympian. Modesty was not one of Allegra's faults and her lack of inhibition ranked high among her virtues. She danced and pranced.

"As you can see, I'm still unexplored territory . . . just a few sea horses, three angels, a sea serpent, a sexy mermaid, and an energetic young Neptune."

"Playful and nicely rendered," Paddy said. "You also have a special start on your upper back with this eagle. That is my favorite symbol of power and freedom."

"Mr. Clarke, do you consider the wager complete, and all bets cleared?" Shannon asked. She held her gut, which ached due to laughing under her breath from the sidelines.

"I do indeed, and admire you all for your taste in art," Paddy said.

Shannon handed the blouses and shirts to her three pals.

Now they stood, dressed as before, with hats still in place.

"There is, however, one part of the deal we didn't tell you, Mr. Clarke," said Allegra as she touched the anchor tattoo on Paddy's upper right arm. "Remove your shirt or we rip it off with gusto."

Before he could respond, three women and six hands held the bottom of his T-shirt.

"Okay, okay. Let me take it off," he said.

What happened next was entirely unexpected. Paddy stood next to a floor lamp, clicked it to the highest wattage, removed the shade and slowly removed his shirt.

The women were slack-jawed.

Paddy's muscled torso, inked as a parchment vest, depicted a sixteenth-century world map with fragments of the Mediterranean; Atlantic coasts of the Old and New World; the Caribbean, South China Seas, and the Pacific islands.

A fierce golden dragon sat on his right shoulder; a compass rose and a navigation star sat above the seascape. Sea serpents attacked square-rigged ships. Sharks and whales menaced other vessels. Watercraft anachronisms from three and a half millennia sailed strategically on the map—a Phoenician ship, a Roman galley in the Mediterranean, Viking ships off the coast of Newfoundland, dugout canoes and Indians in the seaways and along the coast of Maine and a Spanish galleon by the south coast of Florida.

Shannon joined the inspection and traced her index finger to the *Mayflower* anchored off Cape Cod, Chinese junks off China, a US destroyer by the coast of Vietnam in the South China Sea, and an American aircraft carrier by Hawaii.

"What does the golden dragon signify?" asked Gael.

"I know," Marcy said. "A sailor who has crossed the international date line."

Paddy stood like a statue with the four awestruck women around him. "Nothing to say, ladies?"

Shannon whooped and hugged her uncle.

Gael, Allegra and Marcy held their glasses high. Marcy gave the toast. "Bon voyage to the gentleman adventurer and his first mate."

LUCID

A t Boston Logan Airport, Shannon and Paddy boarded the first nonstop flight to Miami and sat comfortably in first-class seats. It was a remarkably empty flight for a Friday.

"This is classy," said Shannon.

"We can talk freely here," Paddy said. "That was a fun party last night. Your pals are good sports. I thought to give them each a gift after the card game, but when they ripped off my shirt, compensation didn't seem in order."

"You left them inspired and appreciated. I know so little about you. Is your tattoo of the US destroyer the one you were on?"

"Yes. From not long after I joined the Navy in 1959."

He told of how he was assigned to the USS *Edson*, a new Forrest-Sherman-class destroyer built at Bath Iron Works in Maine. That ship became known as "the Grey Ghost of the Vietnamese Coast." President Johnson wrongly claimed that the North Vietnamese had attacked American destroyers in the Tonkin Gulf, which led to open war with the North Vietnamese, and escalation of the war. In 1964, the *Edson* was recognized for meritorious service. She was shelled by Vietnam land forces and friendly fire from US Air Force jets.

"Holy mackerel," said Shannon.

"I was trained as a systems engineer to ensure performance to fend off attacks in many engagements. After experiencing that, you realize it is pointless to worry about stuff unless you're in a life-or-death situation." He gave Shannon a wry smile. "The Navy was good to me. I learned a lot and made lifelong friendships."

"What made you leave the Navy?"

"I became chief petty officer after twelve years. I had enjoyed leading work groups as a hands-on type. As CPO for a couple years, the extra money and perks were nice but didn't like the job."

"Why not?"

"When you finally get in the goat locker and deal with all the departments and the brass, it becomes a management job."

"Goat locker?"

"Sorry, that's a Navy term for the chief's mess. Most CPOs are 'old goats,' as the oldest aboard a Navy ship. I was a young chief and not interested in being a career Navy man."

"I'm glad you didn't turn into an old goat."

"Actually, the term comes from the old sailing era before refrigeration, with livestock on ships providing crew with fresh milk and eggs. To keep the supply of milk safe, they kept the goat in the chief petty officer's quarters. Anyway, I think all management jobs involve goat shit in some way or another."

"So you gave up a promising officer's career to do what?"

"A friend got me into the US Merchant Marines. The money was better, and it was less regimented with more shore leave. I had time to pursue other interests."

Shannon sipped her coffee. "What was that like?"

"For the fifteen years I was in the merchant service, it was a Cold War, peacetime operation. I liked the electronics and navigation part. We did milk runs to the Caribbean and back. It was a dream job, getting paid to be on a light crew in warm waters, delivering cargoes, with time to read, study, gamble, explore different ports, and stay in shape."

"Milk runs?"

"Short-haul trips loaded with fuel trucks or cargo from the East Coast to Puerto Rico, Jamaica, other Caribbean ports and back."

"I could get used to a job like that. What then?"

"After an unpopular war and seeing the economic impact of our policies in the Caribbean and politics in general, I was ready to move on as an independent businessman, investor, and collector of naval antiquities."

"And vagabond sailor," said Shannon. "Did you have a plan for all that?"

"I was about your age. My plan was to find compelling new things, focus in, and catch a second wind. Midlife is a fabulous time to embrace new challenges."

"I always liked the expression 'second wind.' I used to run road races and swim-race point-to-point off our beaches, coves, and harbors. Just when you are beat, that extra kick comes. I think it's a physiological thing."

Paddy rubbed his beard. "Some say metabolic switching. Others say early release of endorphins, or just mind over matter. It's a good metaphor for life."

"How so?"

"After years of reading and contemplation, I concluded the meaning of life is about living, loving and learning. I call it the three *Ls*. Or you get rootbound."

"I like your way of looking at things," said Shannon. "For me, I like to live in the present. What I don't do much is plan ahead."

"Planning ahead is good to a point, but it can be self-limiting."

Shannon jerked her head back. "Go ahead."

"I'm a planner, but I had to learn to stay flexible for opportunities. In my fifties, I found that pace and intensity diverge. You can still have high intensity at a slower pace. It becomes more important to plan how to invest your energy, and sharp goals bring focus."

"That's a lot to think about. My goal is to get my captain's license."

"It's nice to be able to adapt to change, Shannon, but if you don't have a plan, you become part of someone else's plan."

"Yeah, be captain of my own life."

Paddy squeezed Shannon's hand. "I couldn't have said it better."

They opted for an egg breakfast, accepted the complimentary glass of champagne, read magazines and watched the news.

The pilot announced that the weather in Miami was a sunny 84 degrees with light winds and the flight was ahead of schedule. To Shannon, it seemed they had just taken off.

She tugged Paddy's sleeve. "I have a strange question to ask."

"Shoot."

"Since you told me about my ancestors, I've had vivid dreams and daydreams about Anne Bonny with Calico Jack Rackham, and about Captain Jonathan Haraden. Not like my nightmares or surreal dreams over the years. It's like my ancestors are wrestling inside me—like I am actually there—and when I wake up, can't tell if it was a dream or a real event just happened."

"That's understandable, given the new information you've heard about your family tree during the past four days."

"No . . . this is like Anne, Jack, and Jonathan are talking with me. I feel and experience them and what they've done in the past."

"That's a description of a vivid dream—so real you can't distinguish it as a dream. Would you call your dream lucid?"

"What's the difference?"

"Have you been able to interact with the characters in your dreams or impact the action?"

"Definitely."

"Lucidity is when you gain insight with increasing awareness of your dream, especially when you take some control over it. Researchers say it relates to rapid eye movements and false awakenings."

"Wow. I'd like to learn more."

Paddy raised his eyebrows with a mischievous smile. "Tibetan Buddhists practiced dream yoga back in the eighth century and learned to take control over terrifying dreams and extend pleasant ones."

"How do you know about this?"

"Curiosity and lots of reading. I tried dream yoga and failed. I was never a good sleeper; don't often remember my dreams, and wish I could."

"I don't sleep well either, but I dream plenty, and some of these dreams go way back," she said, and twirled a circle with her index finger by her temple. "I'm a nutty cuckoo bird with ancestors in my head and coursing through my blood."

Paddy laughed. "Life is full of mysteries. Our understanding of the unconscious is so limited."

"How so?" said Shannon.

"The universe is about energy, matter and information. The given purpose of genes is to gather, store, and transmit information. I believe you are experiencing ancestral memory served up from unconscious and semi-conscious states."

"How can that be possible?" asked Shannon.

"There are trillions of events in the brain every second. Ancestral experiences may resonate in our neural networks, affect our temperaments, and inform our choices."

Shannon perked up. "I like the word *inform* rather than *determine* our choices."

"Why would we not have sense memories or personas from ancestors available to us? That is certainly not the absurd channeling of ghosts or spirits."

"Whoa," Shannon said. "So I'm not going nuts, and can engage the past as a lucid dreamer."

"I believe it," Paddy said. "You have nothing to worry about."

Shannon leaned back. "Hey, if Native Americans smoked peace pipes and communed with their ancestors in altered states, then tapping our brains naturally can't be too dangerous."

Shannon and Paddy collected their bags and took a cab to Miami Marina, a deepwater port strewn with large boats, a marketplace and loads of tourists. Nearby, the Bayside Marketplace of international shops, restaurants and cafes and the American Airlines Arena hugged the boat basin like a gateway to Miami's commercial center, luxury high-rise residences and offices.

Shannon scanned the bay. "What a beautiful place to sail. Everything you need within walking distance of the dock. But so many idle boats and yachts."

"What do you say we enjoy a couple days of luxury before our voyage?" said Paddy.

"I can't wait to get on the water."

"Of course, but keep in mind, when we're on board with crew, you call me Captain Patrick, or Captain Clarke."

She smiled, "Aye, Captain, where is the vessel, sir?"

Paddy pointed forty yards to the right. "There, nestled with the large yachts."

"Wow, a small tall ship." Shannon ran halfway down the dock toward a square-rigged ship with reefed sails but stopped short. A cocoa-skinned woman in a white pantsuit stood on its deck. *This must be a mistake*, she thought.

Paddy strolled past Shannon with the driver and full cart of luggage to the dark-hulled 1700s-period sailing ship with a broad white stripe between its wales, at rest among sleek white fiberglass yachts. He boarded, turned and motioned for Shannon to follow. She froze when Paddy and the young woman embraced.

This woman is impossibly beautiful, thought Shannon, admiring the long black hair, heart-shaped face, large brown eyes, and pearly white teeth. *Not much older than my daughter.* She approached with a welcoming hand.

"Hi, Shannon! I'm Daniella Clarke, Paddy's daughter from Jamaica. I've wanted to meet you for a very long time. Has Paddy been messing with your mind?" Daniella took Shannon's hand. "Welcome aboard the *Second Wind*. White wine or rum?"

"Definitely rum, thanks," Shannon gazed over the vessel to take it all in.

"First cousins we are," said Daniella, serving Shannon a tumbler of clear rum, "with Irish blood and more."

"Indeed," said Shannon, but her gut tightened. *Does Daniella know about Anne Bonny or the treasure?*

"I'll show you the living quarters," Daniella said. "Later, Paddy can do the technical tour." She rolled her eyes. "That will take much longer."

Shannon smiled and started counting her steps the length of the deck. "Nearly seventy-feet long with an eighteen-foot beam," she said. "Wide enough for comfort below and sleek enough for speed with a large sail area." Turning to view the vessel from another vantage point, she sipped the rum. "The woodwork and carvings are beautiful. I can't get over how new—yet old—it looks."

They returned to the raised aft deck by a linen-set table nestled in a cushioned seating area under the Bimini top. An American flag flapped over the stern and a dinghy swayed in a tucked and winched position below. The protected exterior helm station had matching cushions on bench seats right and left.

Shannon stood between the bench seats with her hands on the ship's wheel and surveyed the foredeck, masts, yards, sheets, halyards and rigging. She smiled in a friendly stare-down with the pale yellow eyes of a large brown pelican perched on the starboard gunwale. "I'll bet you're quite a fisherman."

Paddy and the driver emerged from below deck. Paddy gave Shannon a big hug. "So special to have you and my Danny together on the *Second Wind*. I'll see the dockmaster, grab a few things, and be back in forty minutes." Shannon saw him skip down the dock and thought she heard him whistle the Popeye song.

Daniella continued, "Paddy is a maritime history buff and fascinated by naval architecture. This vessel was his pet project ten years ago; he wanted to build a replica brigantine sailing ship with the latest technology hidden away. It was his antidote for stagnation."

"I envy his energy," said Shannon.

"My mother, Jenny, thinks testosterone is not all bad," said Daniella. "I hope to have Paddy's energy when I'm seventy—"

"Two," they said simultaneously and laughed.

"Mae West had it right," said Shannon. "'It's not the men in your life . . . it's the life in your men.'"

"I knew I would like you, Shannon," said Daniella with warm eyes. "Anyway, Paddy worked with a naval architect in the States on every design detail of the *Second Wind*, and oversaw its construction in Thailand. Skilled craftsmen built it to specs at a competitive price. He's been living and sailing on the vessel for seven years."

"That's wild. I am just getting to know him. Do you see him much?"

"He stays at our family home in Jamaica about half the time now. His trips are getting shorter. Paddy has been very good to us. Jenny was a single mom who had just lost her ten-year-old boy in a hit-and-run accident when they met."

Daniella sipped her wine and went on. "Neither of them was marriage material, but they developed a deep bond. When I came along, he was still with the Merchant Marines and home several weeks at a time. He bought the house for us and kept his quarters in a guest cottage in the backyard with his gear. He would come and go, and Jenny lives every day to the fullest.

"Paddy is a great dad and we did a lot together. Now, every November, I cruise with him to Miami where I went to law school. Jenny hates boats—or, more correctly, men's obsessions with them."

Daniella motioned Shannon to the low-profile pilothouse in the aft deck. They stepped down to an internal helm station with two seats. Doors faced forward on the left and right of the helm to the outside. A companionway in the back of the pilothouse took them to a well-appointed galley saloon. Daniella waved at a large dinette attached aft of the galley and pointed up to a darkened skylight.

"That's the glass tabletop I set with linen up on deck."

"Nice layout. I like the external and internal helm setups for any kind of weather and fast access forward, back, up and down. Plenty of seating."

"It gets better," said Daniella, and ran her hand over a gimbaled four-burner range, a cold box, large sink and cabinets, and then stepped through a passageway with a large built-in freezer, washer and a dryer.

"Two bathrooms, two showers."

Shannon followed Daniella past the engine room to the captain-owner's quarters with a queen-sized bed, a finished work space and cargo area, a small stateroom, crew cabin with sleeping for four, and plenty of storage for gear. Shannon's luggage sat on one of the bunks.

"Paddy will show you the rest. What do you think?"

Shannon laid her right hand over her heart. "I'll get to know this vessel until she talks to me."

"I'll read up on deck while you settle in. Paddy suggested we do a sunset sail. He wants you to experience the *Second Wind* before you learn her anatomy. Sound good?"

"Very good. See you topside in a few."

Shannon was relieved to see her unopened FedEx package on her bunk. The quarters were suitable, with an adjoining bath, cubbies and storage spaces. She began to unpack her luggage but then stopped to sit on her bunk and reflect. *This is all happening so fast. Daniella speaks proper English—must be her university law education, but there's Jamaican music in her.*

Shannon jacked her digital music player into the onboard audio system in the galley, and selected Wagner's "Ride of the Valkyries." She raised the volume. *This piece's energy and sense of adventure is dear to me.*

She unpacked Anne Bonny's short sword and other items from the FedEx parcel. *Paddy may not approve that I brought it, but descendants of Anne Bonny do what we want.* Shannon held the sword and moved with the music of Valkyries riding into battle on flying horses. *That was a rush.*

Shannon wrapped a towel around the sword and placed it under the bunk in a compartment with her cargo shorts, cutoff jeans, underwear, and T-shirts.

Shannon did some stretches to loosen up, brushed her hair, switched off the music and rejoined Daniella under the Bimini on the aft deck.

"Nice choice. I like Wagner," Daniella said.

"Do you get a bit randy on this pirate ship, Daniella?"

"Funny you should say that," Daniella said as she gazed at a man installing new equipment on a white yacht nearby. The man waved to her with a big smile.

"I'll take that as a yes," Shannon said. "You're a lawyer?"

"My specialty is admiralty law, and I let the male partners think I'm a prude."

"So, who is the dude over there with the power drill? He looks like an actor from some Italian or Spanish movie set."

"That's Caesar, an independent marine mechanic. Been here the past three days. He delivers new and used boats to people taking ownership. Not really my type. He loves the sea. A man like that can't love just me. His free spirit is damned fetching, but I have a fella back home."

"Is the one back home a lawyer?" asked Shannon.

"Yes, real estate."

"Two lawyers? Sounds like a recipe for acrimony."

"That's what my mother would say. I'll make my own mistakes."

Daniella and Shannon shared Paddy stories and drank lemon tonic water. They stole glances at Caesar's graceful movements on the 120-foot yacht nearby—running tests and cleaning his work areas. Latin jazz swept over the water from portable speakers by his toolkit. Daniella's shoulders swayed slightly to the music.

Paddy arrived with a few grocery bundles. "Glad to see you two getting to know each other. I'll put together some snacks for our sunset sail."

Shannon watched Caesar finish his project, adjust his tool pouch and lug a toolbox toward the center of the marina with its adjoining plaza of open-air shops. Shannon knew he would have to pass by and straightened her posture. As he approached the *Second Wind*, she noted his gaze upon her.

"*Ciao, piacere!* Nice to meet you." His dark brown eyes locked on hers. "I am Caesar Rossetti."

She was speechless. *Chez'a-ray Rrro-settee* echoed in her head.

Daniella responded, "This is my cousin, Shannon."

Shannon shook his hand and looked down. "Nice tools. Oops." All three laughed.

Caesar motioned to the plaza. "Will you two join me for espresso and gelato?"

Paddy overheard the exchange and poked his head out the pilothouse. "Hello, I'm Daniella's dad; I need them back in an hour."

Daniella shook her head. "Thanks, Caesar, I'll stay. Shannon, please bring me back a lemon gelato."

Paddy sat next to Daniella. "I'd like one too, Shannon. Danny and I will set the sails."

Shannon thought how cool it was that Paddy called his daughter "Danny."

Shannon and Caesar walked together toward the plaza shops. Forty minutes later, after a shot of espresso, a crème gelato and an eyeful of Mediterranean man, Shannon returned to *Second Wind* with lemon treats. Daniella peered at her from the bow, her eyebrow raised, smiling crookedly.

Shannon raised a gelato cup. "Caesar interviewed me like I was a candidate for an award dinner. Then he wanted to know everything about fishing off Gloucester, lobstering and the tuna catch. We joked around some. Then, *wham*, says I'm his type and his type is hard to find."

"What did you say?" Daniella asked.

"I told him I might be hard to find but harder to take. Do you really think he's after a woman seven or so years older?"

Daniella laughed. "I can see how he may find you beguiling."

Shannon came aboard and handed over the gelato cups. Paddy cleared his throat. "The pretty sailor man ruffles your feathers, too?"

Shannon turned to Paddy and saw the *gotcha* look on his face.

"Now I have two crew members to tease," he said.

As planned, they cast off by five o'clock to cruise Biscayne Bay into a typical northeasterly breeze with good weather. They motor-sailed south past rows of millionaire homes, skirted along Miami's South Beach and out to open waters of the thirty-five-mile-wide lagoon.

Shannon and Daniella stood on the port side under the reefed and pivoted square-rigged sail of the foremast to enjoy the misty spray and rhythmic pull of sailing closer to the wind as they tacked east.

The *Second Wind* nicely damped the roll and breathed into her sheets:

gaff mainsail and topsail aft; mainstay with a large fisherman topsail; square foretop sail, royal up high on the foremast; inner and outer jibs forward; her large square-sail reefed and angled.

Several boaters hailed the *Second Wind* as it glided past. Shannon and Daniella waved in return. A rare, classic Chris Craft fiberglass and wood-trimmed twenty-three-foot Commander Lancer sped smoothly alongside. A stately man with a white linen shirt and senatorial hair stood at the helm. His white West Highland terrier stood fast in the passenger seat with front paws on the gunwale. The man patted his show dog, smiled at Daniella and Shannon, ran his hand through his own white mane, and held his hand on his heart.

With one hand on the Lancer's steering wheel, he casually took a camera out of his shirt pocket and snapped a few pictures of the women. Shannon thought him extremely attractive and reflexively blew him a kiss. She wondered what her free reaction meant. *Does it matter? I feel so alive.* With a smile and a low bow, the man waved, patted his pup, and sped away.

A pod of dolphins escorted the *Second Wind* past a cruise ship at anchor, loaded with noisy passengers at happy hour facing bright western skies over Miami. Paddy headed the *Second Wind* to nearby Key Biscayne, the southernmost part of the Atlantic barrier islands, and by the northernmost extent of the Florida Keys at Elliott Key. Paddy navigated slowly along the shallows and sea grasses of the bay side of Key Biscayne.

Pleasant memories without words formed as the Miami skyline shrunk slightly in the west. Shannon hugged Daniella next to her with one arm. The Cape Florida Beach lighthouse on the southern tip of Key Biscayne came into view as they cruised for twenty minutes. The historic ninety-five-foot lighthouse loomed large and Paddy piloted the *Second Wind* about the southern tip of the key toward the one-and-a-half-mile ocean-facing beach at Cape Florida State Park, considered one of the finest beaches of Florida.

Paddy nodded to Shannon to help set the anchor. He went below and returned to pop two beach-size towels on the bench chairs by the exterior helm. He lowered a rope ladder and dropped two flotation lounge chairs onto the water. Only two chairs were necessary. Daniella did not swim in deep water.

Shannon and Paddy splashed and swam in the warm water along the waterline of the brigantine. Paddy got into one of the floating loungers and Shannon backstroked to join him on the other.

Way better than the freeze we left in Gloucester this morning, she thought.

By the time Shannon and Paddy toweled off on deck, Daniella had set out Paddy's finger food plates and uncorked a bottle of brut champagne. As they ate, there was no need for words. With plenty of daylight left, they weighed anchor and sailed twelve miles south to view Boca Chita Key with its iconic and picturesque lighthouse, built as an ornament by a private owner.

Paddy piloted northeast for ten miles, tacked westerly for Miami and slowed the *Second Wind.* He gestured to Shannon to take the helm for the first time. She put her hands on the ship's wheel and widened her stance and her smile. He lowered and righted the large square sail on the foremast. The Dacron lungs of the *Second Wind* filled with the northeasterly winds. Paddy motioned to Shannon with a single slash gesture under his neck with his hand and she cut power to the engine. *Only sail, spray, rudder and wind now,* she thought, and held her arms out to embrace the world.

The sun lowered above the Miami skyline with its sparkling buildings, boats, bridges, waterways, and lights. The sunset did not disappoint, with changing hues of pink, purple, red, orange and yellow. Stars emerged and sprouted over Miami skies, reminding Shannon that new worlds form as others age and collapse.

Three days ago, Paddy said we would be sea dogs in a world of possibilities. My life is fresh and new. The Second Wind *will be familiar as my best friend, the ocean. That's why Mediterranean Man knows I'm his type.*

THE NOVICE

The next morning, Paddy, Shannon, and Daniella gathered for a full breakfast in the comfortable dinette below deck. Shannon had slept soundly with sea air flowing into her quarters.

Shannon prepared a Gloucester breakfast favorite known as a "dory scramble," with sausage, bell pepper, egg and home fries. She set out a bottle of her favorite hot sauce from home. Paddy made toast and coffee, and Daniella prepared fresh fruit cups.

It was Saturday, but Paddy was all business. Several manuals and a three-ring binder with a dramatic cover picture of the *Second Wind* lay on the table.

Clearly, this is a breakfast meeting, and the man has a plan, Shannon thought. Daniella sat back, quietly amused with her father in Captain Daddy mode.

On a nautical chart, Paddy previewed their trip, with stops in the Bahamas, a sail around the east end of Cuba, and on to Kingston, Jamaica.

Shannon focused on his every word.

"In the morning, Shannon, we set sail for Key West, arrive at Conch Harbor Marina by late noon Tuesday. Friday morning, we'll assess the weather, and head back up the keys to Miami."

Shannon studied the chart. "I've never been to Key West. Awesome, but why not go straight to the Bahamas, then Jamaica? It's shorter."

"Great question," he said. "This way you get your first watch on an overnight sail, close to land. Official hurricane season lasts until the end of November. Hurricane Sandy seems the last of it, and we'll find our weather opening from Miami."

"Especially with a trainee," Shannon said.

"Your coastal boating and offshore fishing experience makes you an advanced beginner for blue water sailing. By the time we get to Jamaica and back, you'll have your sea legs." Paddy looked at Daniella. "My fair-weather-cruising lawyer daughter is still game to share technique."

Daniella nodded. "I peaked at the third-level: competent."

"What levels?" asked Shannon.

"Father adapted the five-level Dreyfus model for skill acquisition, used initially by the US Air Force for training pilots: novice, advanced beginner, competent, proficient, and expert."

"Danny, this time I'll be a more patient teacher," Paddy said.

"She can handle it."

Paddy cleared his throat. "I want Shannon to enjoy the Bahamas and the best cruising grounds of the Caribbean under the best conditions. Along the way, we will determine how much beating into the easterlies we want to do. She will learn the ropes at a pace that builds confidence."

"Don't baby me," Shannon huffed.

Daniella leaned over and kissed Shannon on the cheek. "I'm happy for the two of you. I am no seafarer."

Paddy folded his arms and sat back with a grin. "Daniella takes her bounty on land, fighting sea battles of justice in admiralty courts."

Daniella pulled earbuds from her pocket and tapped her mobile phone. "I do love to crew with my dad and now you. Heavens, I sound like Dr. Seuss. Anyway, I'm taking a walkabout in town—beach and waterfront."

"What are you going to listen to?" Shannon asked.

"A women's reggae band, and some dancehall music. See you both by three."

Paddy smiled at Daniella, opened his arms, and puckered his lips.

"Too grown up to kiss Daddy?"

She gave him a hug and kissed his cheek. He gave her a gentle pat on the back on her way out. "Be careful, Danny."

Paddy sat back down and gulped the rest of his coffee. "The path to master mariner is steep. My approach is immersion more than training. At best, we educate humans and train animals. Expect targeted instruction with specific readings. You will shadow and model my methods but mostly do what's necessary to become a talent on board."

Paddy drummed the table with his fingers before he spoke. "You will keep a journal, follow my lead, ask questions, make mistakes, and not repeat them." He folded his arms on the table and leaned forward. "Any questions, mate?"

"When do we start?"

He grinned.

After tidying the kitchen and dinette, Shannon and Paddy refilled their coffee mugs and sat at a corner table in the saloon to review the three-ring binder he created for charters. It included pictures, history, news clippings, design details, technical drawings, and features of the *Second Wind* and her ports of call. She noticed a striking picture of Paddy in a fanciful pirate's outfit on the deck of the *Second Wind* with some guests.

Paddy tapped a pen on the table. "Let's start with the functional and technical details of the *Second Wind* and cover expectations for your training, with assignments to prepare for scenario planning and drills once you have attained a basic level of seamanship.

"Before we tour the vessel, we should discuss the attributes and merits of motor-sailers as seafaring vessels and liveaboards. Sailors can be snotty about them as inferior sail craft with their wide beams, small sail area and too-bulky shapes for good wind dynamics. Power boaters, on the other hand, prefer convenience and comfort you can't get with a sailboat."

"You're right," said Shannon. "Most of the time, my sailing friends back home wait for weather and sit at the dock or motor their boats close to shore with sails furled."

Paddy nodded. "Sailors and power boaters dismiss the motor-sailers as 'neither fish nor fowl.' For the past fifty years, they were mostly right, but here you have a vessel that is a champion under sail, or power, or both. In fact, the *Second Wind* is faster running with sail and power and with good fuel economy."

Paddy pointed to pictures, drawings, and bullet points in large type in the charter presentation binder. He sipped his coffee and Shannon did the same, her mind open for his words and experience.

"I had a demanding set of requirements to build this historic 1700s, smallish naval vessel in appearance and function. Lots of design and engineering challenges." He sat back with a wistful look. "It would have been a lot easier to buy a powerful sailing yacht with a spray hull, or build a full displacement vessel with a trawler hull and fishing boat heritage."

He rubbed the back of his neck. "The *Second Wind* is more—a symbol of freedom." Paddy tapped his foot on the floor with his words. "A true brigantine," he continued. "A two-masted ship most favored by Colonial traders, pirates, freebooters, privateers, and for blockade running in the 1700s up through the American Revolution. With maneuverability and plenty of room, it was an easy vessel to outfit with heavy cannons, cargoes, and fighters."

"*Second Wind* must be quite a magnet for tourists and a moneymaker for charters," Shannon said.

"Any boat worth owning should pay its way," he said.

She nodded. "For most people, a pleasure boat is a sinkhole for their budget."

"Full-time life aboard is not for everybody, or for every phase of life," he said.

"It sure looks good to me," Shannon said.

Paddy seemed pleased as he paged through the thick binder. "This contains most secrets of the *Second Wind*. I think of her under sail with the ancients' elements of life—earth, wind, fire and water."

"So that's what you meant in a voice mail before your visit. You made me curious and kept much for surprise."

"Otherwise, no surprise," he said.

She heard his foot going again on the floor—*tat-tat-tat, rat-tat-tat.* "Go on, please. The four elements."

Paddy got up and paced. "The *Second Wind* has hardwood from deep forests, glass fired from silicon, and a steel hull born from iron ore, carbon, oxygen and alloying elements fired in blast and electric arc furnaces. Her masts are made of aluminum."

He leaned against the bar by the saloon. "By the way, in descending order, oxygen, silicon, aluminum and iron are nearly 90 percent of the earth's crust." He pointed down to the engine room. "In there, a turbocharged, fire-breathing, water-cooled diesel engine and exhaust manifold."

His hands were animated as he spoke, as if painting a seascape on canvas. *Surely a family trait,* Shannon thought.

"She sits at the waterline between sea and sky," he said.

Shannon took a deep breath and thought how nice it could be if a young seafaring man spoke such love for her as a woman. "What's the difference between a brigantine and other sailing ships?" she asked.

"Let's go up top. A brigantine has raised fore and aft decks with two masts: the foremast square rigged for extra driving power and the mainmast both fore and aft rigged."

Paddy pointed down to the hull. "She has a period-specific black hull with a white stripe with natural wood trim on deck. A white hull would be better for handling the heat of the tropics, but I wanted an old-world look. The portal windows and the cooling and ventilation system diminish the extra heat generated with a black hull here. The good news is that interior condensation is not a problem for this vessel."

As they stepped around the deck, Shannon asked, "What makes the *Second Wind* so able to achieve the best combination of power and sail in any situation?"

"Glad you asked," he said. "Mostly hull design with the proper displacement, a controllable pitch propeller with the right engine and management system. Other factors for sailing dynamics and roll reduction are center of buoyancy, materials, weight, properly calculated total sail area and rig design."

Paddy pointed back at the pilothouse. "Notice the low profile for less drag." He then turned around. "The higher bow faces the weather."

He stepped to the middle of the vessel. "Here at the low waist of a brigantine, you can swing cargo or board other vessels. From here, you can see the key relationship of beam and freeboard length. I'm happy to say we achieved the optimum ratio for space, agility, and speed."

"How do you know?"

"Before you build it, it's all engineering and guesswork. Then, seven years of fine tuning in almost every condition. The *Second Wind* took five awards in regattas, not to mention several thousand dollars I won from personal bets with sailors who said she couldn't compete with them under sail alone."

"Cool. I might actually enjoy reading the manuals," said Shannon. "What about ease of handling for only two people?"

Paddy spoke faster on this topic. "She has a much more simplified sail rig than in the 1700s, and you can run her from the internal helm station with the remote control panel for the controllable pitch propeller, in varying conditions, without changing engine speed. You can also set different speed modes. Electric winches help. I forgot to mention, and this is very important, she also has a large rudder to rely less on square-rigged seamanship."

"No big crew needed. What an advantage."

Paddy continued the highlights tour at the helm with its instrumentation, navigation and communications gear and then proceeded to the engine room below. He pointed out mechanical systems, HVAC, tool cribs, safety equipment, supplies, storage lockers, hatches and cubbies, valuables, the safe, and other secret compartments.

He set out a stack of preprinted checklists for the captain's log, trip provisioning, maintenance schedules, spare parts and passenger trip guides for Shannon.

"It will be important for you to study these."

Standing by the rear companionway, Paddy went on, "Here is an important secret to keep. Only you, Daniella and I know it." He ran his fingers along a teak trim board in the wall and stopped on a short piece of trim. He motioned to Shannon to twist it counter-clockwise. An LED-lit digital keypad sat in a recess.

Paddy tapped a code. With a faint click, a panel opened revealing a Mossberg 930 semiauto shotgun, Glock .45 auto pistol, Taser, stun gun, mace, Army Ranger knife, baton, and tactical spear. He motioned for Shannon to close it and reset the trim board.

"Wow. The *Second Wind* is ready for anything," she said. She clicked the trim piece in place. "Speaking of secrets, does Daniella know about my connection to Anne Bonny or possible treasure?"

"No. She knows only the Rackham side at this point . . . a matter of timing. I completely trust Daniella, but your connection to Anne Bonny, the artifacts, and documents from your maternal side must remain confidential for your safety and hers.

"The treasure, if we do find it, was Rackham's and Bonny's. Daniella will get an inheritance. She is set, financially. I want you both safe. You will know the right time to share the story of the life of Anne Bonny. It could be years."

Paddy opened a compartment inside the pilothouse containing a mounted fire extinguisher, air horn, axe, rope, small bolt cutter, grappling hooks, pliers, and a hammer with knife-edge. With a gleam in his eye, he said, "Some common tools have interesting dual uses."

He plucked out a demolition utility wrecking bar from the bottom of the compartment and spread his grip on its handle. "This is a personal favorite, the Stanley Fat Max Fubar. Few will mess with you when you're wielding this."

Shannon drank in every word of Paddy's tutorial, which included the boat's sixty tons of displacement requiring a seven-and-a-half-foot draft from the waterline to get through most waterways, and adjusting the aluminum mainmast to clear bridges.

"Those are the key elements," he said. "The rest you'll pick up as you go along."

Shannon gathered up manuals, binder and checklists in her arms. Smiling, she said, "I have a boatload of homework here."

Back in her cabin, images of bins, lockers, tools and weapons floated in her mind. She would study the manuals over the days to come. She wanted to know more and commit details of the *Second Wind* to memory. *I must know how to operate the vessel in every possible condition.*

As Shannon organized the materials, she wondered how soon Paddy would initiate scenarios and drills for safety, bad weather, collisions, or threats. She remembered Washburn's words to "be afraid out there and never be complacent."

Shannon lay down to rest on her bunk. Then it hit her. As a performing artist, she recognized how Paddy spoke of the *Second Wind.* He was speaking in a rhythmic meter like a sea shanty, Homeric poem, or the beats in Samuel Taylor Coleridge's "Rime of the Ancient Mariner," which Shannon recalled:

> *Day after day, day after day,*
> *We stuck, nor breath nor motion;*
> *As idle as a painted ship*
> *Upon a painted ocean.*
>
> *Water, water, everywhere,*
> *And all the boards did shrink;*
> *Water, water, everywhere,*
> *Nor any drop to drink.*

Sitting up, Shannon searched her purse for a pen, fumbled it, and settled to capture Paddy's description of the brigantine and its secrets in her diary. After scribbling, filling, and ripping out nine pages, she captured the *tat-tat, tat-tat* rhythms of Paddy's foot as verse came to her. *I'm no Coleridge, but let's see where this goes with a 4-3-4-4 beat.*

Second Wind by Shannon Clarke

A Second Wind
Gusts anew
At water lined,
Sea skies of blue.

Shannon tapped her foot to the beats.

Trial, by error,
Forebears bent
Hardwood and steel
Designs well meant.

A shipwright's vow
Never fail
Embark upon
The Age of Sail.

Dark hulled, white stripe
Brigantine—
Seafaring type
So libertine.

Bolder than most;
No limit.
Sailors do boast
Cozy in it.

Art and Science
Navigate
Seas of freedom
Bounded by fate.

A ship to live
And to love
Aboard to work
The pleasure of.

Full temperament
Male, female
With mast and curve
Sweet heart of sail.

The Second Wind
Brigantine
Spread great sea wings
So libertine.

The poem released from her mind, Shannon lay back in her bunk and drifted into dreamy relaxation. She imagined six degrees of roll, pitch, and yaw of old wooden ships, with captains and crews. A chantey-man solo with sailors' chorus coordinated hard and short pulls on heavy ropes to raise a masthead or trim the sails. Capstan shanties sung to raise anchor, give joy to their work, and take drudgery from their tasks.

Ancestral images of pirates Rackham and Bonny and patriot captains Jonathan and Nathaniel Haraden smiled upon her as another verse sounded into consciousness.

Pirate, Patriot,
Captains Stand
Old Salts Return
With Second Wind.

Fully awake again, Shannon sat up and tapped on the wooden edge of her bunk with the back of her pen. A tiger yawn grew as she said the words while stretching her paws in the air. She tapped the beats and wrote:

Thank You, My Mates
Precious few
Again, Again
We Sail Anew.

SAILOR MAN

Shannon removed a yellow waterproof boater's box from the compartment where she secreted Anne Bonny's short sword. She pocketed her mobile phone, wallet, and Kershaw stainless steel assisted-opening knife. Shannon always carried a knife specific to the task, fishing or boating. The Kershaw was small and sharp, easy to clip on, hide, or slip into a pocket, and opened like lightning with one hand.

She mused how the knife was more sophisticated than the sturdy Buck she carried for protection as a sixth grader. Her mouth twisted at the memory. The school principal took the knife when he accused her of dealing drugs after school and inspected her purse. She thought him silly to lock it in his desk and tell her to sit still until he returned. After prying open his desk drawer, she took the knife and ran away from school for good. Not long after, she ran away from home. The knife was her only possession when a friend's family took her in.

Shannon secured the thin-bodied Kershaw with its stainless clip in her back right hip pocket and went topside. Paddy inspected his scuba equipment on deck next to an open locker. He nodded to Shannon and dialed his mobile phone.

"Hi, Danny. You headed back from your walkabout? Good, meet me at the marine supply store and we can pick up some things at the market on the way back."

"I can come and help, Paddy," said Shannon.

"No need; finish your examination of *Second Wind* and the offshore checklist for discussion later."

"Okay."

Shannon sat in the U-shaped seating on the aft deck to review all the checklists. She noticed Caesar working on the same yacht again but scolded herself to concentrate without distractions. The offshore checklist broke into sections: boat survey, rigging and sails, navigation, electronics, safety, first aid, tools and marine items, ground tackle, spares, water supplies. Over 200 items listed.

Shannon's introspection continued. Paddy knew the checklists would raise questions for her. She liked to learn by trial and error, doing things on her own, but a captain's job required forward thinking. Deepwater crossings were more complex than running fishing boats or sailing with friends along the coast. She was out of her depth and made a how-to list for what she needed Paddy to teach her:

How to do inspections.

Test safety and electronics equipment.

Prepare the vessel for a squall.

Schedule a boat survey.

Pre-assess rudder, and through-hull fittings.

When to get a technician to recalibrate instruments.

How to navigate when the electronics fail.

She knew it was necessary for Paddy to observe and guide her through the pre-departure process. *I will need his help—days and days of it. I hate to be weak or helpless. My marriage would have been stronger if I let Eric know I needed him. Delphina does that and gets anything she wants from everybody—got no pride at all.*

Shannon's investigation of *Second Wind* halted with the inviting sound of flamenco guitar music pulsating from Caesar's portable speakers.

Take a break, brew some iced tea, and visit Caesar. No, just say hello, thank him for yesterday and offer to make iced tea. I'll brew it first, walk over with mine in hand, and then ask him. Geez, I'm thinking like a schoolgirl.

She grinned as she poured unsweetened iced tea into a tall tumbler filled with ice, added a lemon wedge and crimped a straw. She parroted Mae West's famous line in a smoky voice, "When I'm good, I'm very good. But when I'm bad, I'm better."

She set an empty matching tumbler on the counter and shoved two sugar packets in her pocket. She sprinkled a half packet of raw sugar on top of her drink and sauntered over to chat with the pied piper.

Caesar carefully drilled holes to attach fittings for a domed awning system for sun protection. The long tubes, stays, and fabric lay off to the side. *A two-person job for sure*, she thought.

"Do you ever take a break?"

"Ciao, Shannon, *va bene*."

"Thanks for the gelato and espresso yesterday. Want some brewed iced tea? I just made it."

Caesar glanced back at his tools and squinted at his diver's watch. "I'd love to b—"

"I'll bring you one. Some sugar?"

He pinched his index finger and thumb together. "*Piccolo, grazie.*"

Three men passed Shannon on the dock as she returned to the *Second Wind*. The first was the youngest—Mr. Cool, with dead eyes, cropped black hair, goatee, Nike muscle tee, long basketball shorts and gray Converse All Star sneakers. She did not like the way he got close, stared her over, and sniffed. *This guy is creepy.*

The second man wore dark wraparound sunglasses like a slick-hair bouncer from a Latin nightclub, but in day-job khaki work shirt, camo-cargo pants, and ankle boots.

The third was trim, fiftyish, with a straw fedora, pencil-thin mustache, aroma of young leather or Cuban cigars, a yellow shirt, tan sport coat, Rolex watch, beige slacks, and two-tone tropical shoes. Shannon shook her head. *That one looks like a Caribbean banker out for a Sunday walk in the park. I'm not in Gloucester anymore.*

She returned to the galley of the *Second Wind* to fill another tumbler with ice and tea and overheard an argument in Brazilian Portuguese along with American English. *It's those guys with Caesar, and that cocky Mr. Cool's foul mouth is out of place for yacht-land.*

When she poked her head out from the pilothouse, she saw the three men facing Caesar on the white yacht. Bouncer Man swept open his hand as he said something, and then folded his arms. Mr. Straw Fedora stood away on the dock puffing a fat cigar. Mr. Cool got in Caesar's face, making some kind of demand.

Caesar pitched his head forward and swept his long arms up to walk Mr. Not-so-Cool back two paces. Caesar held up four fingers. Mr. Cool widened his stance, held up two fingers and folded his arms. Caesar shrugged and put his thumbs in his pockets.

Mr. Straw Fedora nodded at Caesar, glanced at his Rolex, and gestured for his associates to leave. He smiled with thin lips at Caesar and turned to follow his associates back along the dock. Caesar tapped his smartphone for a few minutes, and sat to gaze the waters of Biscayne Bay with his chin resting on his fist.

Caesar brightened as Shannon approached with a full tumbler in each hand. He rose to meet her. "*Bella carissima,* come aboard." He took the tumblers and set them on the table.

As she stepped onto the white yacht, Caesar placed his hand on her hip, gently pulled her toward him, and surprised her with a kiss on both cheeks. "I have admired the *Second Wind* for days and, now, here you are."

Shannon handed him a packet of sugar. "Is that your standard greeting for an American female acquaintance?"

Caesar took a long sip of the tea. "I save my affections for special people. Besides, how do you know I haven't dreamt you for years?" He ripped a corner of the sugar packet and flicked it playfully over the ice cubes floating in his tea. With his eyes locked on hers, he took a sip. "*Molto bene.*"

She smiled. "No cultural barriers here."

Caesar pointed at the *Second Wind.* "I am curious about that beautiful sailing ship. Daniella said her father owns it. Are you family?"

"Yes, he is my uncle, and I only met Daniella yesterday. Caesar, you looked a bit unsettled after seeing those guys. You don't have to tell me about it."

Caesar rubbed his hand over his stubble beard. "They bring me jobs. I maintain, repair and deliver boats anywhere for wealthy customers who are buying or selling." He frowned. "They pay well and expect me to drop everything. Luiz is a broker-dealer, moneyman with big connections. Victor is a boat handyman who does the overland and hauling work. Franco coordinates the jobs."

"So, Franco is the one with the muscle shirt, goatee, and attitude?"

"Yes."

"What's the problem? You have other customers."

"I also have my own pet project—a money pit. I bought a used trawler to renovate, live aboard for fishing, and for hire by research organizations. I took a loan from Luiz. Now he expects to be the boss."

Caesar sipped the tea and set the glass down. "I like to work alone, but I can team up with a network of freelancers and other captains, depending on the job." Caesar pounded his fist into his other hand. "Taking that money was a big mistake."

"What does he want that's stressing you out?"

"Deliver a boat to Tortola, in the British Virgin Islands. A nice job, but I'm booked with work. I agreed to do it for them in two weeks." He sighed, rubbed his chin and looked at her with dreamy soft brown eyes. "At least I have some local days until then."

Shannon thought of her own youthful follies, and the importance of picking her battles and not biting off too much. "That's a lot of pressure. Tell me about your trawler."

"It's a seventy-foot fiberglass Morgan in lay up at the old Merrill Stevens shipyard on Miami River. Got it at auction, and doing the work myself."

"What will you do with it?"

"Ecotourism and sponsored research. My interest is discovery and application, which is the hardest money to come by. I worked for a research organization, and there are knowledge gaps that interest me."

Shannon drank the last of her iced tea. *Caesar is such a dedicated guy,* she thought. "What were you doing before?"

"I worked at NOAA Southeast Fisheries Science Center after I graduated from Miami's Rosenstiel School of Marine and Atmospheric Science."

"That's impressive, but where I come from, most fishermen hate NOAA."

"I was on the science end, and you are right, policy and implementation is a big mess. I didn't want a career at NOAA, or to become a regulator or a professor, or work for an oil company. I have my own ideas for independent marine research, education and activism. We need solutions. My hero was Jacques Cousteau."

Shannon remembered a fortune cookie proverb that young men had visions and old men had dreams. She admired Caesar's shag of black hair and stubble and imagined how it would feel to run her fingers through his locks and lie with her cheek next to his.

"I loved Cousteau's documentaries," she said. "It sounds like a great lifestyle, and your vessel a real workhorse. Will I have to call you Captain Nemo? I would love to see it, but we won't be here long."

"I have pictures of my trawler on my mobile phone. It would be easier to see them in the shade," Caesar said. "Can we get more tea under that Bimini on *Second Wind* and a quick tour?"

"Sure, but only for a peek into the galley. Uncle Paddy hasn't really met you yet."

"Of course, he is captain. It is his home—a beautiful vessel, and one of a kind. I studied the evolution of sailing ships since I was a boy."

They strolled over to the *Second Wind.* Caesar boarded and walked past the waist of the brigantine, along the scuppers to the forecastle. He stopped at the bow, turned and craned his neck to survey the sail rigging. Shannon sensed he was inventorying every feature, making calculations, and assessing seaworthiness.

He spoke with his hands moving. "I want to get to know your uncle Paddy and voyages of the *Second Wind.*" He entered the helm station and peered down into the galley. "The layout is fantastic."

Caesar and Shannon walked to the aft deck and sat under the Bimini top. Caesar showed her pictures of his expedition trawler. He spoke of its capabilities and the progress of his modifications and retrofitting.

"Having a bow and a stern thruster is awesome," Shannon said. "I wish the *Second Wind* had that. I'm anxious that I will mangle my uncle's vessel the first few times I dock it."

Caesar smiled. "Not much to worry about with a steel hull, just embarrassment. I think your uncle will enjoy teaching you. You will do well."

He held his hand up with a space between his index finger and thumb. "A little performance anxiety is a good thing. So, what do you think of my project?"

"You got a good deal for a commercial quality trawler. Perfect for what you want—a crane and diving deck, sleeps nine, three bathrooms, big workroom, plenty of seating in the galley and flybridge, mahogany trim."

Caesar shifted his feet and took a deep breath. "A pig for fossil fuel and I will have to keep her working all the time. It will take another hundred fifty thousand to finish it."

Shannon cocked her head at Caesar and smiled. "I would have to get used to having a boat loaded with people all the time."

"The *Second Wind* is a seafarer's dream, but I love research and being around people dedicated to preserving coral reefs, bottlenose dolphins, and spotting environmental dangers like mercury in the waters. When you have hard data, educating the public in an entertaining way can influence positive change."

Shannon lit up as he spoke. This was clearly Caesar's calling. "Jacques Cousteau left a legacy for studying the sea, and Carl Sagan for the heavens."

"You understand me, Shannon." He put his glass down. "When can I see you again?"

She looked into his eyes. "I would like that, but we're off to Key West Sunday, leave for the Bahamas Friday, and then to Jamaica. I have never been to Key West. We won't be back in South Florida for weeks."

"No problem. I have a small job to deliver a Hunter 30 sailboat to Key West. Please, make time for us. I can show you around." He reached into his back pocket, retrieved his wallet and pulled out his business card.

Shannon pocketed the card without looking at it. "I'll text you my contact info."

Caesar collected his tools and left the marina. Shannon kicked off her sandals and sat at the exterior helm of the *Second Wind*. She studied Caesar's laminated white business card with blue seascape. "I think Paddy will like him," she murmured, and fanned her neck with the card.

KEY WEST

After two and a half days at sail, the *Second Wind* berthed at Conch Harbor Marina in Key West—just ahead of schedule at 11 a.m. The marina sported a clover-shaped pool, two restaurants, and nifty conveniences for upscale boaters near historic Duval Street.

Shannon, Daniella, and Paddy had split the four-hour night watches. Now they tried to make up for lack of sleep. Paddy snoozed in his quarters while the newly bonded first cousins catnapped in palm-shaded loungers by the marina pool. A server cleared their lunch plates and offered complimentary margaritas for them as new arrivals.

Daniella flipped through a women's fashion magazine while Shannon journaled about her first night sail. She noted how Paddy conducted himself in every place and situation on the ship. He easily switched between his roles of captain, mentor, and family member. He was mindful of her status as an advanced beginner and Daniella's competence at sea. Twice he ordered Shannon to her bunk to rest for night watches.

Shannon wrote how they had shortened the sails before dark, put on warm clothes, and used flashlights to read in their bunks without the cabin lights. They ran under power and sail with LED deck lights. They dimmed instrument panels, navigation lights, autopilot, chart plotter, radar, and VHF radio to minimize power drain. The CP control panel guided *Second Wind* to Key West. Shannon enjoyed the passage under the stars with Paddy, and overlapping with Daniella's watch.

When her mobile phone vibrated, Shannon set her pen and journal aside to read a text from Caesar.

> *Meet you and Daniella 1030 AM?*
> *Cuban Coffee Queen, 284 Margaret St.*
> *Walk town, Pirate museum, lunch . . .*
> *I drive to Miami at Midnight*
> *Ciao.*

Shannon showed the text to Daniella. "What do you think?"

"We should go tomorrow. A unique place to walk about, and I have not been in Key West since law school in Miami. Caesar is referring to the Mel Fisher Maritime Heritage Museum. After we stop there, I'll split after lunch."

Shannon perked up. "Tell Paddy I'll devote Thursday to preparing for our next sail."

Daniella nodded. "Maybe you should read this." She flipped open the women's fashion magazine to its cover article and tossed it onto Shannon's lap—"Ten Sex Tips for Mr. Happy."

"Ten?" said Shannon. "Men aren't that complicated. This article must be for teenagers." She glanced at it briefly, chuckled and picked up her diary. After a few scribbles, she tapped Daniella's arm with her pen. "What's at the pirate museum?"

From a fully reclined position with a ball cap over her eyes, Daniella answered, "Millions in recovered gold, silver, and gems from wrecks off the Florida coast. Shows the history of Mel Fisher's treasure hunting family and how it found the treasure wreck of the *Atocha.* "

"Really?"

"Yes, the museum store sells pirate jewelry, reproduction coins, and authentic silver pieces of eight. They even let you handle some of the items."

Shannon imagined what it would be like to hold pirate gold and silver. Her dream of Jack Rackham and Anne Bonny frolicking off Marco Island flashed into mind. *Very soon, I may hold my own pirate gold.*

Daniella pushed back her visor and propped up on her elbows. "As an admiralty law student, I found Mel Fisher's story fascinating. His family and investors suffered tragic losses of life and savings. They followed all the salvage rules but spent years in over a hundred court battles to keep what they found. Many jurisdictions claimed rights to the treasure. He finally prevailed in the Supreme Court of the United States."

"There are no friends of treasure," Shannon said, wondering when she could share the secrets of her pirate ancestry.

The margaritas arrived and soon Shannon and Daniella sipped a second round. "Daniella, I can't believe we're already friends and family."

"Good friends," said Daniella. "I can talk about anything with you."

Shannon pulled a trifold travel brochure from her diary and studied the contents for a minute. "What do you say we rest here for a couple more hours, take a walk along the docks at Key West Bight, then check out the Historic Seaport area? Tonight, I'll take you and Paddy out to dinner."

"Perfect," Daniella said, as she rose to take a dip in the pool. Shannon closed her diary and fell asleep in the gentle afternoon breezes of Key West.

The next morning, Shannon and Daniella walked to the Cuban Queen Coffee Shop. They had passed it the day before. Shannon saw Caesar through the restaurant window. He slowly stirred his coffee. Next to him sat Victor, the "Bouncer Man" she had seen with Caesar on the yacht in Miami. Victor's head rested on the back of the booth, his expressionless face hidden behind dark wraparound sunglasses.

Caesar looks like an unmade bed, thought Shannon. *So handsome in that crumpled white Bahama shirt, layered wavy black hair, and silver mariner chain necklace. It must have been a tiring passage on a Hunter 30 sailboat.*

As Shannon and Daniella approached, Victor rose with a polite nod. "*Bom dia.*" Turning to Caesar he said, "I will nap on the beach. Franco and Mateo arrive in the van this afternoon. We leave at midnight."

Victor adjusted his sunglasses and left the restaurant. For a big man,

Victor moved more like an agile circus performer than a boat hauler with a wrench. *I doubt he misses a thing from behind those sunglasses,* Shannon thought.

Caesar got up and greeted Daniella and Shannon, the faint Mediterranean scent of Armani Acqua Di Gio wafting around them. Shannon inhaled deeply as he gestured for them to sit and pointed to the beverage menu board.

"I recommend the Sunrise Special—half a Key Wester sandwich and *cafe con leche.*"

Daniella slid into the booth first, allowing Shannon to savor each moment next to Caesar.

His choice of cologne reminded her of a good man she met when sitting for Cape Ann artists as a female model. He was a famous local Italian portrait artist who wore the same Armani fragrance when it debuted in the mid-1990s. It sat on a shelf in his bathroom, where she changed for sittings in his small studio. *Maybe Caesar is as kind and wonderful,* she thought.

Caesar excused himself. He returned moments later from the lavatory, wide-awake with his wet hair pushed back. After comparing experiences of nautical night voyages, the three left the restaurant to visit places and sights familiar to Daniella on their way to the Mel Fisher Marine Heritage Museum.

Inside the small museum, they viewed glass-enclosed exhibits of heavy gold chains, religious gem-studded crosses, and various artifacts in blackened rooms. Caesar held Shannon's hand in a warm easy clasp, his long fingers wrapped fully around. It had been a long time since a man had held her hand for the fun of it.

The pirate jewelry at the museum store was strangely seductive for Shannon but held little interest for Daniella as they stood looking at glass-cased treasures for sale. Caesar flipped through salvage and dive books on the other side of the shop.

Shannon fixated on a silver *real* coin pendant from the *Atocha*, set in a fourteen-carat white-gold diamond mount. "Sixteen thousand dollars is more than my life savings."

Caesar rejoined Shannon as they left the museum through a narrow doorway. He suggested they order sandwiches to take to the Green Parrot. Shannon knew from sightseeing the day before that it was a local dive bar off the beaten tourist path of Duval Street.

Daniella approved. "The Parrot is the best place in Key West for live music in the evenings. I think the only food served is free popcorn."

"Weekday afternoons are the quiet times there. It's the oldest bar in USA," Caesar said.

They ordered pulled pork sandwiches from a barbecue joint and headed to the bar's open frame building with funky wood signs, folk art, hanging guitars, and rotating ceiling fans.

Relieved to get out of the sun, they entered the establishment and sat near a pool table and dartboard to eat, and ordered cold beer. There were only two dozen people inside. Most were drinking, snacking, storytelling patrons and friends that fed the jukebox to satisfy their taste for blues, classic rock and oldies.

Daniella finished her sandwich and licked her fingertips.

"I thought that was an American habit, Daniella," Shannon said.

"Maybe it's catching on."

Shannon washed down the last of her sandwich with a Sam Adams beer, sat back and looked around at the patrons. "Look who's here, Caesar."

On the other side of the room, Mr. Cool-Franco sat at the bar with a slouched colleague and two inebriated women. One of the women stroked Franco's thigh. Franco stared at Shannon with a squint. She stared right back and turned with a smile to Caesar.

"What drinks are those barflies knocking back so fast?" asked Shannon.

"Root beer barrel shots, an off-menu special here," said Caesar. "They fill a highball glass with Miller Light and drop a shot glass with root beer schnapps inside."

"Ah, like a boilermaker," Shannon said. "Your associate over there with the two women doesn't like me."

"He is jealous I'm with you and you're too good for him," Caesar said. "That is Mateo Dias with Franco; Victor and I will ride back with them to Miami. I hope Victor keeps them out of trouble. Franco and Mateo hang out here in Key West. Mateo came from a tough neighborhood in Jamaica." Caesar took a long sip of beer. "We deliver resale boats here, for clients who drive or fly into Key West International, to take vacation with a Caribbean departure point. The vessels and paperwork must be right and ready. Key West is the only American port in the Caribbean that people from the States can drive to."

"That's an interesting business. I hadn't thought of Key West as a Caribbean port," Shannon said as she rose from the table. "I'll be right back. Need to use the restroom."

She ignored Franco and his cohorts on the way to the restroom, but Franco made ignoring him impossible when Shannon passed by again.

"Nice hooters, hot stuff," said Franco. "I'd like to get some of that."

Shannon stopped in her tracks, facing Franco. "Not in your dreams, you—"

Franco cut her off and called Shannon a name that would rile any woman. Nearby patrons gasped.

"That wasn't called for, asshole," yelled a nearby man.

Franco stood and sneered at Shannon. "Aww, did I upset Captain Shorty?"

Shannon glared at him. "Try to be imaginative. Is that *it*? I'm *short*. That's *all* you got to say?" She stood, arms folded, waiting for his reply.

All heads in the bar turned to the instant adversaries.

"What of it?" Franco replied.

"A minute ago you called me something that begins with *C* and rhymes with *runt*. Do you care to repeat that for everyone?"

Franco was speechless.

"I didn't think so."

The uneasy silence broke with guffaws from the patrons. Daniella and Caesar turned to the fracas.

Shannon said to Franco, "I'm short, yeah, but that's an *under*statement."

The patrons laughed.

"I know, I'm *beneath* your contempt," she continued.

Louder laughs. Franco sat fuming. "Fuck you," he said.

"Oh my," Shannon said, and covered her mouth in faux shock.

The patrons chuckled. Caesar stood with folded arms, but Franco ignored him.

Franco stared back at Shannon with his face flushed and eyes like hot coals.

Shannon spun away from him to the people crowded in the middle of the room and put her hands in the air. "Behold the shorty pants captain, Puss and Booty."

Cheers went up, and curious passersby piled in from the sidewalk.

"Get her a drink on me," said a customer to the bartender.

"Keep it going," another shouted.

Shannon faced Franco. "Come on. Let's have some fun. What about this?" She veered again to the audience and waved her hands as though starring in a musical. "Behold, the female version of Bilbo Baggins. Attention—the marine store in town has a sale on booster seats. Get three for only ten dollars."

Laughter ran through the place, with all eyes on Franco, who steamed like a hot volcano.

She moved next to a round table of chuckling drinkers, stepped up on an empty chair, pitched her head at Franco and leveled eyes on him. "The circus pays me very well. But clowns get even more."

From her perch, Shannon's attention turned to Franco's sidekick, Mateo, slouched low in his chair. "Sit up, laddie. Maybe you need a booster seat too!"

The crowd gathered close, totally with Shannon, and looked to Franco. Caesar opened his mouth but pressed his lips together and put his hands on his hips.

Shannon hopped off the chair and gestured to Franco and the two sultry women. "This poor man is drowning amid an ocean of ignorance."

Franco took a long sip of his drink before sitting back with a scowl.

His thin, monkey-faced sidekick, Mateo, clasped his hands behind his head. She noticed his intense round eyes, short forehead, flared nostrils and muzzle mouth.

Shannon looked back at Franco. "We're just getting started here. Let's see, you have two lovelies with you." She tapped a finger against her cheek as if deep in thought. "Oh, I know. How does a pirate get his mast up?"

Franco crossed his arms.

"He uses a wench."

The crowd cracked up. Daniella and Caesar looked at each other with consternation.

Franco stood up and squared off. "Puss and Booty, what smart-ass names do you have for me?"

"Rat-eating bastard comes to mind," Shannon said. "Who cares about you anyway?"

A few patrons clapped while the rest sat in suspense.

Caesar folded his arms and leveled his eyes at Franco.

The room quieted with a few snickers rippling through as all eyes turned to Franco's steaming scarlet face.

Franco pointed at Shannon as if taking aim with a gun, popped it back and walked toward the exit. Monkey-faced Mateo trailed behind. Shannon noticed how Mateo leaned forward with his short torso and long legs, his trousers pulled to a high waist.

Caesar intercepted Franco and Mateo and spoke in a booming voice to the patrons, "Let's all toast and thank Shannon and Franco for the skit."

"Hail, hail" echoed in the room and people returned to their seats. Franco sat back down with his friends for a drink. Shannon rejoined Caesar and Daniella.

"You were playing with fire, Shannon," Caesar said.

Daniella pulled Shannon close. "Your acting skills could be useful in a courtroom, but watch out for that hothead."

Caesar and Shannon shared backgrounds as they walked to Higgs Beach. She learned Caesar came from La Spezia, Italy, an ancient maritime and fishing village that became a commercial shipbuilding port, cargo terminal, and hub of the Italian navy. She could imagine such a place with Caesar's captivating description. She learned that La Spezia sat at the eastern end of the Italian Riviera, with remains of ancient fortifications.

He described his time as a cadet at the navigation school, involved in Mediterranean patrols for environmental and humanitarian activities. The dual-use navy rescued many desperate refugees in the Mediterranean. He crewed on the *Amerigo Vespucci*, a full square-rigged ship used as a training vessel for Italian navy cadets.

After the navy, Caesar participated in regattas with private and navy-owned tall ships. He returned to Italy in 2007 to crew on the *Nave Italia*, a 185-foot brigantine built in 1993 in Poland, now owned by the Italian navy and operated from the Genoa Yacht Club.

He held her hand as they walked along the pier. She did not object.

Caesar's parents divorced, and his teenage years were split between living with his father, who worked in a shipyard in La Spezia, and his mother in Florence, where she had rejoined with a former lover. His mother was wealthy and sponsored Caesar to go to the United States to the University of Miami.

Shannon snugged next to Caesar on the powdery sand of Higgs Beach under a stand of palm trees. "Now I understand your fascination with old sailing ships and my uncle's brigantine."

"It was funny how you joked like a pirate at the bar, but the way you put Franco down can be dangerous. In Italy, the woman is the power behind the throne. But in the States that pretense is gone."

"And so is romance, it seems."

"I'm still a romantic," he said, "and so are you."

"You're right, but I've had a family already." She paused. "I'm not sure how a romantic friendship works, or I'm not ready for a soulmate."

Caesar gently touched Shannon's face and brushed her hair back. He drew closer to her, looked into her bright blue eyes, and kissed her on the lips. "Don't think so much; I want to be with you soon."

Shannon savored the kiss and pushed him back onto the sand. She looked down into his eyes. "When I return from Jamaica," she said.

KINGSTON, JAMAICA

Paddy took in the mountain views and seascape of Kingston Harbor from the veranda of the sunny, rustic family compound he shared with Daniella and her mother, Jenny. The house was set on two fenced acres with three cottages. Paddy kept one of the cottages for his own use. Red tiled roofs and awnings accented the cream-colored frame and stone buildings surrounded by trees, wildflowers, and gardens fruited with pineapple, naseberry, ackee, banana, and breadfruit. The water tank, outdoor kitchen, and fire pit accented the casual, rural charm. Jenny stood next to an easel on the porch in a bathrobe and bare feet, finishing a portrait of Shannon and Daniella—a picture of them was tacked to her easel.

"Another coffee, sweetheart?" Paddy asked.

Jenny swirled her brush on a palette, with wide eyes on Paddy. She walked to him and painted a heart on his forearm, then tousled her black hair, and flashed open her robe. "Patrick, my man, come back to bed."

When they emerged from the bedroom dressed for the day, they sat on the porch rockers holding hands.

"I love that painting of the girls," Paddy said. "Where do you think we should hang it?"

"It's a gift for Shannon," Jenny smiled with a raised eyebrow. "Maybe it's time I did a family portrait of the four of us."

"Fantastic," Paddy said, rocking his chair.

"That one stays here for good," Jenny said.

Paddy had a gleam in his eye. Lighting his pipe, he said, "Maybe I should, too."

Jenny smiled and squeezed his hand. "Yes, about time, lover boy."

They waited for Daniella and Shannon to return from food shopping in town, keeping an eye on the rough mountain road. Daniella had insisted on making breakfast before Shannon departed with Paddy on their sail back to Key West. Paddy spotted Daniella's blue Toyota van lurching up the rocky road.

"I'm going out back for a minute," he said.

Paddy inspected the wooden structures and targets in his agility training area in the yard. He kept a fitness regimen and practiced martial arts.

He was impressed with the breadth of skills Shannon acquired in the three and a half weeks since they sailed from Key West. His niece was a contrast to Danny, who had little interest in the seafaring life. Daniella, a lean, logical perfectionist, and Shannon more like Jenny—sensual, artsy, individualistic. He cherished was happy they had become close.

At breakfast, Jenny asked Shannon, "What did you enjoy most on the sail from Key West and your visit in Jamaica?"

"Getting to know and love a whole family I didn't know existed." She looked at Jenny and her cousin. "Your cooking is awesome, too." Shannon paused and looked at Paddy. "The close combat training in the backyard was fun. You do take a mean punch."

Jenny, Paddy, and Daniella laughed and embraced Shannon.

"Thank you so much," Shannon said. "Someday, you'll get to know my kids, and Grandbaby Paula."

After breakfast, Daniella and Jenny insisted they would clean up the kitchen. Shannon penned a few notes in her diary. Her thoughts streamed with glorious days at sea with Paddy, hanging out with Daniella, scuba diving the Port Royal ruins, learning the history of the Bahamas and Jamaica, and painting local scenes with Jenny. She set her diary back with her luggage and vowed to journal most days.

Shannon wandered out to the gardens and into the backyard. She gathered Paddy's throwing knives, axes, and four spears that they handcrafted together from old tools. The tips were shaped and hammered from a lawnmower blade, an M16 bayonet, and a used chef knife.

Paddy watched Shannon from the shaded porch.

"Time to go, Shan," he said.

"Not yet," Jenny hollered from inside the house. "Get in here so I can take some pictures."

They assembled in the living room facing Jenny's digital camera mounted on a tripod with the timer set.

Paddy cherished each moment with Jenny, Daniella, and Shannon without words on the short, bumpy ride to the Royal Jamaica Yacht Club (RJYC) in Kingston. He would miss Daniella and Jenny but was excited for the quest ahead.

At the club, he left them to get their coffee inside while he went down to the dock to inspect the *Second Wind*. He had tied up at the visitors' dock, which had plenty of depth and space for large vessels. He moved about the vessel, a pencil tucked behind his ear and clipboard in hand. He checked and rechecked provisions, systems, paperwork, and readiness for sail. Squinting at the skyline, he looked at cloud formations and boat traffic.

Shannon had been a substantial help preparing for the return to Florida; she took initiative and showed promise. With a favorable set to the weather they could enjoy a good run with the easterlies.

Paddy checked supplies of fresh batteries in his quarters, and opened a box containing a metal detector he'd purchased in Miami. A high-end detector might make short work of finding treasure on one of many Calusa shell mounds.

He finished assembling the metal detector and sat at his desk to upload his camera to the laptop. Paddy and Shannon had kept a digital photo gallery file to share highlights of the trip. Some of the best prints made in Kingston sat next to the computer in a plastic folio. He clicked through pictures of Shannon with her Gloucester mates; snaps of Shannon, Caesar, and Daniella in Miami; and shots of Shannon and Caesar outside the Mel Fisher Museum in Key West. He remembered how Shannon had sat and meditated on the spot in Nassau where Calico Jack and Anne Bonny met.

Paddy appreciated the images of Shannon and Daniella at historic sites, museums, and the National Archives of Jamaica. He held a favorite picture of Shannon sporting a huge smile, hoisting scuba gear with university archaeologists and students at the sunken city of Port Royal. Known as the world's richest and wickedest city in the Age of Piracy, it was now a quiet fishing village. Daniella had worked the right channels to get Shannon on the dive group in the restricted ruins area.

A massive earthquake had sunk thirty-three acres of Port Royal in 1692. Much of the pirate city's sunken shelf remained intact and level less than forty feet below sea level. One in four of the stone buildings were brothels, boarding houses, or drinking establishments.

Shannon explored the underwater structures and was reluctant to leave at the end of each day's dive program. The young university divers struggled to keep her pace. Few had her natural ease in the water. None could have her secret passion to discover her pirate ancestry.

Calico Jack Rackham had met his end in Port Royal, his tarred body hung in a gibbet at Gallows Point, now known as Rackham's Cay. There was still much more to be learned about Jack and his English family. The only chance of doing so was to obtain Anne Bonny's memoirs in Charleston or Yorktown.

Paddy studied a picture of Jenny and himself surrounded by Daniella, Shannon, and local friends gathered for a festive hog roast with music and an open fire two nights ago at their Jamaican home. Daniella had embraced Shannon and shared the multicultural richness of Jamaica. Shannon would always have a place at his Caribbean home.

Paddy shut down his computer, set down the picture prints, and hustled toward the clubhouse to let Shannon know that they needed to shove off soon. Another boater dressed in a blue polo shirt and pressed white slacks detained him by the dock.

The man said, "I've been admiring this vessel for two days. How old is it?"

The man seemed like a local but dressed like a recreational sailor. "She's less than ten years; designed it with a colleague." Paddy continued walking. "We're departing shortly."

"I'll follow you, sir. Just a couple of questions, please."

The man got in front of Paddy and walked backwards like a reporter talking to a VIP. He stopped on the walkway in front of Paddy. "How many do you need to crew this vessel?"

"I can handle it myself, but two works fine."

They ascended the stairs to the club. The man lost his balance, but Paddy steadied him.

"How fast can she run under power and sail?"

Paddy thought this too much information but answered, "Fourteen knots."

"Wow." The man straightened up. "Why a brigantine?"

"Just look at her! Thanks for your interest. Good day."

While waiting for Paddy in the clubhouse of the yacht club, Shannon dashed notes to friends and family on six artsy postcards purchased from a Jamaican shop. *Snail mail is nice to get*, she thought. She had hardly used her mobile phone since Key West. Two weeks earlier, in the Bahamas, she replied to texts and emails. Last week, she emailed Caesar a picture of herself scuba diving in Jamaica. Caesar texted three days ago from Tortola in the British Virgin Islands and wanted to fly to Jamaica to meet her before returning to Florida.

"Wish I hadn't missed that," she said. She wrote back that they would have to wait to see each other in Key West before she returned north for the season, and she added the itinerary for her sail back. *Que sera sera*, she mused.

Shannon looked out the yacht club window at the marina. *It's about 570 miles to Key West from here as the bird flies, or an 800-mile sail. It will be a great sail. This time, I want to catch fish in deeper waters, away from the reefs. Maybe catch a billfish, but a school of mahi-mahi would be nice.* She held her hands on an imaginary rod, lowered it, pulled it up quick, reeled in with a downward stroke and pulled up again. *Catch and release; no need to risk* ciguatera *poisoning. Don't have to worry about that in cool waters back home.*

A thin young local walked past the window of the building with a hat pulled low on his face. Something about him looked familiar and made Shannon anxious. She may have seen him with the same T-shirt in Kingston, two days earlier when she and Daniella were shopping. She wondered if he was tailing them but shook her head—it was the sun and heat.

Shannon collected Daniella and Jenny, who had finished their coffees, and they walked to the *Second Wind* by the visitors' dock. Paddy was sitting at the helm, ready for all to say their goodbyes and exchange promises to keep in touch. Jenny gave Paddy a long hug and he whispered something in her ear. Jenny whooped and smiled.

Daniella and Shannon exchanged quizzical glances. Daniella said, "Mom is happy about something even though Dad's leaving."

Shannon said, "If something good is meant for us to know, we will."

Paddy lit and stoked his pipe before guiding the *Second Wind* out of Kingston Harbor. Shannon waved to Daniella and Jenny until they were no longer distinguishable across the water. After Shannon adjusted the sails, she stepped back to the exterior helm. She noticed that the cover on the dinghy was loose around five of the grommets and cinched the rope tight with a double square knot. With everything tidy on deck, she relieved Paddy at the helm. Paddy relaxed near her and puffed on his pipe.

Shannon asked, "What is my level of seamanship now, Captain?"

"Competent," he replied.

The *Second Wind* plowed on, sails full with easterly trade wind. Shannon entered a flow state, relaxed in a timeless moment, with keen awareness and agility. *Piloting a priceless vessel in the Caribbean on a superfect day*, she thought. *It just does not get better than this.*

However, Shannon's brain served up the image of a man with a high waist and a forward tilt in his walk. "Monkey-face!" Shannon said aloud. "That creep Mateo Dias is up to something in Kingston." She remembered Franco pointing his finger gun at her in Key West, with the Jamaican, Mateo Dias, at his side.

Shannon motioned to Paddy to step down with her to the interior helm station and took control of the vessel from there.

"Lovely topside; what's up?" Paddy asked.

"I screwed up."

Paddy raised his eyebrows and removed the pipe from his mouth.

Shannon continued. "I'm sure I saw one of Caesar's questionable associates, Mateo, walking near Daniella and me in Kingston, and then at the yacht club before we shoved off, but I didn't place him until a few minutes ago. He had a hat pulled down a bit over his face."

"Who knows about our float plan?" he asked. "Does anyone know where we are going?"

"Caesar, but I trust him." Her mouth felt so dry she struggled to get out her words. "He delivered a boat to Tortola and I got a three-day-old email this morning from him that he wanted to fly back via Jamaica."

"Why are you concerned with this Mateo guy?"

"Daniella, Caesar, and I had a beer at the Green Parrot bar in Key West and two of his associates, Franco and Mateo showed up and got drunk. They said something that triggered me to humiliate them." She paused, the cold reality of her actions settling in. "I pushed it way too far. They were pissed, and everyone at the bar laughed at them."

Paddy rubbed his beard. "It could be nothing, but now you know not to share your float plan with strangers. I should have been explicit on that."

Shannon took one hand off the ship's wheel and said, "Please take over, I need to sit down. This is my bad. Caesar has to deal with all types of marine freelancers to serve his customers. But Franco and Mateo are downright creepy."

Paddy stood at the helm. After a few moments with only the sounds of wind, ship and sea, he said, "In situations like this, I think of the worst, the best, and everything in between. For all we know, the creeps may have Caesar's phone and you have not been communicating with him at all. You don't know Caesar well, either."

"Yikes. Caesar is trustworthy, but I didn't consider his mobile being hijacked. Maybe I don't know so much."

"I felt something was amiss with a man who distracted me back at the yacht club," Paddy said. "He may have been a spotter. There is a lot of crime off the coast of Jamaica. I made the mistake of breaking the need-to-know rule, and we may live to regret it."

"Holy shit," said Shannon.

"Calm down. You're the one who sensed danger. Now we are ready. That's a big advantage. We must be vigilant for the next eight to ten hours."

"What should we do?" asked Shannon.

"Stay alert, don't overreact. Watch the radar; keep your eyes peeled for any fast boats approaching us." Paddy scanned the seas around them and gave Shannon a look she could only think of as intrepid—the same word ascribed to Captain Jonathan Haraden. "We will be fine. Take back the wheel," he said. "I have a few things to do."

"Yes, Captain."

CARIBBEAN COWBOY

Shannon and Paddy took turns at the helm for six hours, with watchful wariness of vessels in their vicinity. Only the occasional yacht, cargo, or cruise ship were visible.

"It will be dusk in two hours," she said. "I'll make dinner."

Paddy nodded and took the last few puffs from his burled pipe before tapping the cherry tobacco ashes out over the water.

Shannon took in the sweet aroma mixed with sea air before going below to prepare a simple dinner of tuna sandwiches, tangerines, four of Jenny's macaroons, and fresh squeezed lemonade.

Paddy's eyes widened when she brought the platters topside and placed them on the aft deck table.

"Looks delicious, Shannon. Didn't realize how hungry I was. Take a seat. I'll stay at the wheel for a while." He put his extinguished pipe in his pants pocket and grabbed half a sandwich without taking his gaze from the radar and instrument panel.

"You look pensive," she said.

"A vessel five miles due southeast has maintained an average distance of four miles for the past hour. Could be a fishing boat, but I keep changing speeds every twenty minutes and it does not fall behind. Keep an eye on it."

Shannon looked up at the radar antenna on the mast. "The radar can spot images up to six miles. Why is the antenna set only twenty feet above sea level?"

"This is a line of sight technology, mostly for collision avoidance. The military has had over-the-horizon radar for decades. If you take this radar and put it up much higher, you wouldn't get much gain from it, and you need the beam aimed just off the bow to work in close."

"A six-foot person standing on shore can see a horizon up to three miles," Shannon said.

"From up there in the crow's nest, Shannon, you'd see more like ten miles with clear weather."

Shannon took the ship's wheel to head for late afternoon sun as cool air flowed over them. Paddy went to his quarters and used his iridium satphone email service to message Daniella to run a check on Mateo Dias. He returned topside and stood near the bow with his hands braced on halyards to ride the wave action. It wasn't long before he came back to join her at the helm.

"Slow to seven knots for twenty minutes, watch the radar. If no change in distance to that vessel, run full out for twenty."

"Got it, Cap."

"I'll take over at that point and see if she gives chase. With a sustained speed of fourteen knots, we should know if we have company."

Just before sunset, Shannon saw a pattern. "Paddy, radar shows the vessel gained a bit on us on the same heading at lower speed but fell back significantly when we ran full out."

He moved into position next to her at the helm. "I'll take it back to eight knots and see how the distance closes. Most trawlers can only manage about eleven knots. A go-fast boat can cruise over ninety-five. The boat on the radar may just be a fishing trawler, but adjusting speed in relative position to us is suspicious. I expect to confirm that either way in the next half hour."

Shannon sat in the bench seat on Paddy's left in the exterior helm station and gazed at the sun, waves, radar display, and instrument panel. Paddy's confidence calmed her. He checked his watch and the radar display every ten minutes.

"Now we have something to be concerned about—a second vessel on the radar, moving fast."

Shannon tensed. "What do we do? Call the Coast Guard?"

"First, take evasive action. We change heading southwesterly, pick up the pace, see what they do. Then—"

A thump on the back deck startled both of them.

"That won't be necessary, Captain Clarke."

Shannon spun around to find muzzle-faced Mateo Dias with a pistol aimed at her forehead. The cover to the suspended dinghy was off.

Paddy lunged toward the cubby closest to the ship's wheel. Mateo fired a shot in the air. Paddy froze.

Mateo swept his gun back and forth at their foreheads. "Don't make me use this. Two boats are coming. Do what we say, nobody gets hurt."

"What do you want?" Paddy demanded.

"This is business. You take us for a ride. Do what we say. We let you go." Mateo threw a pair of handcuffs at Shannon. "Put on him, hands behind. Do it!" Mateo said, with his gun trained on Paddy's chest.

Paddy nodded. Shannon fidgeted with the handcuffs as she put them on. She noticed a key dangle from a black spiral wristband pushed above Mateo's elbow.

"Tighter," Mateo said to her, keeping his gun aimed at Paddy. The cuffs clicked shut.

"Empty his pockets and put in this mesh bag."

Mateo tightened the handcuffs and forced Paddy onto the deck away from the helm station.

"Get down on the deck over here," he ordered Shannon.

Shannon remained standing.

Mateo put his gun to her head, "Now."

She stood firm. "Screw you."

Mateo smashed the butt of his gun on her forehead and shoved her, and quickly fit the ties onto her wrists and ankles. He patted her down as she held her breath.

Shannon pushed her back up against the front edges of the U-shaped seating area, her wrists bound behind her. A bruise swelled on her forehead.

After putting a long cable tie around Paddy's ankles, Mateo turned off the engine and secured his gun in the back of his pants.

"What now?" Paddy asked.

"We wait for my friends. You cooperate. We take this rig to Gulf of Mexico. You go home and forget it."

"If we don't cooperate?"

"Not good for anyone you care about. I don't get involved in that, just transportation."

Shannon worked the small Kershaw knife out of her back hip pocket, thankful Mateo missed it when he patted her down. She gingerly worked the sharp blade across the plastic cable tie while trying not to slash her own wrists.

Mateo explored the helm station and found Paddy's loaded Glock in the cubby. He checked the action and tucked it in the front of his belt. He mocked a sad face at Paddy and patted the gun. "Better to use on you."

"Are you really a killer or just a thief with a Caribbean cowboy act?"

"Shut up," Mateo said and turned to the radar display. "Ha, two boats. Now you meet interesting people."

Shannon clipped her Kershaw knife under the back of her cutoff jeans and held her arms back as if still tied.

Mateo explored compartments in the deck area and collected items into the mesh bag. He looked into the tool bin, wagged his head side to side, then replaced the cover.

"Nice stuff, but we leave the boat how we find it. You get your things back if you don't do something stupid." He grinned and shook the gun. "It's a short ride to the bottom of the sea."

Mateo aimed Paddy's Glock at Shannon and pulled Paddy to his feet. "Hop over there. We may need you for assistance." He pressed the gun to

Paddy's back and pushed him away from the exterior helm. He unlocked the left handcuff and tightened it onto a stainless deck loop. Paddy was now out of reach to the helm station, his right hand shackled to the gunwale.

That is my chance, Shannon thought. A flush rose in her body, her lungs pumped oxygen to her muscles and her fists balled.

Mateo assessed his captives, then stepped below deck. Shannon heard him rummaging compartments and cabinets. The heat of Anne Bonny's ire rose within. Paddy's eyes bulged when Shannon freed her hands and crab-walked low and quiet to him. She pulled out the wrecking bar and small bolt cutter from the tool bin. With a swift movement, she snapped a link of the steel handcuffs with the bolt cutter to release her uncle.

Paddy grabbed the knife-edged hammer from the tool compartment and held it behind his back as though still shackled, awaiting Mateo's return.

Shannon scrambled atop the pilothouse with the wrecking bar in one hand, and hunched low on the roof above the external helm station. She flipped back her wild red hair, crouched in wait and spread her hands on the wrecking bar. She coiled, ready to smash Mateo's head when he emerged from the pilothouse below.

She waited. Time stopped. Paddy kept looking up to her and back down into the galley. He shrugged. She turned to see if Mateo came up the cargo hold from the scuttle amidships. Nope. She heard a thump down in the vessel and resumed her stance.

Paddy whispered, "He's still down there."

They waited and waited for Mateo's next move.

Shannon tightened her grip on the wrecking bar and began to sweat.

"Behind you!" Paddy yelled.

Too late. Mateo already hopped up onto the pilothouse behind Shannon with his gun.

Shannon let loose a bloody hellcat scream, landing the wrecking bar on Mateo's left shoulder. She reversed the bar and pitched the pry blade to his stomach. He cried out, partly deflected the move, and reeled back.

Then Mateo steadied, slammed the butt of the Glock on Shannon's forehead, and kicked her off the pilothouse roof. Shannon fell hard onto her back, knocking the wind out of her lungs. Her head slapped the deck by Paddy's feet.

Paddy held back in position with the knife-edged hammer behind his back.

Mateo rolled his shoulder and groaned from atop the pilothouse. He kept his gun trained on Shannon as he eased down to the aft deck and put his foot on her neck.

"You bitch. Nobody was supposed to get hurt." She blinked through a double image of Paddy swinging his knife-edge hammer at Mateo, and then she blacked out.

Ꙇ

Paddy propped Shannon up on the bench seat in the helm station. She loosened the blanket on her shoulders as she became more alert. Paddy checked her eyes, neck, and palpated her back and ribs. *The fall knocked the wind out of her,* he thought. *Possibly a concussion; some bruises but no broken bones.*

"No time for bravado, Shannon. Play more hurt than you are."

Her eyes fluttered, so he assumed she heard him but could not be sure she understood. Paddy cleaned the swollen wound on her hairline above the left eye and applied a dressing from a first aid kit.

Mateo lay hogtied on his side, moaning. "My shoulder . . . my hand . . . wrist is killing me." A bloodstained bandage covered his right wrist and hand, the one Paddy had broadsided with the hammer.

Shannon looked at Mateo and back at Paddy, squeezed her eyes shut, then widened them with raised eyebrows. She scowled at her attacker and pushed her hair back.

"See this face, Mateo? Payback really is a bitch."

Mateo's left eye was swollen shut. Stepping over to the captive, Paddy slowly pulled him up against the bench seat.

Paddy twisted Mateo's wrist as he interrogated him. Mateo quickly confessed the plot, muttering, "Don't tell them about the operation. What I told you."

Franco and his heavily armed gang were on their way to hijack the *Second Wind* and use it to illegally transport people and drugs to Miami.

The sun was slipping below the horizon. Decisions had to be made. Looking at the radar again, Paddy estimated that the boats would arrive within minutes. There was no time for escape. Any boat would be able to overtake them.

Paddy prepared as best he could with his Glock slung underneath his denim shirt, and he pocketed the ammo clip from Mateo's gun.

Shannon interrupted his thoughts. "Captain," she said groggily. "What the plan? Let's get the *Second Wind* out of here . . ."

"Can't do that, Shannon; they're just a few hundred yards away," said Paddy. "We're going to take our chances. If Mateo is telling us the truth, we're outmanned and outgunned. Let's hope all they want is to 'borrow' our ship for a bit."

Thunder from the go-fast boat erupted behind them. Paddy saw the outline of a trawler farther back.

Mateo sat terrified and malleable. He pleaded with Paddy. "Please, don't tell them I let you tie me up."

Paddy stepped back to grip Mateo's wrist again.

Mateo cried out, "No . . . don't . . ."

"Just a reminder, Mateo, a deal is a deal. I'm taking a gamble here—I help you, and you help me. I want my family safe and my ship back. You want to finish this caper and keep your job. You tell them you nearly killed us, right?"

"How did you know I wouldn't shoot?"

Paddy tapped his temple with his index finger. "I knew right off you weren't a killer, and confirmed it after you shot into the air and put your safety on."

Paddy went to helm station with Mateo's gun and relished the defeat in Mateo's face.

"I am going to let them board my way, Mateo. I do the talking. Now that I know their intentions, manpower, and firepower, I will cooperate after a little showmanship."

Paddy saw five men on the deck of the fast boat as it swept by the leeward side of the *Second Wind*. The boat's deck lights flicked on. Paddy recognized Caesar seated on the boat, handcuffed. A young man with a goatee stood over Caesar with a handgun. Two masked men targeted Paddy with assault rifles. A third masked man, smaller in stature, did not appear to have a weapon. Paddy wondered if he had made the right decision to leave his Mossberg auto shotgun out of the equation; he could make two deadly shots but not three or four.

Shannon muttered, "The guy with the goatee is Franco."

"Get down, Shannon."

Paddy held Mateo's handgun low to the side and spoke every word clearly to the men on the fast boat. "I will cooperate. Mateo said you would not hurt us. My niece needs medical attention."

"Where is Mateo?" asked Franco.

"He's tied up at the moment. I have a question."

"Drop the gun first."

"Tell your men to lower their weapons and I'll keep mine low until you answer my question. No need for murder, Franco. Certainly you can handle this situation."

Franco kept his gun trained on Paddy's head and nodded to his two large associates. They lowered their assault rifles. The smaller unarmed masked man stepped back, looked down and shook his head. Paddy figured Franco was making his bones as a tough guy.

"Your man, Mateo, almost killed us. Can you assure our safety?"

Franco squinted back at him.

"Answer my question," Paddy said.

"We're only making a transport," Franco said. "You will be confined until we reach our destination, and released."

Paddy tossed the gun down with a huff, held up his hands and stood by Shannon. The two large masked men boarded the *Second Wind*. One frisked Paddy and took the Glock. They cleared Shannon and untied Mateo.

Franco stepped aboard the *Second Wind* and squinted at Shannon. "Later, I'll teach you and Caesar a lesson. Now, I am cruise director, responsible for safety of guests. This is a business trip. Our guests stay below and identities are not your business. We liberate them to unite families."

Franco looked at Mateo and then back at Paddy. "Mr. Clarke, one of our men will handle medical problems and gather what you need while on our vessel. Caesar will pilot the *Second Wind* and you will answer his questions."

In less than thirty minutes, team Franco transferred seven blindfolded passengers with black duffel bags, three large coolers and five hard-sided suitcases from the trawler to the fast boat and to the galley of the *Second Wind*. Paddy figured the blindfolded guests to be five men and two women.

One of the armed men gestured with Paddy's Glock for Caesar to come onto the *Second Wind*. He guided him on board and gave Caesar a walkie-talkie. Caesar studied the instruments and controls in the exterior helm station before looking at Shannon and Paddy.

"I am so sorry about this," Caesar said.

Paddy, Shannon, and Mateo were shuttled onto the go-fast boat for a short ride to the trawler. One of the husky masked men had handcuffed Shannon and Paddy, but they were quickly separated. Franco nudged Paddy to the flybridge of the trawler where they sat in twin helm chairs. He handed Paddy a walkie-talkie as the fast boat thundered east.

Mateo spoke to the smaller unarmed masked man. "Doc, I need bandages, pain killers, and rest."

"Let's go below," Doc said and took Shannon's arm. The three descended where Mateo entered and closed the cabin door.

"You can call me Doc," the trim man said as he guided Shannon to a forward cabin. "I will return with your things, remove your cuffs, and give you medical attention. First, I must ask some questions. What is your name? What happened to you? What day is this?" Satisfied with her answers, he said, "This room will remain locked. When in my care, Shannon, I will protect you."

Doc returned with a medical bag and other items. He propped her head up and provided ice packs for her forehead and the back of her head.

She was ultra-sensitive to light and had a throbbing headache but no queasiness. He assured her that Paddy was safe, then exited the cabin and sat outside her door with a practiced military posture. He checked on her every twenty minutes with repeated questions regarding her status. After two hours, he gave her a Valium and Shannon nodded off.

Franco piloted the rust-bucket fishing trawler westward. Behind the shabby façade were powerful new engines, electronics, and large fuel tanks. Paddy sat next to Franco on the dual helm chairs of the trawler's open flybridge. Franco tested the chain that connected the handcuffs on Paddy's wrists to the leg irons on his ankles.

The walkie-talkie clipped to Franco's belt chirped and annoyed him. He had monitored the chatter for the past half hour and was growing tired of the stupid jokes being told by his men. He yanked the walkie-talkie from his belt and pressed the side button.

"Men, limit chat to updates. Caesar, you will do what you are told. Mr. Clarke will answer questions about that old sailboat. I want status reports every fifteen minutes."

Paddy demanded to see his niece.

"Later," said Franco. "Drink this coffee, but I'm not in a talking mood."

Franco kept the trawler two miles behind the *Second Wind* as they headed for the east end of Cuba. He knew Caesar did not require navigation assistance, and his masked associates were pros. Franco pressed the talk button on his walkie-talkie: "Doc, come up to the flybridge. Bring the fast-acting stuff."

"Ten minutes," said Doc. "I'm finishing a check-in with Shannon. She has head trauma."

When the Doc arrived at the flybridge with a syringe, Franco grabbed Paddy's arm. "If you care about your niece, take the sedative without a hassle."

"Give it to him now, Doc; take the helm, and keep an eye on our Mr. Clarke."

Paddy yanked his arm out of Franco's grip, turned and drove his two cuffed fists into Franco's diaphragm like a battering ram. Franco doubled over, struggling to breathe. Doc zapped Paddy with a stun gun and injected him in the arm.

"I hate guns, Franco," Doc said. "You are losing control here."

Franco coughed and moaned. "That old fucker is dangerous. Do your fucking job, I'll do mine."

"Show respect, Franco. If you have internal bleeding, you will beg for my help."

Franco sat on a side bench in the helm, held his stomach and started to move his hands around his diaphragm in regular rhythms. After a slow deep breath, he strained to cough, and then straightened up.

Paddy convulsed on the deck from the stun gun. Franco kicked him three times in the ribs. "You sucker-punched me, you prick."

Franco folded his arms and watched Doc prop up Paddy's deadweight, cushion his head, and drape a blanket over his torso.

"Stay on the heading, Doc," Franco said. "I'll check on Mateo and the princess."

Franco exited the flybridge and tiptoed two flights down to a private cabin. Mateo was sleeping on his back, his arm covered with a cast and angled up in a sling. Repeated doses of pain medicine, snacks, water, and bathroom breaks would keep him out of trouble for a while. Mateo's black-and-blue eye was ghastly. Franco had seen injuries like these aplenty. The eye would turn yellow by the time his pal returned home to their associates in Jamaica.

Franco grabbed a beer in the galley of the trawler and went to his stateroom for a long hot shower. He soaped up, toweled off, got into comfortable camo fatigues, and spread tactical combat gear on his bunk. He picked up a black stun gun and tested it. The battery was good. He shoved a length of nylon rope in his pants pocket.

An assortment of nasty persuaders lay on the bed: a retractable baton, leather-covered slapjack, and a set of titanium offshore fishing needle-nose pliers in a nylon sheath. He slipped the pliers on his belt and clipped on the stun gun. He retrieved a 1,000-lumen metal flashlight from the cubby next to his bed, set it to a tight beam, and ran it past the mirror. More than enough power to blind a raging bull.

"The bitch is in for some serious payback," he said aloud, as he toyed with the slapjack in his hand. "No more of her smart-ass talk." He slid the slapjack into his back pocket and stepped quietly through a passageway to Shannon's cabin door. "This time, I'll have all the fun."

RATLINES

Shannon rested in darkness, half asleep in a dream of frozen unpreparedness. Paddy was in trouble. She could not move her limbs to protect him or the *Second Wind*. Her head pounded with stars sparkling behind closed eyelids. The drugs were wearing off. A blinding light shined upon her like a hundred suns. Her arm jerked up to cover her eyes.

Franco stood over her with the tactical flashlight. "You don't look so good, bitch."

"You aren't real," she said in a hoarse whisper.

"Here I am, the rat-eating bastard."

Shannon groaned at the painful blaze of light and tried to sit up. "What do you want? Where is my uncle?"

"Don't worry, be happy. It's playtime."

Franco pushed her back on the bunk, gripped her throat and straddled her body.

"No!"

He slapped her face. "Stupid bitch, now I punish you for Mateo." Franco set down the flashlight and began to pluck the buttons off her light blue denim shirt with his needle-nosed pliers. "You don't need to get hurt."

She struggled and kicked against his weight until he crackled a stun gun in front of her eyes. "All right, okay," she said. "I need to breathe. Let me stand up and I'll take it off."

Franco shoved back and shined the flashlight over her body.

Shannon kept her eyes averted and rose slowly. Once her eyes adjusted from the torrent of the tactical flashlight, she untucked the front of her shirt slowly and pulled it open. She was not wearing a bra. Franco's eyes fixed upon her. She pulled the sides of her tucked shirt up a tiny bit at a time, and kept her eyes leveled at him with an impassive look. Anne Bonny and Captain Jonathan Haraden flashed in her mind. She needed their strength, fierce and bold.

Franco leaned back against the cabin door as Shannon released the top button of her cutoff jeans. Her Bonny blood boiled, but her senses were Haraden keen. The grogginess was gone and adrenaline quenched her pain. She felt power rising in her.

She reached back with both hands to pull up the tail of her shirt, and her right hand grasped the Kershaw knife hidden between her cutoffs shorts and briefs. She wagged her shoulders slightly back and forth to hold his attention.

Franco put his right hand on his hip and danced the flashlight beam across her body. Shannon held his gaze and swayed in her stance with both her hands behind her hips. She stepped forward, waited, and stepped back, continuing her flowing motion. Franco came closer. Just before his next step, Shannon rotated her hips lower and planted her right foot back. She looked up at Franco. He came closer.

Shannon flicked open the Kershaw knife and rotated it in a reverse handgrip behind her back. Pushing off her right foot, she smashed her fist-knife up to Franco's jaw. The perfect arc of power popped Franco's head back as her fist caught his jaw and the blade followed deep through his cheek to his nose. She reversed to slam her elbow back in a bony smash to the other side of his head.

Franco howled. "You fucking whore!" He swung the stun gun toward the flesh below her collarbone, but it collided off her rising forearm. He returned with a tight jab into her ribs with 200,000 crackling volts for a full five count.

Shannon came to with sharp waves of pain slapping the back of her head but could not compel her body to move. Dim cage lights rolled past overhead. A steel corridor took shape. She struggled to free her bound hands as Franco dragged her like a potato sack by a rope around her ankles. Her head bumped again as he yanked her over a threshold to a dark, dank cargo hold.

Cage lights shone from the corridor into the squalid chamber, and she glimpsed Franco in the doorway. Blood streaked down his face from an angled gash. A red-soaked towel hung from his collar. His shirt, arms, and hands were painted with blood. He threw a plastic bucket, cheap flashlight, two candy bars, a plastic bottle of water, and a blanket at her. He stepped in to cut the rope off her wrists. "Conserve water. You'll need it in hell."

Shannon grumbled under her breath, grabbed the flashlight and untied her ankles.

Franco bunched his towel and wiped blood off his face. "Caesar will regret ever meeting you." He turned to the door and looked back with her mobile phone in his hand. "No password, stupid. Your family is easy to find if you provoke me again."

"Leave my family alone."

The steel door slammed, followed by a heavy *clunk*. Shannon directed the weak beam of the plastic flashlight into the damp smelly blackness. She was not alone. A family of busy rats moved about peaks of ripped rubble trash bags. The steel door was as unyielding as the humid filthy air. Shannon pushed herself into a corner by the door and pulled dirty linen laundry bags in a semi-circle around her as a bunker. To dry her territorial moat, she grabbed more bags from the room, inspected them, laid down rags and pushed them outward as a dam. She wrapped her legs with the least offensive cloths. She rinsed her mouth with bottled water and took a few measured sips and set the candy bars, water bottle and the bucket next to her, then took cover with the blanket and turned the flashlight off. It would be easy to remember the geometry of the dark dungeon from its bow shape.

The trawler bobbed and rocked side to side. The gentle roll calmed her breath; senses faded on the edge of sleep. All existence became breath, detached from physical reality—consciousness without content, then nothing at all.

A voice rang in the darkness, stirring Shannon. It was Anne Bonny.

"Do not despair, Shannon. I spent five months in cruel, close confinement in a filthy jail facing certain execution. You, too, will survive and thrive. Your adversary is a mere peacock; a fool for respect. You gave none, and none is what he deserves. This is all so familiar. Watch out for the rats, be they with four legs or two. You will prevail."

Shannon held her breath and began to rock forward and back. The scuffling sound of critters resumed. She flicked on the flashlight and peered out beyond the blanket. Curious rat eyes peeped from mounds of trash only six feet away.

Her headache pounded back, her body ached, the air still acrid. But her coping skills returned. *Stay awake. The Doc will return. Find Paddy. I'm a mother who will protect her cubs.* Anne Bonny's throaty words rang back to mind: *Do not despair.*

FISHING FOR CLARITY

The *Second Wind* swayed like a drowsy ghost ship, her sails reefed, without a soul on deck. The hijackers, their cargo and the fugitives had all disappeared in the night. It had been six days since Paddy and Shannon sailed from Jamaica, with no communication with the outside world since their abduction after leaving Kingston.

It was morning. Paddy had been marginally awake on his bunk for hours, struggling to consciousness with a whopping headache from heavy sedation and dehydration. His ribs hurt plenty from Franco's kicks. He forced himself up to swig a few sips of water through his parched lips. He wobbled to Shannon's bunk, checked her pulse, the bandages on her head, neck, hand, and ankle. She moaned and drifted back to sleep.

Paddy pulled himself topside in the early light. Thankfully, the vessel and instrument panel seemed okay. His body loosened a bit when he determined they were at anchor, twelve miles off Marathon Key, Florida.

With slow, steady breaths, Paddy meditated to a safe place, and relaxed to a point of calm where he could frame the bizarre tapestry of the past five days. The hijackers were transporters for a smuggling ring with a triangle trade of cocaine from Brazil, guns from Miami, and illegal persons collected from the ninety-mile-wide Mona Pass between Puerto Rico and the Dominican Republic. More boarded from Jamaica and Cuba. He gave the interlopers enough trouble to keep their ugly bargain and leave. Thankfully, their medical man, Doc, did his part to keep the brutality in check as Franco departed with his team, the goods, and human cargo.

As prepared as Paddy and the *Second Wind* were for defense, it was no match for armed and organized high-tech smugglers, thugs, and pirates. Paddy had followed news reports of smuggling and doings in Caribbean waters. He was well-read in the techniques of historic pirates amid the triangle trades of goods and slaves in the Age of Sail. The game had changed but was as ruthless as ever.

Cocaine now moved easily from Peru and Columbia through Bolivia and Brazil's porous borders to eastern Caribbean ports, flowing through Jamaica to Cuba and the Bahamas on the way to US and European markets. Cash and easily procured guns out of Miami swung through the Caribbean and to South America. Illegals and migrant immigrants were like bonus cash on the return, funded out of Miami and bound for the US.

Paddy figured Franco's team had netted over a million dollars for their ten-day circuit. Considering their vessels, manpower and security, medical services and coordination, a high-paying clientele bankrolled them.

Resting in the pilot chair of the exterior helm, he drummed his fingers, desperate to know what happened to Shannon in that trawler. The masked doctor had taken quite a risk to protect her. He had glimpsed Doc and Caesar in a shouting match with Franco as they all left on the go-fast boats toward the Southwest Florida Gulf Coast. *A mess of pros, amateurs, and malcontents*, he thought. *The sedative Doc gave to Shannon did its job, but no telling her state of mind when she wakes, or the trauma she endured.*

Paddy considered the way forward. *Should I ask Shannon questions, or just reassure her and see what bubbles up?* He stood up, rubbed his ribs lightly, sighed and sat back down. Ten minutes later, he went below to brew some coffee, checked on her again, and returned topside to put a fishing rod to work. *Maybe that will help. She is fish crazy. If she is stable, I'll try to get a rod in her hand today.*

Big fish in the Gulf came within fifteen miles of the Southwest Florida coast for the warmer waters. The action was strong near Marathon Key. Paddy pulled up baitfish, cut them up, and poured the bits over the side. He hummed, "Chum-hum and they will come." Soon he felt a strike on the line, played it right, and pulled up a large redfish. He set it snout down in a white five-gallon pail of seawater and placed a wet towel over the top.

He went below to bring coffee to Shannon, waking her as if it were just another day. He sat on the bed and held her hand. She lurched up. "No . . . Stop . . ." She rubbed her eyes. "Paddy?"

"It's okay. It's me; they're all gone."

She hugged him and sobbed. "I thought they killed you. I dreamt the worst. Franco threatened my kids. What happened?"

"Let's go slow, Shannon." He coaxed her to sip the coffee and gave her biscuits. It was a relief to see her eat.

He put his hand on her forehead, and took her pulse with the other. "What . . . how do you feel?"

"Beat up and shaky." She ran her hand over the back of her head. "Throbbing bumps everywhere. What are these bandages on my hand and ankle? It stings under there."

Paddy examined the lump on her forehead and bruises on the back of her head. "The bruises look like you were hit repeatedly with a blunt weapon."

"I was tied and dragged with my head bumped over steel compartments," she said.

Paddy growled, punched his fist into his other hand, and stood. "I'll clean the bruises and get more ice packs. What else can you remember?"

Shannon paused and pulled a bandage off her hand. "Shit, a rat bite. Hurts like hell. Franco put me in an infested dungeon after I knifed him in the face. He was going to rape me."

Her face contorted, her head and shoulders drooped. She heaved silent breaths. Paddy winced, his face heating in anger, and lowered to put his arm around her. His thoughts ran to revenge and his Mossberg automatic shotgun. He muttered, "Someday, Franco will get what's coming."

They held hands in silence. Shannon coughed and cleared her throat. She took in a breath and pushed her hair back. She asked for more coffee. *A good sign,* he thought.

Paddy returned with chamomile tea and honey. "I think this will be better."

"Thanks." She shook a bit. "This is my fault."

"No, we both own it. What's the last thing you remember?"

"Franco beat me with a slapjack—locked me in a trashy hold. I tried to stay awake and keep the rats away." She buried her face in the bunk.

Paddy tried to pat her shoulder, but she groaned at the touch. "Get more rest, then I'll get you up walking and tend those wounds."

"Help me up now," she said.

After a few steps with Paddy's support, Shannon staggered to the head. "I really have to pee."

Paddy got dish soap, a bowl of warm water, hydrogen peroxide, cotton balls, antibiotic cream, and fresh gauze. He sat her at a table in the galley and got to work.

"First, I'll wash the rat bites with soap and water. Then apply hydrogen peroxide, which is going to sting, and a dressing."

He dripped and dabbed solution on the three deep rat bites.

Shannon grimaced. "More."

He dried the wounds and applied antibiotic cream. "You will need oral antibiotics after we get through customs."

She nodded.

"If it's any consolation, Shannon, Franco isn't looking too good. Doc stitched him quick, but his face is scarred for life. You also made a mess of Mateo's shoulder." He gave her a studied look. "You did admirably." Paddy handed her a glass of water and three ibuprofen.

"What about you, Paddy?"

"I'm fine. Let's go up on deck. I have a surprise. Let's get you comfortable up there. It's a beautiful day."

ဢ

Shannon insisted on pulling her own way up from the galley. Near the top, her threadbare bathrobe caught on a hook. She stumbled sideways into the helm station. She grumbled and tossed the robe down into the galley, retied her gray sweatpants and rolled up the sleeves of her son's Gloucester Fisherman ice hockey team sweatshirt.

She squinted at the late morning sun and sat near Paddy in the U-shaped bench seat. "I need a drink. What the hell happened?"

He handed her a pair of sunglasses. "The bar is closed."

She noticed fishing rods, tackle, and a white five-gallon bucket sloshing across from her on the deck. Pointing, she gave him a questioning look.

He stepped to the bucket, removed the wet towel, and lifted up the large redfish. "Tonight's dinner."

Shannon opened her mouth with a silent *wow*.

Paddy baited a rig and handed her a rod. Shannon moved slowly, studied the wind, currents, and rocky structures just above the water. She leaned slightly over the rub rail and flicked a cast. She jigged the rod absently with her brows knit.

"I'm fishing for clarity here. Tell me more."

"I figure you were in that hold for thirty-six hours before the Doc guy got you out of there. He kept you on IVs, sedated you, and he did his best to protect you. When we neared the coast of Matanzas, Cuba, an open boat brought ten Cuban nationals to the *Second Wind*."

Shannon blew out her cheeks. "I don't remember any of that. I do remember Franco threatened my kids. What else happened?"

"We were press-ganged by smugglers who used the *Second Wind* as a decoy to move illegals and drugs. Mateo squealed like a pig when I interrogated him. Franco was a foreman in the operation. He played it safe staying on the trawler for the switch in cargoes close to US territory. I think he was trying to prove himself to an organized syndicate."

Shannon scratched over the new bandages. "What else?"

"Stop scratching," he said. "From the men's chatter, I gather they have connections beyond South America, the US and Caribbean, to Eastern Europe."

"That scares me more."

"Trust me, Shannon. You and your kids will be okay."

"How can I be sure?"

"We take the threat seriously and get on with living."

Shannon sighed. "I hate being scared of anything. What can we do?"

"The most important thing is to avoid contact, let things cool down. Franco has more to deal with than chasing down your family. He told me to keep our traps shut on this, or he will retaliate. They did not intend to hurt anyone, and they did set us free. We survived."

"That's it?"

Paddy set his chin with a grim smile and put a hand on her shoulder. "Yes, and stay out of it."

"All right. But I need to see my kids."

"Okay, let's take it easy today, get some rest tonight, thoroughly check the *Second Wind* in the morning, and report to customs in Marathon. When I think you're ready, we'll visit Delphina and Grandbaby Paula in North Carolina."

"You are the best." She blinked back tears and shuddered in relief.

Paddy took her fishing rod and reeled it in. "Remember, we leave when I'm convinced you're ready. Don't obsess over Franco. The Doc was the adult supervision on that squad, and clearly disgusted with Franco. The big bosses will surely learn what happened. They will squeeze Franco to stop with the theatrics and wasteful vendettas. They have a profitable business to run."

"What about that drink now?"

Paddy wet his lips. "A little grog would do us both some good."

The next morning, Paddy rose before dawn, sleep-deprived from a full night watch on Shannon. Lying on his bruised and possibly fractured ribs was excruciating. He took shallow breaths and painkillers. At least he slept on his back through most of the night. Paddy examined his aching ribs, stretched slowly and rotated his torso as best he could. He knew they would be slow to heal.

Paddy decided to risk a dip in the water to relax his muscles. He lowered himself carefully down the rope ladder, using the strength of his legs. Taking light breaststrokes around the *Second Wind* energized him and confirmed his assessment that X-rays were unnecessary.

He toweled off and the sun dried his skin. Meditating beyond the horizon, he tried to fathom Shannon's state of mind. He was happy to hear her movements in the galley below. She soon came up the companionway in her blue robe with a mug of coffee and carafe he had prepared.

"Good morning, Captain," she said. "I had a long, hard sleep."

"You needed it."

Shannon gasped for air. "Felt like I swam underwater all night." She squinted. "It's so bright . . . my head aches."

Paddy gave her his sunglasses, held on to her hand, and smiled. "You're healing. Let's sit at the helm station."

"Sorry I didn't bring up a mug for you," she said.

"I'm set. Want to know how you are doing."

"Good enough to be useful," she mumbled and looked intently at Paddy's illustrated torso in the bright daylight. "After I study your tattoos and finish my coffee, I'm ready to work. What's up?"

He smiled to note her fighting spirit. "The brig needs a thorough search from stem to stern, a straightening up, and cleaning till we get to dockage in Marathon. My quarters are all set. I'll check the rigging and instruments."

"That's the least my sorry ass can do." Shannon traced her finger in the air from his collarbone, across his sternum, to the side of his abdomen. "Speaking of the *Second Wind*, I see her image sailing toward your belly button."

"That's the finishing touch of the design."

"Meaning?"

He grunted and chose not to answer.

Shannon changed tack. "It's a masterpiece, but a tattoo on the stomach had to really hurt."

"A pint of rum helped," he said. "The artist is from Nassau, the best in the Bahamas; learned from a pro in Miami, keeps a clean shop, and only uses organic pigments."

"I want to get one there."

Paddy swiveled in the pilot chair. "Great to see you bounce back. Now we get to work; search the vessel, every compartment, every inch."

"Roger that, Captain," Shannon said, stepping down the companionway.

Moments later, Paddy chuckled as he heard her curse as she rummaged below.

"Where's the soap?"

Dishes and glasses clinked in the sink.

"The head's filthy."

Doors, drawers, and compartments were rifled through and shut firmly.

"Bunch of pigs."

Water cascaded into a bucket and a mop sloshed.

"Smells like a friggin' locker room."

Cabinet doors sounded open and shut.

"No fresh food."

He smiled as he listened to more movement and sounds of searching.

"Good, nothing broken . . . Arrgh."

A thud sounded like a fist hitting a wall.

"Where the fuck is it? You thieving son of a bitch, Mateo. My ass you wouldn't take our stuff."

It got quiet. Paddy heard more thumping and movement. He peeked into the galley, strewn helter-skelter below. Shannon was somewhere in the fore of the vessel. *Anger is a good sign,* he thought. *She is crawling out of her emotional dungeon.*

Paddy checked the instruments but mostly waited for Shannon to come up on deck. Now he heard what he expected from below— Shannon's raging scream.

"The monkey-faced bastard took my birthright."

"What do you mean?" he yelled back.

"Anne Bonny's short sword."

"You brought it here?"

"It was a bad call. I'll search the planet for that prick, Mateo, and get it back."

Paddy listened to more of her rummaging and cursing. He broke out laughing.

Shannon came fast up the companionway with a red face. "This isn't funny."

"Oh, yes it is, mate. Maybe you should check the weapons locker. Do you remember the combination?"

"Arrgh," she growled.

Shannon ran her hand along the teak trim board, located the hidden keypad and entered the code. The pad beeped and the compartment door clicked open. Shannon slid out Anne Bonny's sword, secure in its decorative scabbard, and held it to her chest. She sprang up the steps and laid it on Paddy's shoulder.

"You prankster—you put it in there and knew I would freak out. Stop with the smug face."

"Some lessons have to be earned, Shannon. Mateo learned his the hard way. He won't mess with us again. The black mesh bag in there has the rest of your personal stuff."

She turned and trotted about the deck holding the sword over her head. "I got my mojo back. Yo, Anne."

She settled and handed the sword to Paddy. "Please put it back. I'll get to work in a few minutes." She stepped up onto the gunwale, walked a few steps as if on a balance beam, and dove into the water in her wrinkled T-shirt and shorts.

Paddy said, "Hey, get back up here. Too soon to be doing that."

She swam around the *Second Wind* three times and climbed back aboard, dripping wet. Paddy shook his head and averted his eyes.

Ninety minutes later, Shannon and Paddy finished their task list and raised the yellow Q flag to signal request boarding and inspection. Paddy called US Customs and Border Protection under the Small Vessel Reporting System and referenced his filed float plan. Since there was nothing to declare, they cleared in without an inspection. Deemed a low-risk boater, the in-person visit was not required.

Shannon overheard Paddy's call. "That was easy."

"The Marathon Port of Entry with customs still isn't ready after years of planning. I'm glad we didn't have to go into town and be told to take a bus to Key West to answer questions," he said. "With all the coordinated Homeland Security high-tech monitoring, and Coast Guard patrols, I thought we'd be asked about unusual activity around our vessel. I should have reported the incident but made the choice not to. We have too much to lose—too many questions to answer about our own reasons for being out here."

"I get it. What's our plan now?"

"A marina slip awaits us at the entrance to Boot Key Harbor."

"Are we talking hot showers, restaurant—a hot meal?"

"Is that the best checklist you can think up?"

Shannon looked at him, wide-eyed. "Now you're just busting my ass."

"Sometimes it's good to shock back to normal. By the way, the marina has the depth we need, a fuel stop, pump-out, fresh water, and laundry."

Shannon poked him in the ribs. "Gee, that's all?"

Paddy groaned in pain and tried to cover it up.

Shannon looked Paddy in the eye. "You okay?"

"I'm fine, just pulled something. I could use some rest though. By the way, the marina has internet, cable, twenty-four-hour security, and a pool."

"You do spoil me."

"Too bad you aren't up for some fishing. The restaurant and bar prepares the catch."

"You just don't let up," she said.

"One other thing, Shannon. I called Delphina."

"You did?"

"She was thrilled to hear from us. We'll sail tomorrow afternoon to Marco Island and get you to the walk-in clinic there. Then we rent a van and drive to your daughter's place in North Carolina."

"What's today's date?" she asked.

"We will be with Delphina and Grandbaby Paula for Christmas."

GINGERNUT

With the *Second Wind* secure at Marco Island Marina, Paddy and Shannon were on their way to her daughter's apartment in Woodfin, North Carolina, in a rented brown van. They hustled to get ready for the twelve-hour drive and would Christmas shop on the way. Shannon had a headache, was shaky, and her large joints ached. The welts on her body were healing. Nothing would override her determination to see her family—it was the only goal that mattered now.

"I'll drive," she said.

"Are you sure?"

"It's all highways. It'll focus me."

Paddy switched seats with Shannon at their first gas stop. Shannon put a fresh bottle of water on the console and adjusted the driver's seat and mirrors. She gulped down the penicillin and ibuprofen from the clinic they visited earlier.

"Nine hours to go," she said.

Paddy sat tall in the passenger seat. "Did the doctor at the clinic really say you're okay to drive?"

"No restrictions."

"What did he say?"

"Mild concussion, early onsets of rat-bite fever. The rash around two of the bites, joint pain, the shakes, and headache will pass."

He sat back. "A two-hour shift for you. That's it. Stop sooner if you're tired."

"A good captain knows when to step down."

"All right," he said.

Shannon stared at the blanket of green leafy vines covering the trees along the highway. "What is that growth all over the trees?"

"That's *kudzu*—it's a vine introduced from Asia by our farmers in the late 1800s and by the government to control soil erosion. It can grow a foot a day and chokes trees throughout the southeast."

"Friggin' invasive stuff. Next time I want to say the *F*-bomb, I'll use the word *kudzu* instead." Shannon pressed her lips together and took in a long breath. "About that kudzu rat-bastard, Franco, and his threats: do you think I should get Delphina a new phone for Christmas? She'll love it if I pay for a family plan."

"Good idea; get new numbers. Might avoid intimidation tactics by Franco, or having to give Delphina information about what happened."

"It's still a no-win. If I tell her, I'm not protecting her. If I do, she'll freak out for what could be nothing. If Franco knows people are looking for him, he may do something. I'm still thinking about it."

"Figure it out. Let me know what you decide. I don't think he'll do anything if we don't provoke or implicate him."

Shannon looked at the kudzu choking another large tree. "I suppose I could tell her I was accosted by thugs in a Miami hotel. They stole stuff, took my phone, and said their pals would go after me and my family if we went to the police and identified them."

"Not bad."

Paddy suggested they stop for dinner in St. Augustine, drive on to Savannah, Georgia, and stay at a hotel. "A good night's sleep and scenic five-hour drive to North Carolina will be a reward for our long day today."

"I can't wait to see Delphina and Paula. Grandbaby turns four in January. I'll get her a teddy bear and a mermaid or dolphin puppet."

"You might want to get something for Alex and Eric as well."

"They'll be there?"

"Delphina wanted it to be a secret, but we can't show up empty-handed, can we?"

Paddy and Shannon arrived at Delphina's small apartment in Woodfin the next afternoon. Shannon hugged her daughter and grandchild tight. As Shannon lingered on the floor with little Paula, Delphina got reacquainted with her great-uncle Paddy. The four-day family holiday was a warm blessing. Shannon was relieved to gather with her far-flung family.

Dinner on Christmas day brimmed with everyone's favorite dishes. Shannon and Eric's separation was remarkably normalized. Eric flew down the day before with six lobsters from their friend, Captain Steve. Ever modest, Eric casually mentioned a promotion with a yearlong assignment in Connecticut. He was gracious during the visit. It was wonderful to still be a family. Shannon realized that their grown kids had adjusted before she did.

She took comfort that Delphina liked living in the Blue Ridge Mountains, and her son, Alex, was enjoying his freedoms in California. Alex shared pictures of himself and new friends surfing California beaches from Half Moon Bay to Rincon, Malibu, Huntington, and Black's Beach in San Diego.

When little Paula saw the pictures of Alex surfing she asked, "Is that Glosta? Home in Glosta?" This, of course, annoyed Delphina. Delphina loved her new stylish mobile phone with Mom's subsidized calling plan. Everyone goaded Paddy to talk about his family in Jamaica and share stories of his *Second Wind* voyages. He enjoyed playfully chasing little Paula while she dragged the new teddy bear about by the ear and kept her new dolphin puppet tucked under arm.

The day after Christmas, Paddy treated everyone to lunch and an afternoon family swim at the indoor pool of the hotel where he, Eric, and Alex were staying. Shannon observed her strong-willed granddaughter take easily to the water. The fiery little redhead had a big belly laugh with an Irish attitude. Her nickname, Gingernut, fit.

Shannon stayed in Paula's room with the little snoozer next to her each night. Paula held fast to her teddy. The stuffed dolphin peeked out from her pillow. Paula turned over in her sleep and rested her little hand on Shannon's face. Shannon had never thought it okay to have a separated family, the way other families had become, but now accepted it.

She considered humanity's history of empires, ravages of war, disease, eras of exploration and migration that caused painful family separations. Today's communications are more immediate but face-to-face time more rare. Shannon knew her family bonds would stay strong. Her concept of family was evolving with her quest for the truth of their seafaring ancestry.

CHARLESTON

The five-hour drive from the Blue Ridge Mountains to Charleston, South Carolina, allowed Shannon and Paddy time to plan their investigation of Anne Bonny's life after piracy as Anne Burleigh. Shannon lowered the passenger side window and hung out her elbow.

"What do you think we can accomplish in Charleston?"

"This is a three-and-a-half-day research mission. We have the location of Anne Bonny's old stone boarding house," Paddy said. "But we can't arouse suspicion or reveal our true focus."

"We need to get smart on the history of that house," Shannon said.

"Yes, but we go wide first. Recon outside-in, get the relevant history of Charleston, the times of Anne's life, what local records might show about her father, William Cormac, the plantations, and homes in the historic district."

"That's a lot in three days."

"You and I have skills. We identify sources, ask the right questions."

After they checked into rooms at a bed and breakfast in Charleston, Shannon made phone calls while Paddy obtained walking guides from the lobby, got coffees to go, and waited out front on the sidewalk. Shannon had a smug face when she joined him.

It was a clear, breezy day and holiday lights swung over the streets. Ornaments and tinseled trees graced hotel lobbies and storefronts.

"Oh, thanks for the coffee," said Shannon as she joined Paddy on the sidewalk.

Paddy was already on the move. "Let's stretch our legs along the stately streets of Charleston."

Shannon looked up and down the roadway, getting a feel for the place. It seemed a bigger version of Gloucester's Main Street during Christmas week. The walking guide displayed the orientation to the harbor. She barely caught up to Paddy when he picked up the pace again.

"Hold up, Paddy. I'm still on a holiday buzz."

"I've only visited this port to refuel, and for pub meals by the waterfront. Now we have the chance to soak in the local history of tidewater aristocrats, farmers, slaves and pirates."

Shannon stopped by a park bench. "Let's sit here for a minute to enjoy our coffee."

Paddy sighed. "Okay."

They watched people leisurely pass on the sidewalk. There was not much street traffic. She noted the tranquility of the place and the politeness of the people. When they resumed their walk and turned onto Church Street, Shannon stopped short, spilling some of her coffee on her hands and shoes. "That's the Bermuda stone house, Anne's old headquarters. Let's go around the block to see it from all sides."

"Today, we want the big picture," Paddy said. "Tomorrow we split up the city records research, historical tours, museums, and library stuff."

"Paddy, I need to tell you something; I've already jumped the gun."

Paddy squared his head to hers. "What?"

"Call it initiative or stupidity, but I got the number of the owner this morning and reached an older family member of the house. His name is Hancock."

"Our cover is blown."

"No, it's okay. We will get an appointment before we leave. Mr. Hancock said it was now his daughter's place and her decision for us to see it. He was very polite, said we came a long way, and their holiday guests are leaving tomorrow."

"What exactly was your story, Shannon?"

"I am doing hush-hush site research for an independent film company on a Revolutionary War film that pays well for a few days of shooting."

"That's a whopper."

"I'm an actress, not a liar. If it makes sense to film the place after seeing it, and agree on compensation, we don't have to actually finish a film project later."

"That's solidly in the fiction category, Shannon."

"I offered to pay for the short tour. He said it wasn't necessary and his Christmas guests would be gone. Apparently, the building has an owner's section and three rental apartments. Most everyone is out of town. He seemed interested in the money for the film shoot."

Paddy shook his head and laughed. "There is Haraden blood in you. Captain Jonathan Haraden overtook larger British vessels with bluffs instead of bloodshed."

Shannon beamed.

"Maybe your ruse will work," he said. "But the next time we agree on a plan, we negotiate any changes."

"I'm crazy to find out what's there."

They rounded the building to an alley on the north side.

Shannon bounced in her steps. "Imagine, Anne's place of business here by Colonial Charleston Harbor."

"Bonny knew what she was doing when she bought the place," said Paddy. "It's a short walk to the Old Exchange and Provost Dungeon."

Paddy and Shannon soon put some of the pieces together with their research. The stone building, built in 1704, was near St. Phillips Cemetery, associated with the Anglican congregation formed in South Carolina in 1681. The first royal governor of South Carolina, Robert Johnson, was among early prominent Colonial figures buried there.

Johnson had set up a naval force to resist pirates Blackbeard and Stede Bonnet, who preyed along the Carolina coast. Bonnet and his crew met their end in Charleston and were hanged at high tide, their bodies dumped into the river.

The Bermuda stone house survived horrific fires, wars, and hurricanes. St. Phillips church had burned and was rebuilt across the street. Laborers in the West Indies cut the pinkish coral into blocks, which became ships' ballasts and were imported to Charleston's French Quarter as building material for several early buildings. Exposed to the weather, the stone hardened and remained in good condition. A secret tunnel once connected the basement of the house to the battery near the historic waterfront.

Local legend held that pirates used the tunnel to get from the harbor to the house in the early eighteenth century.

In the 1930s, a city development project redirected its sewage system, filling the Colonial passageways with sand. The local pirate stories at the house were undocumented, but, with Anne's letters, Paddy and Shannon knew them to be true.

Anne and her new husband, James Burleigh, became owners of the property around 1736. She was thirty-seven, with a respectable identity, a growing family and a thriving business. Anne's storehouse in the basement had a vaulted room to the south side of the building underneath a courtyard that bordered the St. Phillips Cemetery. One of her letters alluded to a vast collection of curios and the fruits of her labors stored below.

Shannon and Paddy lingered outside the wrought iron fence surrounding the courtyard of the building.

"This place seems familiar."

"Of course," said Paddy. "You saw pictures of it on the internet days ago."

Shannon rubbed over her heart. "The pictures only showed the front. I recognize the features all around, like I've been here before. Look at the heavy stone that covers the raised well in the courtyard. I'll bet anything that Anne's vault is below that wellhead."

After a long walk around the historic district and a stop at the Visitors Bureau, they strolled over gravel walkways at White Point Gardens—originally named Oyster Point for the mounds of sun-bleached shells at the southernmost point of the city where the Cooper and Ashley rivers meet. Adjacent was the Battery, a landmark defensive seawall and promenade.

"This wall is where the tunnel from the house led," said Shannon as they passed a number of military and historic monuments on the promenade.

She stopped at a monument marker of pirate Stede Bonnet's dishonor, the hanging of him and crew 1718. She surveyed the beautiful views of the harbor and the shady live oak trees, with their thick, short trunks. Widespread canopies with Spanish moss draped over low branches. She imagined the working Colonial waterfront come to life.

Shannon had much to process at bedtime, and the fresh air of Charleston's historic district and harbor mingled into a night of unforgettable dreams. She transformed as spirit time-traveler from the waters of Colonial Charleston Harbor by the Battery. The date, December 3, 1773, rippled past on a floating broadsheet. Men hustled boxes from a wooden ship to the dock and up the hillside. Shannon could not understand the muffled utterances of the men as she hovered over the scene. Then she recognized Anne Bonny's face from an earlier dream, now a regal woman with a large hat and trailing scarf, standing like a monarch under a live oak tree on a bluff. Anne peered back to Shannon with a smile. Anne stood with a middle-aged man and youthful female in her twenties. They shared a family resemblance.

Anne Bonny Burleigh's gown was pleated silk; the man was her eldest son, James Burleigh, Jr., in a riding jacket, standing by her granddaughter, Elizabeth, with a pouf cap and brocade silk dress. Anne laughed and chided anxious men who scurried past them to haul a refused shipment of English tea back to the Exchange Building.

Turning to James, Anne said, "Tea is now gold. The people are insane for tea and filled with hate for the new Tea Act. The British think us all scoundrels and smugglers, but the squirmy lizards in the House of Lords are the true pirates. Tensions will reach the breaking point. Every levy they lay on us works to our favor. Our merchants have agreed to refuse the tea. Fellow citizens demand the boycott."

James put his hand on the shoulder of his daughter. "We are just bankers and merchants supporting our right to trade."

Anne finished her rant with a smile. "Over 90 percent of our tea and other goods are acquired elsewhere. Corrupt and powerless customs officials turn a blind eye. Half of the English business in high goods is to our colonies. With resolve, we shall gain the upper hand."

Elizabeth smiled at her grandmother. "One day we will be rid of these bastards and live in a free land."

Anne squinted at Elizabeth. "Remember what I said about loose lips." Anne surveyed the town, looked directly at Shannon and then back to her son. "A siege will certainly be upon us here. The British will make Charleston an easy target as strength grows in the North. You must both go tomorrow. James, take the trunks I prepared for each of you. Get Elizabeth to the Lee House in Yorktown to stay with our friends. Make haste to Boston with the mail pouches and report status to our cohorts. Elizabeth can rejoin you up North after things unfold. I will await your letters. Give blessings to our relations in Ipswich, and Squam in Gloucester."

James protested, but Anne stayed him with a gloved hand. "I'll be fine here and amused to see if this matter of tea be the spark that lights fires of freedom."

He accepted her word and assured her of his conviction. "Whether tea is stored, stolen, or dumped into the harbors, our merchant proxies bought it, are indebted to us, and fear for their skins with the British. We will pinch some of that English drug tonight to add to our storehouses."

Ann rubbed her hands together. "The tea will sell for a dear price along with our other acquisitions and, in time, finance revolt. I will keep a sharp eye on our affairs from the country house." She held Elizabeth close. "I have provided you a bequest of important writings and valuables in your garment chest. They are for you to cherish, safeguard, and to pass on to the eldest or ablest daughters of your descendants. My instructions are clear. Godspeed."

Shannon's dream shifted to the Bermuda stone house. She saw Anne holding a lantern as James moved a few cartons of British tea into the basement, its stone arches flanking a passageway to a vaulted room full of wine, deerskins, rifles, weapons, a harpsichord, antiquities, gold, silver, silks, fine linens, carved ivory, gold jewelry, plus racks of documents and bound booklets. Dusty masonry tools sat upon a stack of red bricks next to a partially completed wall under the arch to the vaulted room.

Anne handed James two leather letter carriers. "We have documents to expose or control our enemies." Then Anne turned to Shannon. "Yes, you too shall enjoy and pass on my bequest."

Shannon awoke, sitting up and running a hand across her face. "This is way beyond a dream . . . beyond lucidity."

DÉJÀ VU

Shannon rose early the next morning to use the inn's guest computer and printer. She wondered whether the lucid dream was too crazy to tell Paddy. *It was like floating in a movie set,* she thought. *Maybe his theory of genetic resonance and dynamic ancestral memory does explain it.*

She entered the date and location from her dream into the search engine: December 3, 1773, Colonial Charleston Harbor. Charleston's first tea party, thirteen days before the well-known Boston Tea Party, popped up.

She viewed a real estate site that gave the current market estimate of Anne's old headquarters at $1.5 million and annual property taxes of $50,000. It had been in one family for years, and they had converted the building into rental units. *No wonder the man was interested in the money for a film shoot.* Shannon resumed her work on the computer to create a cover story.

Paddy and Shannon divided their work for the day. The job fell to her to conduct city records searches on the historic Church Street homes and investigate the old walled fortifications of Charleston and the sewer and water projects in the area of the Bermuda stone house. She would do the schmaltzy pirate tour in the afternoon. Paddy would research at the museums and take the historic home tours. By dinner, they would have a context to case the Bermuda stone house. Shannon confirmed an appointment the next morning for her and her "associate, Mr. John Kelly," to tour the owner's section and common areas of the residence. She got permission to take a few pictures.

Shannon and Paddy compared notes over take-out dinners in their adjoining rooms. They uncorked a California pinot grigio.

"It was a good day," said Shannon. "We know what we know and what we don't. I breathed plenty of stale air in the municipal building basement, reviewing utility and sewer project diagrams, property information, birth, death and marriage records."

"How was the pirate tour?" asked Paddy.

"It was fun the way the guides ham it up. Most of it was familiar. They did mention the Bermuda stone house, pirate lore and secret tunnels, but were quick to say there's no evidence of pirates being in that historic home."

Paddy sipped his wine. "I hoped to locate the plantation of Anne Bonny's father and their country home where they grew indigo and rice. Most of the plantation homes on the historical register were built in the 1800s and well inland by a river. Anne's father, William Cormac, had a plantation near the Charleston coast in the early 1700s. It might be the Oakland Plantation, about twelve miles from the Historic District. It was owned during the right timeframe by an Irishman, John Perrie from County Cork, Ireland, who became governor of Antigua. He passed it to a daughter. It was known for indigo and rice. A coincidence, perhaps, but Anne Bonny was born in County Cork. I wonder who Perrie really was, and his relationship to her father, Cormac."

"With Caribbean connections, too. Is the plantation open to the public?"

"No. Descendants of two families have owned it for two hundred years. We'll tackle it on a future trip to Charleston."

"We figured there'd be some dead ends in public records, but I found something," Shannon said. "Charleston has one of the most advanced systems on the planet to convey water, wastewater, and storm water. I have a drawing of the closest underground access points of the new system built over the past few years and older tunnels still open nearby."

Paddy leaned in. "Anything else?"

"We can believe the story about Colonial underground tunnels for smuggling."

"Tell me."

"Charleston has had tunnels dating back hundreds of years. There is a unique fossilized limestone under the city and rivers called Cooper marl, which is soft enough to tunnel and dense enough to transport water without pipes. When it is cut and exposed to air, it hardens like cement."

"You are crazy to get inside that house, Shannon."

"Like a dog chasing a bus."

"So what does red dog do when it catches the bus?"

"The dog knows it's something good," said Shannon.

Paddy folded his arms.

"I'm highly optimistic."

"Tell me what you know," he said.

"I'll explain tomorrow."

The next day, Shannon approached the Bermuda stone building with Paddy in tow. She wore a stylish form-fitting dress with a sweater over her shoulders. It was 10 a.m. and an older man sat with a newspaper on the stoop of the front entrance.

"Mr. Hancock?"

"Good morning, Ms. Packard." The man stood. Turning to Paddy he said, "I assume you must be Mr. Kelly."

"Call me John," said Paddy, who wasn't entirely comfortable with the pseudonyms.

They shook hands. Mr. Hancock turned to Shannon and stopped in place.

"My daughter is away. She asked me to request a business card before we begin."

Paddy cleared his throat and his eyes widened.

Shannon said, "Of course." She pulled a card from the pocket in her purse. "Here you go."

Hancock read the card. "Independent Film Services, Sharon Packard, Director of Location Research." He looked up with a smile. "Thank you.

So, let's do a tour. Do you have a business card for me, Mr. Kelly?"

"Not with me."

"John left his briefcase on the plane," Shannon said. "I have something else for you, Mr. Hancock." She reached into her tote bag to present a pastry box from a local bakery containing four fresh cranberry-raisin scones.

"Ms. Packard. How could you possibly know those are my favorite?" Gesturing to the house he added, "I have coffee brewed for you both, if you like."

Shannon looked at Paddy. "Yes, we would, thank you," she said. "I had a scone yesterday and anybody who lives within ten miles of that shop would want one."

Hancock squinted with a twinkle of mischief. "I try not to underestimate people from New England. Boston and Charleston were sister cities during Colonial times, you know."

They toured the entrance, drawing room and common areas and then got a peek at two of the apartments. Hancock talked mostly about the renovations on the house since it had been in his family for four generations. He grew up in it.

Shannon asked permission for every picture she took and Hancock brightened each time she spoke. He was most agreeable to her manners. Paddy kept in the background and asked her logistical questions about rooms to shoot scenes, angles, and outside shots that would be necessary.

"I like it. Can we see the basement now?"

Hancock hesitated and frowned.

Shannon waited, sweating in her dress. "We were hoping to shoot pictures of the stone foundation for a low-light scene of Colonials meeting in secret with members of their militia."

He rubbed his chin and looked at the floor.

"Is there a problem, Mr. Hancock?" Shannon batted her eyes at him.

He sighed. "The cellar has divided storage areas for the tenants separated with simple wood partitions and stapled chicken wire—a bit of a mess down there. Some sections have padlocks."

"No problem," said Paddy. "We don't mind the clutter. If we decide to use the location, we'll pay extra to store everything and set up a nice new storage center for your residents with secure keypads after the shoot."

"That would clear up a nightmare for me, and the residents." Hancock sighed again. "My daughter owns and sort of runs the place, but it seems I am still the caretaker. She has a demanding job and lives with her husband and college-aged son a few miles from here." Hancock paused. "Wait here. I'll get a flashlight, so we can have a look."

Once he led them down, Hancock turned on the dim basement lights and handed the flashlight to Shannon.

The basement was cool and not as musty as expected. A dehumidifier droned away in the corner. Each side of the foursquare house cellar had a large arch. *Built to last*, she thought.

The east and west arches guarded recessed open rooms nearly six feet deep. *Probably for root storage, preserves, bottled and packaged goods*, she decided. She ran the beam all around and focused on the north and south walls bricked in under their arches.

She turned to Paddy. "John, we'll need to request period lamp fixtures. This place is perfect." She then addressed their host. "Mr. Hancock, it may take months for the film company to get all the investors before we commit, but I can tell you that we will need three to five days of shooting scenes in the common areas, basement, and courtyard at twenty-five hundred per day. We cover hotel rooms for your residents as necessary, and meal service for those who wish to stay in their quarters. We would also get a bid for the new storage system and pay the bill."

They shook hands on the arrangement and left. Hancock resumed his post with his newspaper, scone and coffee on the front stoop as they took one last walk through the courtyard. Then they strolled back to their hotel.

"Where did you get the business card, Shannon?"

"I got a sheaf of business card stock for laser printers at the office supply store down the street, created a file, cut and pasted an image for a logo, printed a few and *voila*."

"Why bother?"

"Authenticity. We're flaky film subcontractors, always on the move."

"Why didn't you tell me about the cards?"

"Either I ran out of time and forgot, or maybe I just thought it was my turn to tighten your jib."

"Ah, payback for me letting you sweat about Anne Bonny's missing sword. But that was a lesson."

"Today's lesson is 'Don't underestimate me.'"

Paddy laughed. "So what did you get out of the visit?"

"The south side arch in the basement has modern brick. That is where the tunnel once led to the harbor. The north side toward the courtyard and graveyard has Colonial red brick the same as in the fortifications around town. Anne Bonny's vault of valuables is behind that wall."

"How can you be so sure?"

"Call it déjà vu. I can tell you exactly what's inside that vault. I mean, if it has not been breached since being bricked up, or pillaged from the capped well in the courtyard outside. We have no idea how long the big stone in the courtyard has covered the well."

They headed to a sandwich shop and spoke softly over lunch. Paddy became convinced of Shannon's information after she sketched a detailed drawing of the vault and a long list of its contents.

"My belief in ancestral memory may get validated," he said.

She whispered, "Paddy, do you think there is a way to return someday and excavate the cellar in five days?"

Paddy laughed louder and louder.

Other patrons glanced.

She faced them. "It's okay; I forgot to give him his medicine this morning."

Paddy roared crazily, rocking his chair back and falling.

Shannon helped him up.

He grinned, keeping his arm around her, and whispered in her ear. "Ms. Packard, you'll need professional bank robbers for that idea—and then clear your schedule for years of jail time. Come up with a better plan, pirate."

"Yeah, I'm a bonehead; too much risk. Right now, our best opportunity is to get back to Barfield Bay and find Jack and Anne's pirate treasure.

BARFIELD BAY

On New Year's Day, Shannon and Paddy made good time driving from Charleston back to South Florida. She toyed with strategies to access Anne Bonny's vault in the Bermuda stone house someday. Getting Anne's memoir and valuable artifacts there would have to wait. Now they would resume their uncertain hunt for Jack Rackham and Anne Bonny's buried chests near Marco Island. Shannon's uncle spent years researching their pirate ancestors and believed the vague vellum note pointed there. The scant description of the shell mounds, keys and cays seemed to fit what was now known as Barfield Bay. Shannon's lucid dreams of Jack Rackham and Anne Bonny were convincing, but she doubted if anything could be there after nearly 300 years. She tried to convince herself that the journey was as important as the destination.

Shannon took her turn driving after a rest stop in Fort Myers. In less than an hour, they would pass Naples on the way to the Marco Island Marina near the big bridge.

"I just spoke to the dockmaster on the phone," Paddy said. "The *Second Wind* is fine at the slip. I asked about the nearest beach. He said it would be a perfect afternoon to explore and swim at Tigertail Beach."

"Fantastic."

"I can tell when you get land sick, Shannon."

"Before Charleston, you asked how many more days we had to do 'land stuff,' and you said 'kudzu' a lot."

"No more kudzu blues—we're going to the beach."

"After that, we line up a backwater fishing or pontoon boat rental for tomorrow. The waters are shallow where we're exploring."

The next morning, they restocked the *Second Wind* with provisions. Shannon put together the checklist for their reconnaissance mission and packed the van with fishing gear, Paddy's metal detector, two backpacks, four duffel bags, and two folding trench shovels from the *Second Wind*. They drove north over the Marco Island Bridge to an East Naples shopping mall to purchase two large white rolling coolers, work gloves, and a folding pruning saw. *More than enough to go operational,* she thought.

Paddy closed the back door of the van. "If we are successful, we'll use our backpacks and sea bags to load booty into the large marine ice coolers. They'll roll nicely off the pontoon boat to our van when we leave."

"What then?" she said.

"We need luggage to conceal the booty if we check into a quiet extended stay place. We can't take it straight back to the *Second Wind.*"

Shannon pointed across the parking lot. "What about that Goodwill store?"

"Brilliant."

They walked out of the Goodwill store with vintage tweedy suitcases in three sizes and two sets of used golf clubs.

"The golf bags are a stealthy touch, Shannon. With big straps and pockets they can handle some weight. We could be carrying millions in gold and people would think us boring duffers on vacation with old clubs."

They got back into the van. Shannon looked at her uncle. "I get it. We disappear in the gray wave of seniors?"

"You do not disappear well, young lady. Do your best, and this time let's agree to follow recon protocol," he said.

Paddy sat at the steering wheel and lowered the windows. He called two marinas about boat rentals. "Florida makes water sports available without hassles. The marina complex in Marco on Bald Eagle Drive has nice rentals, but it's far away and the docks are too busy. The Caxambas Pass Park Marina is close but no suitable rentals."

"What's the problem?" asked Shannon.

"Unlike Gloucester Harbor, where people mind their own business, here's throngs of visitors, authorities, and nosy bystanders. On the way back, we'll stake out the more casual marina by the residences at Isles of Capri. At this point we're just learning the terrain, identifying resources and obstacles."

Fifteen minutes later, they drove through the Isles of Capri neighborhood of modest homes with docks. "This is a sportsman's paradise, and the marina is perfect. It's quiet, with easy in and out by van."

"Nice neighborhood," said Shannon. "Like a mix of Lobster Cove, Wheeler's Point, and Lanesville back home, years ago. Any place that has RVs, boats in yards or canals, with marinas and bait shops can't be all bad." They parked at the marina and walked the dock to scan the area and the boats.

Paddy held a waterways route guide. "Looks like a perfect setup to rent a pontoon boat and motor through secluded cays and waterways with only a few paddlers, party boats, and people fishing."

"Great choice," she said.

"But we have to scrap the idea. They don't allow their rentals to go out in the Gulf even for a short stretch before turning into Barfield Bay. My mistake. Let's grab lunch here, then drive to the Indian Hill neighborhood on the southern tip of Marco by Caxambas Pass. We can view our target locations in Barfield Bay from that hill."

Over a grilled grouper lunch, Shannon updated Paddy on what she had learned in her research of the Caxambas Pass area and the ancient Calusa Indian shell mounds. "We believe that the vellum parchment cached in Anne Bonny's dagger handle pointed easterly from the highest hill on San Marco to the tip of the highest island. Those overgrown mounds are called keys or cays today."

"Right," he said.

Shannon looked at her notes. "Satellite imagery of the Indian Hill area showed a house on the highest point with a vacant lot next to it on the corner of Indian Hill Street and Caxambas Pass Drive. That hill is the highest elevation in Southwest Florida at about fifty-two feet above sea level."

"That is one mighty pile of oysters," Paddy said.

"East of that in Barfield Bay are the mangrove keys we are interested in—Alpha Key, Pig Key, David Key, and Pass Key. Unfortunately, the satellite and geological surveys didn't show elevations."

"Walking Indian Hill will be a good way to scan the bay," said Paddy.

Shannon pointed at the waterways map. "Right here—Pig Key and David Key—appear to be the best targets because of their orientation. Pig Key is east and David Key is northeast from Indian Hill. "

Paddy nibbled a crispy sweet potato fry. "We don't know which key is tallest, and Anne likely used the sun's arc to determine west-east."

Shannon sampled Paddy's fries.

"Help yourself, pirate."

She looked at one of the leaflets from the marina. The Calusa built the shell mounds over 3,000 years ago. Many of the Calusa people were seven feet tall. The women harvested oysters, conchs, clams, and mussels. They filled their baskets and created higher elevations by placing the shells on sandbars and wet soil banks. The growing mounds provided dry shelter, fishing grounds, protection from hurricanes, and burial sites closer to shore. The men used dugout canoes and caught fish using nets made from woven palm fiber, fabricated fish traps, weirs and corrals.

"What became of the Calusa people?" asked Paddy.

Shannon cleared her throat. "They were exposed to the Spanish in the early 1500s, and nearly decimated by the time Anne Bonny and Jack Rackham were in the area. Disease and conflicts with the Spanish, and later with Creek Indians and other tribes, led to their extinction less than fifty years later."

"Three thousand years of a sophisticated aquatic culture—gone," Paddy said.

Shannon nodded. "Some archaeologists believe the Calusa were descendants of the Mayans. They may have been here seven thousand years ago, based on bone, pottery, ancient metals and wooden sculptures found on Marco."

"A sad end to a great people," he said. "Let's go."

They drove twenty minutes to Indian Hill and hiked up a path to a vacant lot next to a sprawling million-dollar home twenty feet higher up.

The soil was a combination of dirt and stony white chunks of eroded shells, with sections of old hardwood hammock and newer Florida scrub. The lot had the remains of a burned house foundation where part of a masonry fireplace still stood. The elevated view out to Barfield Bay was spectacular, with its expanse of islands, cays, and big sky dotted with puffy clouds and flocks of birds.

Shannon pointed out David Key and the longer Pig Key beyond. Pass Key was to their right and two smaller keys sat on the north side of the bay.

"We will have to guesstimate the angle of Anne Bonny's sight line since we are sixty yards from the top of the hill on the next property."

"Tomorrow, we'll get a rental at the fishing village of Goodland and start with Pig Key," Paddy said.

"Why? David Key looks tallest, and closest to Indian Hill."

He folded his arms. "They are both likely targets, but remember that we recon outside-in. You never know what you can run into in unfamiliar territory."

"Aye, me hearty Captain."

The next morning, Paddy and Shannon ate breakfast on the *Second Wind* at Marco Island Marina before they drove to Calusa Island Marina at Goodland. Paddy signed the paperwork for a pontoon boat rental, and at the dock Shannon bought live shrimp for bait. She lingered to speak with local anglers about which fish were running.

Shannon whistled as she walked out of the shop. A perfect January day: sunny Florida, fresh bait, backwater fishing, and chasing a dream.

"There's the Cheshire Cat smile," said Paddy.

"Fishing today is more than a cover story," she said. "If we don't find the trove, I'll catch fish."

They loaded the boat with the gear and rolling coolers from the van, and piloted toward Marco. Shannon checked the setup on her fishing rod with anticipation for her first black drum or king mackerel. She would settle happily for a pompano or sheepshead.

They motored in a mid-incoming tide, cautious of the shallows and flats. Thankfully, they had an onboard GPS depth fish-finder, and waterproof nautical maps.

Shannon trolled from the stern and quickly brought in a small ladyfish, and five minutes later, a feisty crevalle jack. She marveled at the variety of species in the backwaters.

"We need to stop at some good fish holes," she said. "I'm looking for small mangrove inlets with moving currents, where the big lazy fish lurk in the shallows to feed off schooling fish."

A few minutes later, Shannon pointed. "There, that is a perfect ambush hole."

Paddy stopped and she soon brought in a mangrove snapper.

"It's shy of ten inches; has to go back in," she said.

"Nice little fighter, though," said Paddy.

They threaded their way through several keys and stopped long enough for Shannon to catch a regulation sheepshead. They continued through a narrow channel by Ramsey Key where she caught a beautiful silvery snook.

"Quick, Paddy, take a picture of me with this beautiful fish."

Paddy obliged with Shannon's mobile phone.

"My first snook; they hit and fight hard," she said. "If it were in season, we'd have a keeper, and a delicious meal. An angler's delight." Shannon gently released the fish into the water.

Paddy gave a sharp whistle. "Rods up, Shannon. Your turn to pilot and navigate. Head for the channel between Key Marco and Helen Key." He handed her the waterproof chart, got out his pipe and plugged it with buttered Jamaican rum tobacco.

As they approached the oyster bars of Caxambas Bay, Shannon turned into the narrow access to Barfield Bay and maneuvered around the shallows of Pig Key. They anchored back on the east side for privacy.

"Play at fishing. I'll hike up, check it out. Keep the boat nearby and your mobile on." Paddy loaded his backpack with several rocks he had gathered around their hotel, insect repellent, a roll of toilet paper, hand trowel and a small plastic bucket. He tied on a folding trench shovel and held onto his metal detector.

Shannon looked at Paddy.

He said, "The toilet paper is also good cover for why I'm carrying a trench shovel."

"What's with the rocks?"

"I'll explain later."

"Are metal detectors okay here?"

"It's okay. I spoke with the communications manager at the Rookery Bay Research Reserve, which includes these keys on 110,000 acres of pristine mangrove forest, uplands and protected waters."

"Who owns the land?"

"Florida state land, but less restricted than state or national parks. The main issue here is ecosystem preservation, coastal management research, and the history of the Calusa. Animal life and historically significant articles are not to be disturbed. It is also verboten to harm the mangroves."

"Who knows what we will find," said Shannon, "but I read that over years of archaeological research, the most productive finds were at Calusa villages and gathering sites along the coast and mucky lagoons. The small cays and keys in this area of the Ten Thousand Islands had mostly fish hooks and bone tools of the lost people."

Paddy shouldered his pack and entered the red mangroves at the waterline of Pig Key. He steadied himself on thick branches and fought his way through the initial thicket. He marked his progress with orange flagging tape tied at shoulder height as he ascended through the growth. Red mangrove plants gave way to white mangroves, to a higher canopy with vines stringing from the ground.

Hiking under the higher canopy was cooler and easier; the cover blocked sunlight to the ground and choked off underbrush. Paddy stopped to apply insect repellent and noticed a ridge to the high point on the cigar-shaped island. It took about fifty minutes to explore the ridgeline. At the highest point on Pig Key, he used binoculars and a compass to take a reading to Indian Hill to the west. He connected a set of earphones to his metal detector and made multiple passes in the area and along the sides of the ridge and flat spots. The detector didn't chirp, but he recognized an old and familiar *whop-whop-whop-whop* of a low helicopter. Paddy pulled off the earphones as the copter passed overhead. Just then Shannon called.

"The copter is circling this area and a small boat is approaching."

"Relax, I'll be right back. You be the good guy. If they question you or intend to search our boat, tell them I rented it and wait for me to come. I'll do the talking."

"All I know is fish."

Paddy tucked the bright orange flagging tapes from the branches into his pocket. He hustled back to find Shannon speaking with a pudgy uniformed man and an attractive female officer on a Florida Fish and Wildlife Conservation boat that was rafted-up to their pontoon boat. A stately officer stood at the covered helm of the patrol boat.

Shannon held out her mobile phone to the female officer. The helicopter made another pass. Paddy waded through the tide to join Shannon on the pontoon boat and set his pack on the deck. "What's up?" he said.

Shannon looked at the young female officer and back to Paddy.

"Your niece just showed me a picture of her catch-and-released snook. I'm Officer Gomez. FWC is patrolling the area with Collier County Sheriff's Aviation Unit in concert with federal agencies. There has been suspicious criminal activity in the area. Ms. Clarke has been kind enough to show us her catch and demonstrate her knowledge and respect for fish species here. We don't need much of your time."

Paddy cocked his head, narrowed his brows. "What probable cause is there to question recreational visitors to Rookery Bay Preserve?"

The heavyset male officer spoke up. "I'm Officer Higgins; FWC has full police power and statewide jurisdiction as a law enforcement agency and is investigating the movement of people and contraband here. We work in cooperation with ICE and DEA. We will conduct a compliance search of your vessel and ask a few questions."

Paddy folded his arms. "We have nothing to hide. You have permission to board."

Higgins and Gomez boarded and took Paddy's and Shannon's identification and the boat rental contract to pass on to the older male officer on the patrol boat, who called it in.

Gomez and Higgins quickly inspected the pontoon boat.

Higgins said, "This boat is in order but the flares are expired. That's a fineable offense. I will make note of that for the operator. What is your purpose here?"

Paddy reached into his pack set on the seat cushion, produced a roll of toilet paper and a hand trowel and held it at Higgins. "Exploring, exercise, and a restroom," said Paddy.

Higgins shifted his considerable weight onto his other foot.

Paddy's backpack tipped partly over the edge of the cushioned bench. The attached metal detector and trench shovel tumbled onto the deck.

"What else is in the backpack, Mr. Clarke?"

"I think you are taking this too far. You still don't have probable cause to search me."

"We can confiscate metal detectors on protected state land. What are you really up to, Mr. Clarke?"

Officer Gomez gave a slight headshake at Higgins, which he ignored.

Paddy pitched his head toward Higgins. "Some of us do our homework, Officer Higgins. Metal detectors are allowed in the preserve."

Gomez smiled at Paddy.

"I'm going to ask you again, Mr. Clarke. If you have nothing to hide, what is in your backpack?"

"Go ahead." Paddy stood back.

Higgins grunted when he lifted Paddy's backpack.

The senior male officer on the patrol boat interrupted and handed the identification cards back to Higgins and spoke to Paddy. "Are you Patrick Clarke who served on the USS *Edson*?"

"Yes."

"Are you the owner of the brigantine *Second Wind*, at the Marco Island Marina?"

"Yes."

"Did you clear in at Marathon, by phone with nothing to declare?"

"Yes."

The man saluted and said, "Good enough for us, sir. Thank for your service, Mr. Clarke. We're done here, Higgins."

Higgins gazed at the backpack in defeat.

"Take a look. It's okay," said Paddy.

Higgins looked inside the pack, embarrassed when he saw it filled with rocks. He gave Paddy a puzzled look.

Paddy spoke loud enough to Higgins for the senior officer to hear. "I've always liked to weight my packs for exercise, ever since 'Nam, and rocks are good for self-defense."

The senior officer on the patrol boat said, "You do stay in great shape, sir."

Higgins nodded, exited the pontoon boat, and gestured goodbye.

"Don't take it personally, Officer Higgins. What you do is important, but if we don't assert our freedom every day, we lose it."

Officer Gomez looked back to Paddy and waved, and he returned the wave with a smile and nod.

The chopper disappeared toward Naples and the FWC patrol boat sped away.

"I am crazy to find the treasure, but now I understand how recon lowers risk," Shannon said. "By exploring a secondary target first, we learned of patrols in the area. I doubt they will bother us with our routine when we go to David Key."

Paddy slapped his palms together. "And clear that we are on a watch list."

"Gomez liked how you chopped Higgins's ego."

"I liked her class."

"And her curves," said Shannon.

"Maybe I just like competent women in uniform."

LOVERS KEY

T he next day, Shannon and Paddy debated when to resume their treasure hunt in Barfield Bay. They agreed to let things cool down and sail *Second Wind* north along the Gulf Coast for a few days. The first stop was to anchor by Estero Island and explore Lovers Key State Park.

The float plan they left at Marco Island Marina included a cruise up the east side of Sanibel Island via the Florida Gulf Intracoastal Waterway (GICW), with a run by Captiva. They would traverse Tampa Bay with a stop in St. Petersburg before the return to Marco.

Shannon checked entries in the logbook as she piloted the *Second Wind* into Estero Bay. She sighed when calculating her total days at sea.

"Good to resume training for my captain's license."

"You're the skipper for this sail," Paddy said. "You set the pace, adjust the itinerary and the watch schedule. Beware the shallows, and mind the bridge schedules on the GICW."

Shannon smiled. "You got me on edge already."

"You'll master fundamentals on this run. When the time comes, you will breeze the Coast Guard exam."

"You make everything look so damned easy."

Paddy leaned to her. "You're a natural around kids, an artist, a jack-of-all-trades, willing to learn. I think you make that look easy." Shannon relaxed her shoulders as she relished the compliment.

By midafternoon they had set anchor, and they took the dinghy to the pristine white beach at Lovers Key and walked about the remote preserve. Shannon dawdled along the beach picking at shells, sand dollars, and starfish. The clear water, bright white sand, and mounds of seashells were like a remote tropical paradise.

Paddy sat on a shady bench outside the Welcome Center while Shannon poked through the gear and guide maps for fishing, bird watching or kayaking the park's four barrier islands. The ranger answered some of her questions about the fishing.

"So, the fish here are moving in what's mostly three feet of water?" asked Shannon.

The ranger tipped his hat. "Yes, but you may see manatees just off the beach today."

She yelled over to Paddy. "I want to live here."

They returned to the beach and rested on the soft sand. Shannon said, "I can see why Anne Bonny and Jack Rackham stayed here to honeymoon."

Paddy nodded. "They took a break from pirating, and for the crew to repair their damaged vessel after an encounter with a Spanish sloop. Their romance blossomed here, while their shipmates secured timber from far up the Estero River."

"A guide said Lovers Key was named after them and all the other lovers that visited since," she said. Shannon lay flat on the sand and shaded her eyes from the sun with the visor of her baseball cap. "A hundred years ago, there were no roads to this getaway. You had to take a boat."

Sunlight faded to black as she rested her eyes. Soft breezes rustled nearby palm trees, and calls of shorebirds blended with the serenity of the beach. Anne Bonny and Jack Rackham came to her dreamy state of mind.

Shannon saw Anne and Jack haul palm fronds and driftwood to fashion a lean-to, a love nest. Anne's hands became Shannon's own as she lashed driftwood supports. Jack stared at her with gleaming eyes and a wide grin. They hugged and lingered, staring deep into each other's eyes.

"You vex and amuse me," he said.

"I'm getting hot," Anne said, pushing him away. "We must weave the top of the hut and get out of the sun."

Jack made no pretense of captaincy with her. After a few moments weaving cabbage palm leaves and saw palmetto trunks, he laughed, tickled and teased her. She shook a large palm branch in his face. Jack picked up another and yanked off some of the leaves. They waged a mock swordfight and fell together onto the sand.

Jack held her face in his hands to admire her. He grasped her hair and pressed their lips together.

"I am without defense from you, my fiery-haired, fair-sexed pirate."

"Get used to it," Anne said.

Jack laughed and pulled her waist tight to his. "I am doomed by your vivacity," he said. "My father warned me that a young man must consider the precious value of his time and not waste it in idleness, jollity, gaming, or banqueting in ruffians' company."

Paddy spoke, jolting Shannon awake.

"What?" she asked. The word 'ruffian' had brought a smile to her face.

Paddy repeated himself. "Families can enjoy Lovers Key now. It can't get too crowded with so little parking."

Shannon gazed the length of beach and paused. The dream had vanished, but her connection with Anne Bonny at Lovers Key would remain a treasure.

"Paddy, let's rent bicycles for the loop around Black Island. It's connected by a small land bridge to the back of the beach, and we can take a swim on the beach before we leave."

"I'd like that," he said.

The next days tested Shannon's seamanship to monitor conditions, follow marine protocols, use navigation aids, and traverse bays, rivers, and the Intracoastal Waterway back to the open Gulf. Paddy exercised restraint, with minimal coaching. The *Second Wind* bore not a scratch.

When they returned to Marco Island Marina, Shannon put the question of her seafaring performance to her uncle. "How am I doing on the competency scale now?"

"You've grown from novice to advanced beginner, to competent on ocean vessels—power or sail."

She licked her bottom lip. "What will it take to reach level four—proficient?"

"A boatload more experience."

Shannon sighed.

"You need leadership experience out in blue water for at least two full months to develop a deep understanding, see the big picture, and maintain a high standard that becomes routine."

"Like second nature?"

He smiled. "Yes, with vigilance."

"I remember when Washburn said, 'Always be a little afraid out there.'" Shannon paused. "What about level five—expert?"

"That takes years, and few achieve it. A sailing master faces many situations to gain more than required knowledge. They deal with routine events intuitively and improvise in extraordinary situations with grace under pressure."

"Like intrepid Captain Jonathan Haraden . . . that's a tall order."

Paddy looked Shannon up and down. "It won't be long before you'll be ready to pass the Coast Guard exam and know how to operate with a skilled crew."

She slid her hands into her hip pockets. "Guess I won't be single-handing across the Atlantic anytime soon."

"True, but we'll have plenty of Caribbean sailing in blue water between islands before you head home to Gloucester in the spring."

Paddy looked at Shannon as if to continue speaking but gazed up at the sky and clammed up.

"What is it, Paddy?"

He shifted his feet. "Jenny and I are making vows. We're getting married."

"Wow, Captain Freebird is going to settle down."

"More balance. Jenny is ready to adjust her artsy independence, focus her activism, and simplify her social life. We're ready for new experiences together. We have a common law marriage and this is a new beginning."

"What will be new?"

"We've been soulmates with different lifestyles. She wants to travel together, see more of the world and return to focus more on the inner journey." Paddy wore a rueful expression. "Jenny is an islander. She has taken an interest in her Irish and African roots. The first wave of indentured laborers and slaves in Jamaica were mostly Irish men and women."

"Irish slaves?"

Paddy nodded. "Oliver Cromwell put down an Irish rebellion in 1648 and shipped many to Barbados to work under brutal British planters in the Caribbean."

"It seems we all want to learn about our ancestors." Shannon said as she brushed sand off her legs. "I don't see you slowing down, Paddy."

"Slowing down? Jenny and I will fashion a new life together. She wants to travel to Ireland, England, the States and parts of Africa. We will do philanthropic work in Jamaica and enjoy plenty of live music and dancing. There are so many fun new things to learn."

"That's so exciting," Shannon said with a wide smile. "I am so happy for you both. And it's your three Ls—living, loving and learning." She loved the simplicity and power of his mantra. "Can I help plan the wedding with Daniella?"

Paddy hugged her. "We'd love it. More than that, Shannon, I want you to be my best man."

"Count on it. Hey, I also get to be the one to give you away."

Paddy said, "*Best mate* might sound better, though."

"Either way, I'm your man, Captain."

He hugged her again. "Thank you. Do you think there's a chance Daniella will make Jenny and me into grandparents?"

"Don't take that on yourself, Paddy. Daniella said her biological clock was ticking, but she wants her career. Maybe the right guy, family support, and more faith in relationships will help."

Paddy nodded. "That feels right. Maybe Jenny and I become what Daniella had always wanted for herself."

"You and I are changing places, Paddy. I gave my family what I did not have growing up. Now I want to live my dream of a sea captain's life."

He smiled. "Being in the midst of change is turbulent and exciting."

They both sat quietly for a while. Shannon scanned the yachts at the Marco Island Marina. *Some beautiful vessels here*, she thought, *but none compare to the vintage charm of the* Second Wind.

"What do you say we enjoy the facilities, pool, and mix with some of the captains in the barbecue area tonight?" Paddy said.

Shannon stretched her elbows and arms out, yawned, and took in a deep breath. "I look forward to hearing their stories. Tomorrow, we hunt for Jack and Anne's booty on David's Key."

ANNE'S BOOTY

Shannon and Paddy rented a small, fast center-console fishing boat and headed for Gulf waters. By early morning the tide was rising, which would enable them to navigate the shallows of Barfield Bay.

Shannon piloted the boat for forty minutes through mangrove cays to skirt Cape Romano. They ran along the Gulf coastline by Kice Island and stopped by its eastern tip. "That's Dickman's Point," she said, "the place where Spanish vessels in the 1700s anchored to gather fresh spring water for their return to Spain."

Paddy looked at the waterways map and spotted Caxambas Pass across from them. "How did you know about the location of the spring, Shannon?"

"After a dream about Anne Bonny and Jack, I called Caxambas Pass Park. The man who answered said fresh water still flows from the middle of Kice Island just over there." She turned to him. "*Caxambas* is basically Indian for 'fresh water.'"

Paddy widened his eyes with a smile. "Easy enough for Jack and Anne to collect water there and row back and forth to the anchorage of their ship. Now we'll see what that row up to Barfield Bay might have been like."

Shannon took the chart back from him and studied it.

"What's the distance to David Key?" asked Paddy.

She stood self-assured. "Less than three nautical miles over flat water. Jack and Anne could have rowed that in a half hour. No large vessels can get in there."

"Good to hide away a treasure trove," he said. "This saltwater boat for shallow backwaters and the coastline will get us in there."

They entered Barfield Bay, headed around David Key, and hauled up at a crescent sandy beach on its west side. The beach nestled between two prongs of the wooded island spread like a lobster claw, with a ravine running thirty-five feet to the top.

Paddy suggested they stage an umbrella, cooler, and two chairs with towels at the beach. He hiked up the ravine, while Shannon moved the boat to deeper water to set the bow and stern anchors. She cast her fishing rod repeatedly over the shallows, alert to any boat traffic.

Erosion on the east side of the small island made Paddy's trek passable and kept their position hidden from the western views of homes on Marco's Indian Hill only a quarter mile away. He reconned the summit of the pointy island.

Shannon waved to a passing recreational boater and let twenty minutes pass before anchoring back close to the beach. She left a fishing rod by her folding chair and scrambled up the ravine to join Paddy, who methodically swept the metal detector.

He pulled off his earphones. "I've covered most of the crown. Some evidence of overnight camping here at times, but nothing detected yet. We could be poking and digging this key for days."

Shannon sat, faced Indian Hill to the west and closed her eyes.

Paddy waited. "What are you doing?"

Shannon kept her eyes closed, and Paddy waited as she concentrated in silence. After a while, Paddy sat next to her. The area was still, without cloud cover, and getting hot.

"Sweep along the whole west edge." Her voice was firm. "I'm sure of it."

Paddy wiped his brow with a kerchief, donned his headphones and resumed a patterned sweep of the detector along the top edge facing Indian Hill across a stretch of water. Shannon sat cross-legged to watch. A full hour went by, they found nothing, and she began to have doubts. *Too many years have gone by, and they call these Ten Thousand Islands for good reason.*

She blew out her cheeks and thought of her lucid dream of Anne Bonny and Jack Rackham. *This has to be the island; it fits what we know.* She took a towel and put it over her head to block out the sunlight and attempted further meditation of the dream.

Moonlight images of Anne and Jack moving heavy chests over high ground . . .

Shannon flipped the towel off her head and marched over to Paddy, still sweeping the detector on the western edge. "Their boots angled here on the downslope . . . they were slipping."

She tapped Paddy on the shoulder. Startled, he spun round and tore off the earphones. "What?"

Shannon spoke through fast breaths and pointed lower on the hill. "Jack and Anne worked on the slope." She pointed. "Down there."

He squinted at her and winced. "You all right?"

"I just know it."

He shook his head. "Let's take a break, get out of the sun. You look a little—"

She folded her arms. "I'm not crazy."

"Let's drink some water, and now."

They took a short break under some brush, and Shannon guided Paddy back to the same area he had worked earlier. She pointed to a slight ridgeline several feet lower on the downslope. He nodded and marked a line in the crumbly white and brown soil with his foot before moving farther down.

Paddy walked and worked the detector along the steep incline below her, braced on the shoulder of a small ridge. He stopped at times to rest and wipe sweat from his brow. Eventually, he worked past her and shook his head.

"Stop and rest, drink more water," Shannon said.

They sat for a while.

"You all right?" she asked.

"I'm fine," he said and got up. "Just starting to wonder if we even have the right place. Maybe Anne was referring to the land east across the bay, which looks like an island, too."

"Maybe," she sighed. "Wherever you look, there are landmasses and islands as far as you can see. But I just know it's here."

"Let's work the ridge some more."

"This time I'll secure a rope around my waist and to yours. I'll hip belay above you. Less risk of a fall, you'll be more secure and get less fatigued."

"I should have thought of that."

With her feet braced above him on the side of the hill, Paddy continued sweeps with the detector. She moved along above him and kept the rope taut. *He is thorough,* she thought, *but working the same area for too long. He may slip again. How selfish of me to expect him to continue.* She bolted up to call it off.

Paddy ignored or did not hear Shannon as he swept the wand.

She crabbed down to him, shortening the rope. "Please stop, Paddy."

He spun around to face her, smiled and yanked off his earphones. Sweat soaked his shirt and rolled off his face. "We've got strong beeps along this short section and faint ones on each end. Let's get test holes going."

She moved tools onto a blanket nearby. Paddy took a stick and made a rectangular mark. "Start digging gently around this perimeter." He sat down in a shady spot and drank some water.

Shannon used the trench shovel to remove soil from the high side of the slope along the marked area to improve their footing on the lower side. She tamped down a flat space for them to work, wiping her face with a bandanna. The midday sun was unforgiving, with only knee-high scrub around them.

They trenched around the area, alternating in short shifts to conserve energy and cut down the risk of error.

Shannon made a demand. "Take some shade."

Moments later, they both froze when noisy boaters came near the island. They tried to discern what was going on. Laughter carried from the beach side of the key, where their staged furniture was.

"I'll go down there and hang out till they leave the area," she said.

Shannon could see through the brush—two young couples had anchored a shallow sport boat twenty yards off the shore from where the rental boat was beached by the folding chair setup. The couples lunched on their boat. Shannon emerged from a shaded area, sat on one of the beach chairs and tested the reel on her fishing rod. Too shallow for any sizable fish but a good cover act. She watched the couples splash and tease about their sport boat. One of the girls waded toward Shannon and walked onto the beach.

The twenty-something girl in a red bikini stood with her legs tight and scanned the vegetation behind the beach. Their eyes met. Shannon greeted her. "Hi, are you looking for some privacy?"

The girl nodded.

"You need anything?"

"No, thanks," the girl said.

Shannon pointed to vegetation at the far end of the beach.

The girl shuffled away.

Shannon moved her beach chair and fishing rod to the water's edge. She cast her weighted bucktail lure, sat with her feet in the water, and jigged her line. She made multiple casts in the general direction of the visitors. One of the guys waved and gunned the boat closer to the far side of the beach where the girl had walked.

Don't want to be too friendly and encourage them, Shannon thought, *just friendly enough.*

Shannon continued to cast and jig her rod until the boat zoomed away. She waited ten minutes to climb back to find Paddy in cross-legged meditation under the shade near their work area.

"That was a long stretch," she said. She noticed how Paddy had placed tent pegs along the rectangle, with holes along the edge.

"Yeah, for both of us. Let's get more test holes going. This is the only active spot. "

Shannon got to work with the trench shovel.

Three and a half feet into the shell mound, she struck something. "Wicked pissah," she yelped.

"Easy, Shannon. We don't want to disturb."

"This is it. Jack and Anne dug a notch along the side of the hill, set the booty and filled over it."

Paddy took pictures of the site and skimmed the earth away in layers.

"Don't get your hopes up, Shannon. Could just be beer cans, and camp trash. What makes you so sure? We found squat on Pig Key."

"I feel it, dreamt it. Besides, this location fits Anne's note, and the metal detector sang plenty."

Soon they uncovered two iron straps over a caved-in rectangular shape.

They stood speechless. Shannon sifted handfuls of white gravelly soil through her fingers. Paddy dug out three narrow holes on the edges with his trowel to inspect hard layers of shell sediment.

"There is a dark thin layer of decomposed fiber or soot just under the sand," Paddy said. He brushed away more top sand. "Ha, an oilskin or tarred sailcloth was placed over this sea chest before it was buried."

Shannon took pictures of the site as they worked. They heard voices carry from activity nearby. Paddy stood to discern sounds in the bay.

"Go ahead, Paddy. Check on our boat," she said. "I'll work like an archaeologist, and call you before anything comes out of the ground."

"Good," he said. "I'll chill on the beach chair and report. When we're clear, tell me what I need to bring up."

Shannon took special care to trowel and brush soil from the top of the cavity with her hands. She removed remnants of a wooden cover from under the iron straps. A dried animal skin covered contents inside the old sea chest. *Probably a sheepskin*, Shannon thought as she paused. She could not resist the temptation to pull the raggedy skin back. She gasped.

Spanking dirt off her hands, Shannon grabbed her mobile phone and took a picture. Then she called Paddy. "You're not going to believe this. Bring a whiskbroom, towels, tarps, rope, my knapsack, and stuff the blue duffel with two sea bags."

"Be right up. All clear here."

When he arrived, Shannon pulled the rest of the animal skin off and they stared at the folds of a tattered black pirate flag with a smiling white skull and crossed swords. "Calico Jack left his signature."

"It's his all right. This is priceless, Shannon. There are only drawings today of actual pirate flags and this was unique to Rackham—and the most famous of all." He looked at his niece. "May I?"

Shannon nodded. "You deserve this moment."

Paddy lifted the flag from the box. Shannon ogled the weaponry and artifacts below.

"Let's not get ahead of ourselves," said her uncle. "We inspect one item at a time." The flag unfolded to three and a half feet on the staff and five feet on the fly.

"It's single-ply wool bunting," Paddy said. "The emblem patch is sewn on one side and the reverse image painted on the other with oil-based pigment."

"Why do you think he left it?" Shannon asked.

"To cover the booty inside the chest . . . or leave his mark." Paddy shrugged. "Or both."

Paddy examined the flag and its emblem further. "Captains in the day would sketch their designs and have the ship's sailmaker construct the flags, or consign someone ashore to do it."

"Jack may have had spares made," said Shannon. "This could have been his first one. After they finished repairs in Estero, he put a fresh Jolly Roger on the new mast before they sailed again."

"Good thinking."

They gently shook out the flag, folded it, and placed it in a large plastic bag. The top layer in the chest had two cutlasses and a jeweled sword like the one Paddy had given her. They carefully removed the items and wrapped them. She lifted out several more objects—three daggers, two flintlock pistols, and a backstaff for navigation.

Paddy retrieved and inspected a compass and a spyglass. "Can't believe what good condition these are in."

Shannon stared down at a dark wooden box the size of a hefty altar

Bible. She motioned to Paddy. He put down the spyglass, lay flat on the ground and reached in to lift the box with gentle hands. He stood and held it to her. Shannon ran her fingers over the dark wooden box.

"It has an engraved plate."

"Heavily tarnished," Paddy said. "Can't identify what it says."

Shannon took a pencil and small notebook from her pocket. "I'll do a rubbing."

Paddy grinned, "You should have been a detective."

An image emerged: *Henry Jennings.*

Paddy took a step back. "Jennings was a British privateer and early pirate leader of New Providence. Pirate Charles Vane was under his command then. I hope the box is what I think."

Shannon opened the swivel latch to reveal a dueling pistol set.

"Incredible." Paddy held one of the pistols. "It will clean up nice, and easily command over twenty-five thousand at auction, but with Jennings's name on it, many times that."

"How do you know this stuff?"

"I've gone to auctions for years to collect nautical antiques and period weaponry. I'm fussy and only bid for investment grade."

For the next hour, they picked through silver plates and goblets, a gold chalice, and jewelry items kept in decayed canvas shot bags once used for artillery. The jewelry included gold religious artifacts, crosses, chains, bracelets, earrings, amethyst pendants, semi-precious stones and a small pouch of large uncut emeralds.

Shannon put a large gold olive blossom ring on her thumb. "I can't believe this has been buried for three centuries."

"Some time ago, I read about these coastal shell mounds—called middens. Calcium leaches from the shells and creates low-acid soil conditions, which slow the decay of buried objects."

"Anne Bonny sure picked a good spot."

"Definitely, and flood free," he said. "This treasure was safely encased in this dense calcified soil below an earthen layer of plant material since 1720."

They packed the smaller items from the plain sea chest into vinyl sea bags and secured them in their backpacks. The larger items got wrapped in towels and stuffed in the blue duffel bag.

"What do we do with the empty chest, Paddy?"

He handed the metal detector and earphones to Shannon. "Use this first."

She swept the detector over the bottom of the empty chest and shrieked to hear rapid beeps.

They carefully dug around the sides of the dilapidated chest, but it fell apart as they removed it. Below were the tops of two chests embedded in the hard layers of crumbled shells. They bent into the hole to uncover and dig around the smaller one but found it awkward and heavy to free up.

Shannon worked in the depression to dig out each side and secure a rope for them to pull it up and set on the clearing.

Paddy walked his hands over the chest, using his fingers as a gauge.

"It has a raised flat top about twenty by twelve by ten inches. May have been a captain's ditty box that held important papers."

Shannon freed the latch and opened the lid. They both stared in silence. Above them, a screaming red-shouldered hawk on a kill pierced the moment, echoing Shannon's emotion. She blinked several times and exhaled slowly when she realized she had been holding her breath. She rubbed her eyes—but knew what she saw was real. Her skin and hands tingled.

Paddy reached down into the trove. It was filled with hundreds of gold doubloons and small gold bars. "This must be Charles Vane's share when he and Jennings looted the Spanish salvage operation off the coast of St. Augustine to recover gold after the *Urca de Lima* galleon sank in bad weather."

Shannon grinned. "Florida authorities will claim it 'historically significant,' and expect to take it all."

"So, you ready to turn in your half?"

"Kudzu that. Dead men tell no tales. Let's keep digging."

They lifted the chest onto high ground.

"It has to weigh about thirty-five pounds," Paddy said. "Let's say it has twenty pounds of gold. That's three hundred troy ounces. Melted down, it is worth over four hundred thousand dollars. Many times that, Shannon, for doubloons in excellent condition."

She laughed. "The authorities would call that *financial significance*. Let's get at the other one down there."

With effort, they dislodged the third chest and brought it to the surface. Shannon admired its dome top and filigree hardware and then worked to open it. The hardware would not budge, and the chest held together as she tried to pry it open. She wiped sweat from her face and combed her hair back with her fingers. "It's heavy. We can't hide it easily—if we manage to open it."

"It's rugged, all right," Paddy agreed.

Shannon struggled to open it again. "I need something substantial to pry it. It might be nailed shut."

"Leave it closed, Shannon. We can't have it pop open while we carry it down to the boat. Sweep around the dig area one more time. We need to get out of here."

"Roger that," she said.

Paddy wrapped the sealed chest in a brown tarp, tied it over with rope and knotted it to make grip handles. Shannon pulled off the earphones. "That's it, three chests, just like Anne wrote."

"Let's get everything down near the beach. Then I'll load and protect the boat while you tidy up here."

"Okay," she said, "I'll come back to set the first trunk back in the ground like it was, toss in the old sheepskin, fill it over with soil, level the area, and cover it with dead brush and leaves."

"Perfect."

They finished wrapping the smallest chest and brought down the blue duffel and heavy knapsacks. The booty was loaded onto the boat except for the tarp-covered, heavy-domed mystery trunk, which they dragged down the trail to hide in brush above the bank.

Paddy navigated back to Goodland to the public boat park facility where they tied up and waited for a middle-aged couple to finish launching a small boat. Onlookers stood by the concrete ramp where a local captain cleaned and filleted fish for his charter guests at a wash station to the side.

"No keepers," said Shannon to a man who inquired about her catch as she brought the fishing gear to the van.

Paddy wheeled the gold-laden marine cooler to the back of the van and used the strength of his legs to load it.

"I forgot one of the rods out there," said Shannon, loud enough for bystanders to hear. "We have to go back. Park the van at the marina. I'll swing the boat over there to pick you up."

Paddy winked. "Roger that."

They boated back to David Key and pried open the large chest to find it filled with Spanish silver *reales*. "No wonder it was so heavy," said Paddy. "It's all pieces of eight, mate."

Shannon fell to her knees, grabbed up two handfuls of the coins and let them slip through her fingers and clink onto the pile. "That feels so-ooh-good. Let's transfer it to the other big cooler and leave the chest here."

"I agree; it would raise too many questions, and we don't need that when we unload the booty. I'll hide it farther up the slope."

Shannon piloted them back to the marina and sang part of her poem as a lyric.

> *"Pirate, Patriot,*
> *Captains Stand*
> *Old Salts Return*
> *With Second Wind."*

She added another line in a deep-voiced, downbeat chorus:

> *"And Dead Men*
> *Tell no tales."*

Paddy pulled out a flask of scotch. "Let's sing it together."

They harmonized and improvised verses until they approached the marina at Goodland. Paddy returned the boat keys. Shannon backed the van to the welcome dock, helped Paddy load the heavy cooler, and drove North Barfield Drive to Marco Island Marina.

Shannon looked out the driver's side window and spotted a kingfisher diving into open water on the marsh fringe of the Everglades. Her wide grin reflected in the side mirror; her flame-red hair rustled in the wind.

"What now, great rogue?"

"Leave everything in the van. We celebrate over dinner and plot some new moves."

FINDERS KEEPERS

Marco Island Marina was the place to party that night. Shannon and Paddy met three sailing captains and crew at the picnic area who were transients from Australia, England, and Germany.

Every night the band of sailors sampled tiki bars along the Gulf Coast from Fort Myers to Marco Island. They wanted to party at the marina with locals and grill their day's catch from the Gulf.

Shannon offered to take some of the fish to prepare a spicy fish stew. Paddy brought a bottle of scotch. They joined in camaraderie as old friends with magnificent vessels and stories told. *What a way to live,* she thought.

She was eager to hear of their day's fishing in the Gulf. They in turn enjoyed her "Glosta" fish tales and vowed to visit her in Cape Ann someday. Usually such vows were niceties soon forgotten, but she knew they meant it. Full-time liveaboard sailors were a special breed, and they would be most welcome.

At daybreak, Paddy prepared breakfast in the galley of the *Second Wind*. He and Shannon said their goodbyes to their new pen pals, who took early leave of the marina. Now it was time to talk with Shannon in private about the booty sitting under cover in the van.

Paddy poured coffee. "You look weary this morning."

Shannon stared into her cup, bleary-eyed. "I slept off the booze in four hours, paced around the van and strolled around the water park till early light. What's the ballpark value of the treasure?"

Paddy looked pensive. "That's a premature but understandable question. We need to sort it, identify key artifacts, grade, value, catalogue, clean, and pack it in lots. Then we build a strategy."

"What's involved?"

"Decisions on reporting, storing, authenticating, saving, gifting or monetizing the goods slowly through international dealers, auction houses, and other channels."

"What if we had five years to do that wisely?"

"Great question. With time on our side, I believe this trove is worth at least fifteen million," said Paddy. "And if we diversify our shares into investments, we could put a multiplier on that."

"Wow." Shannon rubbed her face. "I am out of my depth here. Let's talk scenarios."

"Good," he said, "and jot down our ideas. I'll put music on to muffle our voices."

Shannon sketched pirate ships, palmy islands, and treasure chests on the margins of a notepad.

Paddy sat back on the dinette with his hands behind his head, staring through the skylight. "Let's start with the sea chests." The one they first opened was the size of a seaman's locker—usually about forty inches long, twenty-six inches wide and eighteen inches high; this was a typical example but with better hardware over the top.

Shannon made notes as Paddy spoke. "Crewmembers used their lockers for all of their clothes and possessions. The simple box served as a seat, rowing bench, workbench, and table."

"Minimalist versatility," said Shannon, "perfect for large crews in tight quarters and work spaces on old sailing ships."

"Indeed," Paddy said. "Back in the day, each chest was personalized by its owner's painting, fancy carved beckets, and ropework handles."

"I think that locker was packed quickly with a mix of goodies pirated from several vessels," Shannon said.

"I agree. Pirate Charles Vane gave cruel treatment to captured captains and crew, but after Rackham succeeded Vane, he'd offer some to stay and set malcontents free, with provisions. Of course, Rackham kept the booty on board."

"Maybe Vane didn't attack that French warship because he had too much of his wealth hidden in his captain's quarters," Shannon said. "But his quartermaster, Calico Jack, figured it out and never told his crew after they deposed Vane."

"A good supposition," Paddy said.

Shannon started writing as she spoke. "That seaman's chest had its day. The fancier domed hardwood chests with tooled metal hardware were for captains, or specialized for documents, armaments, medicines, tools, or navigation."

Paddy nodded. "I think we should leave the empty one I hid on David's Key." Before she could respond, he added, "Did you brush away our footprints?"

"Uh-oh, I didn't think to do that. Maybe we should get new sandals, drop it for now and decide later."

"Just teasing, Shannon, but we can't get too paranoid. I'd like to retrieve that chest as a historical artifact and donate it anonymously."

"Where to?"

"The National Museum of Historical Archaeology in Jamaica. If not, the Port Royal Collection of the Institute of Jamaica. As much as I'd like to keep Rackham's pirate flag, it would do more good to support Jamaica's effort to get world heritage status for Port Royal."

"I like that."

"The whole Caribbean isn't well represented. I'd like Port Royal to be added to the list as a center of exploration."

"That would be good for the economy of Jamaica. Some of the artifacts could go with it."

Paddy nodded. "I'd like to keep the Henry Jennings dueling pistol set too, but that would be the right place for it. He operated in Jamaica when he pirated Spanish vessels. If we reported the find locally, the artifacts would likely end up in a corner of a Florida museum."

He drank the rest of his coffee. "We need to be very careful not to share pictures of us with the trove on David Key or elsewhere."

"Definitely," Shannon said. "But the pictures of the trove could prove valuable later in accounting for the complete find, if not the location."

Paddy nodded and poked his head out of the galley and greeted other boaters walking past on the dock to their vessel. He returned below and closed the hatch.

"Let's talk about treasure laws, and what I know. They are changing all the time, and in many jurisdictions. There are still a lot of gray areas."

"Are we in trouble?"

"Could happen, but let's start with the facts. Our dig did not disturb a burial site, fossils, or bone tools of ancient civilizations that are of archaeological interest. Nor does this site show up on the Florida DHR as an archaeological landmark zone."

"What's the DHR?" asked Shannon.

"Division of Historical Resources," he said. "Archaeologists have increasingly convinced legislatures that they have priority in the waters and on land and get to decide what is in the public interest to keep for educational, research, historic and museum interests."

"You are thorough."

"I'm a collector, not a treasure hunter," he said. "But know it would take a gaggle of lawyers, courts and years to deal with this. Our behavior is important."

"What do you mean?"

"We'll get to that."

Shannon jotted down a note. "So, we didn't disturb burial sites or native artifacts, but we did take a treasure from state-owned land without a permit."

"Correct, and they would have required the dig to be conducted and supervised by a public archeology center."

"Sounds like Big Brother in sheep's clothing. I understand treasure salvage companies get permits and keep 75 percent of the find."

"Actually, Florida claims that it owns all salvaged treasure within its territorial waters, but you are right that they have a practice of giving 75 percent of the value to the finder, keeping 25 percent for their collections. Not reporting it is the problem."

Shannon frowned. "I read that some people remove items and wait over a year before testing their options with an attorney, even if it is on their own land."

"Yeah," Paddy said, "and metal detector enthusiasts under the old rules still proudly display gold treasure coins and artifacts in their homes and never sell them. But they help the public by turning in contemporary rings and watches so people who have lost personal items can claim them."

"What about the fact that this trove was buried intentionally on land by our blood relatives before this country even existed?"

"You'd think that would be in our favor," said Paddy, "but won't make a difference. Until a few years ago, Florida was the place for treasure hunting. New regulations at all levels constrain it, and each state is different."

"That's why you checked the use of a metal detector in the preserve."

Paddy nodded. "I also investigated if the city of Marco has any jurisdiction over Barfield Bay. It turns out they don't yet but are in discussions with the preserve to get it for development and infrastructure."

"What about finders keepers?" asked Shannon.

"On your own property or international waters, that generally still applies for treasure trove."

"How does the government define what treasure trove is?"

"Treasure trove laws refer to coins, bullion, or paper money buried or hidden for so long that the original owner is unlikely to return for it."

"What if I left something like a bicycle somewhere, with no intention to return for it?"

"That would be abandoned property."

"What if I lost an earring in the street and didn't know it?"

"That's considered lost property."

"What if I set an expensive watch to be repaired in a box on the counter in a jewelry store, left the store to take a phone call, and forgot about it for a day or two?"

"That's called mislaid property. You intentionally brought it to the jeweler to be fixed."

"What's the difference in all this?

"Abandoned property and lost property are likely to come under finders-keepers rulings. Mislaid property is expected to be safeguarded by the property owner or place of business where you intentionally left it, and you have a right to it."

"So, Jack and Anne intentionally buried this treasure trove for themselves and heirs, yet we would have to prove and reveal the genealogical connections, notify surviving heirs, deal with prosecution for breaking the law to remove it on our own, and still be at the mercy of the courts."

"Pretty much," said Paddy. "Until now, I wanted you to have plausible deniability. You didn't know the rules. You have the opportunity now to decide for us to turn it all in, and I'll take the heat."

"Kudzu that," she said. "Finders keepers; it's ours. We have pirate blood, and it's nobody's bloody business. We will do good with this, in our own way, and in our own time."

"That brings us to strategy, and our behavior going forward."

"I constantly have to catch up with you."

Paddy threw his head back and laughed. "It's called mileage."

Shannon smiled. "Mileage enough to know that there are no friends of treasure and everyone wants a piece of it."

Paddy cleared his throat. "Yep. Right now we need a secure AOP."

"Huh?"

"Area of Operation. Let's find a short-term condo rental for our inventory work."

Paddy and Shannon located a spacious vacation rental condominium in a gated resort community in East Naples with a garage and lanai, near a clubhouse and pool. There would be no hotel staff checking in on the space. Paddy drove the van into the garage. After they got settled in, they spread the treasure over kitchen counters, tabletops, beds, and floors.

Shannon set up a daily work schedule with time to enjoy the resort, the Naples area, and get out for evening sails on the *Second Wind*.

The first four days were devoted to sorting, light cleaning, photography, description, and inventory of the items. Shannon took a break and rolled on a king-size bed of gold coins with a heavy nine-foot gold chain draped over her shoulders and opulent jewelry on her fingers.

She got up and walked into the kitchen with the massive chain around her shoulders. Paddy stood counting gold coins. Shannon chuckled at his getup. He wore a black T-shirt, black bandanna, a gold pirate earring on his left ear, and a large cross pendant hung from his neck with twine. He made the sign of the cross blessing toward Shannon.

"I just realized something."

"What, my child?"

"The more I handle this stuff, the more desensitized I get to it. I think it is what you do with your wealth that matters."

"What do you want to do, Shannon?"

"Get a cottage in Gloucester with a dock on the Annisquam River. Have my own working charter vessel, good as a liveaboard, and spend winters cruising warm waters."

"Those dreams can come true."

"I want to select family heirlooms to pass on, store my reserve gold and silver, diversify, and contribute to causes I believe in."

"That is evolved thinking."

"You might want to think about getting one of those large rough emeralds cut and made into a pendant and earring set for Jenny as a wedding present."

"I like that idea; she could pass it on to Daniella."

Shannon looked around. "How do we store this stuff?"

"Think like a thief—use multiple locations, bury some on your own property and use private vault storage outside the financial system."

"Stealthy."

He held up a large gold doubloon. "We should get hard plastic coin flips for the best ones, and, for the rest, canisters that don't contain PVC, which can cause chemical action with the metals. We'll rent a temporary storage locker in East Naples with some of the booty in our used Goodwill golf bags and suitcases."

"That doesn't seem very secure."

"It will look inconspicuous once we toss in old furniture, garden tools and housewares. We'll get a metal truck storage box with a hasp and lock as a safe for some of the treasure and put it in with the heap."

"Can your contacts and dealers in nautical antiques help move some of the treasure?"

"Yes, with discretion, and the *Second Wind* can stow a portion of it indefinitely. There's a hidden metal vault low in the hull at the bow." He smiled. "Great for ballast in heavy seas."

SALACIA

Two and a half weeks later, Shannon and Paddy were aboard the *Second Wind*, docked at Marco Island Marina. It was Super Bowl Sunday. She would listen to the afternoon game, in spite of the fact her New England Patriots had lost to the Baltimore Ravens in a home game for the AFC championship. Shannon's revenge was to root for the San Francisco 49ers against Baltimore.

Paddy was out for the day to get provisions for their two-month Caribbean adventure. She took slow breaths to calm her exuberance as she reviewed the ship's logs and checklists.

Her confidence had grown from skippering the recent trip up the Gulf Coast. She daydreamed of island-hopping to Martinique, St. Lucia, St. Vincent, Barbados, and finally Grenada, with visits to British and French islands. It was sobering, however, to consider just how the voyage would test her mettle as acting captain in open ocean waters. Anxious and excited at the same time, she read how the Windward Islands aligned such that easterly trade winds of ten to twenty-five knots prevailed for some of the best-known sailing in the world.

She realized that her wish list for the extended cruise had too many ports of call from the Virgin Islands to the Windwards at the southern end of the Caribbean Sea. They would have a hard stop in Trinidad for vessel inventory and marine services before the final jaunt to Jamaica for

Paddy and Jenny's wedding in late March.

She and Daniella had kept in regular contact to plan the wedding. Shannon's role was to generate creative ideas, handle the groom and groomsmen details, and get Paddy to the wedding on time.

She wondered how Paddy had acquired his skills, the nuggets of useful information at his command, and language for so many foreign ports. Yesterday, he returned from a Naples bank with two large envelopes filled with Eastern Caribbean dollars and euros for their trip.

The afternoon football game was a downer. It was the first time Shannon had listened alone to a Super Bowl playoff on the radio instead of watching a television with a gang of friends.

Paddy returned from the store with grocery bags filled with magazines, coffee, spices, teas, and first aid items.

Shannon grimaced. "You hear San Francisco lost?"

"Yeah," he said. "It was on every station, from the van to the stores. There are plenty of snowbirds from Boston with glum faces around here today. On the upside, the weather opening will be fantastic the next several days."

"What's typical this time of year?"

"The dry season just began, rain showers will become brief, and we should have good winds through March."

"Sounds ideal," said Shannon.

"But we may face squalls with intense rain and winds over forty knots. We'll do some drills for that."

"I understand we have to pay special attention when anchoring between islands."

"Exactly. After a few nights shifting anchor in rough seas, you'll become seaworthy and sensitive to pace and conditions to reach protected harbors."

"We're done with prep and totally good to go," she said. "I'll get drinks for us before we go out for those baby back ribs you talked about."

Shannon brought a tray of lemonade and snacks up from the galley to join Paddy on the aft deck under the Bimini top. She noticed a large man wearing dark wraparound sunglasses approaching their slip. He wore a white sleeveless shirt and black dress pants. She listened as he greeted Paddy.

"Mr. Clarke, I am federal agent Roberto Costa, and I need to speak with you and Shannon."

"Can I see your credentials?" said Paddy.

Shannon studied the man, who held up a Homeland Security Investigations badge. "Victor?"

Paddy shot a puzzled look at Shannon.

"Yes, Shannon," said the agent. "We met in Miami and Key West with Caesar Rossetti. I do more than haul boats. My real first name is Roberto. This visit is to discuss your safety and apparent involvement in an ongoing investigation." He pointed to a large boat docked on the other end of the marina. "Let's talk privately on that vessel."

"Okay," said Paddy. "But first tell us the questions and what you want to discuss."

Costa looked at both of them and sighed. "All right, we need to talk about the hijacking of the *Second Wind*, what you saw, threats made, details, and how we are going to handle it."

Shannon kept her gaze on the agent. "Anything else?"

"We have kept tabs on you both. Interesting movements and temporary living arrangements you've had lately. I don't care about what you two were doing in Barfield Bay, as long as you cooperate."

"Let's have a chat. I'll do the talking, and I'll stop talking when I think we need a lawyer," Paddy said.

"Okay, I am here partly because of inquiries made by a certain woman in an admiralty law firm in Kingston, Jamaica, about Mateo Dias," said Costa. "Then, Mr. Clarke, you made inquiries about Caesar Rossetti and his associates. That all has to stop."

Shannon looked at Paddy with wide eyes. She knew she had made mistakes. Daniella and Paddy could be at risk because of them.

"So much for privacy," Paddy said. "The woman in Kingston was doing me a favor and doesn't know anything."

"Get off the case, Mr. Clarke. We know she is your daughter and submitted anonymous tips to local authorities about those smugglers."

Costa turned to make a casual scan of nearby boats. He continued in a low voice. "We never talked to her directly but intercepted conversations. Be happy about it. We kept her out of it. Thanks to her, Mateo Dias is in custody—and giving us useful information. I doubt he will ever bother either of you again. Especially after the bashing you and Shannon gave him." He gestured to the gleaming white eighty-foot trawler he had indicated earlier. "Let's walk over."

As they boarded the trawler, Shannon scanned the cranes, winches, tanks, and tidy arrangements of equipment on deck. Paddy appeared deep in thought, rubbing his neck. *He's probably figuring out what to say to Costa—formulating a plan. God knows we need one.*

Costa led them to the flybridge, gesturing for them to take a seat, but Paddy and Shannon remained standing.

"Okay, have it your way," said Costa. "What I can tell you is this. Franco Torre has been in custody for two weeks. We expect him to be in jail for a very long time. We netted him and others in an interagency sting with DEA, FBI and ICE."

"I never knew his last name." Shannon scowled. "He should rot."

Paddy put his hand over hers. He tapped his chest. "Remember, I talk."

"Sorry," she said.

Costa cleared his throat. "One of the men involved in hijacking the *Second Wind* took a big risk to spare you two and your ship. He also helped us with a sting of a subsequent smuggling operation. He is now in a witness protection program for the prosecution."

Shannon thought of Caesar in restraints and held her hands to her mouth.

"Is he okay?"

"He's fine," said the agent. "After the trial, he will have a new identity and a new life. He glanced at Shannon and Paddy. "I need to hear from you both what happened on the *Second Wind*."

"You know that we cleared in at Marathon with nothing to declare," Paddy said. "That was true, so what else can you expect me to say?"

"My superiors know nothing about this meeting," Costa said and rubbed his jaw. "You did omit serious details. The lawyers would say nonfeasance, blah, blah, but I'm not recording this conversation."

Paddy folded his arms and squinted at the agent. "It's hard for me to trust this. We have too much at stake for not reporting the hijacking, and I can't risk any credible threat to our family."

"Okay, but I would have to trust you to keep what you learn confidential. And why should I do that?"

"Because we have more to lose," said Paddy.

"Maybe, but I'll take the risk because you have distinguished service to this country, both of your records are clean, and I believe you are victims in this case." Agent Costa softened his look and held up his palm. "Stay here. I'll be right back."

Shannon and Paddy looked at each other. Paddy spread his hands open with a skeptical expression on his face.

Costa returned with Caesar Rossetti, who stepped onto the flybridge wearing a blue fishing shirt and pressed khaki shorts.

Shannon and Paddy were speechless.

"*Ciao*, Shannon, Captain Clarke. Welcome to research vessel *Salacia*." Caesar held and kissed Shannon's hand. "I worry so much for you. Sorry to disappear. Let Signore Costa explain, and you help him."

Shannon hugged Caesar. "I worried about you, too, but wondered if you were a crook. Are you in the witness protection program?"

Costa interrupted. "He refused that. He's actually a hero: played along with Franco, participated in a dangerous sting operation with our agents to gather intelligence in Brazil at the home of a cartel-connected family."

Shannon snarled at him. "So you ran Caesar like a bait fish."

"Yes, but drop the tone; there's more." Costa glanced at Caesar, who kept his eyes on Shannon. "Caesar convinced the man known as 'Doc' to turn himself in to us. Doc gave testimony in exchange for a better life with his family. He is the one in witness protection. The doctor was pressed into the whole affair and couldn't get out until Caesar intervened." Costa nudged Caesar. "Tell her the rest."

Caesar looked down and then met Shannon's eyes. "Franco Torre is my half-brother."

Shannon recoiled, straightened up, and swallowed hard. "Creepy," she said. "So that's why you associated with him?"

"When my mother paid for my education at University of Miami, she had just one condition: that I look out for Franco. He was always in trouble. I spent my teen years with my father in La Spezia. Franco was with our wealthy mother and her rich lover in Florence, but they did not want him. She gave Franco money but no discipline. Franco came to the USA and stayed with me in Miami while I finished university. I found him work, but he met new troublemakers and pretended to be legitimate. He tricked me to meet you on your sail out of Jamaica, then hijacked your brigantine when I refused to go along with his plans to smuggle people and contraband goods." He paused, fear clouding his face as he took her hands in his. "Franco has a personal vendetta against you, Shannon."

"Don't sugarcoat it, Caesar," said Costa. The agent produced a head shot of Franco with a mean scar on his face. "Franco is very dangerous, wants revenge on Caesar, and rants he will come for you, Shannon. The FBI has been tracking you and Patrick since you checked in at Marathon. The agency cannot risk leaks. I'm here because Caesar insisted on this meeting, or he wouldn't accept our deal with him."

Shannon looked at Caesar. "What did you get out of this?"

"Your safety, my freedom, and the *Salacia,*" Caesar said. "She is the perfect oceanographic expedition trawler. I am a contractor to several agencies, with a grant, and have accepted to run private ecotourism research charters."

"The *Salacia* is yours?"

"Yes. The government helped me trade my project boat and finance this, with conditions."

"So you are helping the feds break criminal networks in the Caribbean?"

"Yes. I have no regrets. I cannot fix my mother's mistakes. Franco is not a brother to me anymore." Caesar winced and his chin dipped down. He looked at Costa and turned back to Shannon with a flushed face. "Now they are smuggling young women for *putas*. Franco can go to hell."

He gazed into Shannon's eyes. She softened. "A family is like a hand; each finger is different. Trust me, I know."

Caesar relaxed, pulled her into a hug and whispered, "I will do anything to protect you."

Shannon held him tight and kissed his neck. When she stepped away, Paddy shook Caesar's hand. "I trust you now."

Agent Roberto Costa directed an exchange of information, after which they all agreed to secrecy.

Costa pointed to Caesar and Shannon. "You two must not have any contact until the investigation ends, and that could be months." Costa gave business cards to Shannon and Paddy. "I am the contact. Call me if anything comes up."

"It says Victor Alves, Marine Mechanic," Shannon said.

"My cover," Costa said, "but Victor is my middle name. I'm part Portuguese and Brazilian. As a kid, I came to the US with my parents. To you, I am a boat mechanic. You and Paddy have never met agent Roberto Victor Costa. My office does not know about this meeting. Keep it that way."

The agent turned to Paddy. "Why don't you and I take a walk, have some of that lemonade on the *Second Wind*, talk about life, and give them a few hours to catch up?"

Paddy smiled and nodded. "For us, I think vodka, ice and sparkling water with that lemonade will taste good."

"I'd like that," said the agent. "I'm done with working on Super Bowl Sunday. I heard Baltimore won."

Paddy and Roberto Costa walked to the *Second Wind*.

Caesar held Shannon on the main deck of *Salacia*, his hands softly on her hips. They lingered with a kiss. She ran her fingers through his dark wavy hair, and along the side of his stubble beard. Beads of sweat rolled down her spine. He held her firmly to his body. She breathed in his natural fragrance with a hint of Armani Acqua Di Gio cologne.

"You are my Salacia, goddess of the salty seas."

She gazed at his molten brown eyes. "*Salacia* may not reveal her secrets so easily, but I might be persuaded."

He kissed her on the neck and moved his lips to hers. Their bodies drew close and tongues danced. She felt the excitement in his body and moaned softly.

SEA TRIALS

The next morning, Shannon began her stint as captain for their extended Caribbean voyage. She considered the arc of 7,000 islands and cays stretching from Florida east through the Bahamas to the Virgin Islands, and south to Trinidad near the coast of Venezuela. They would finish in Jamaica, but a major decision remained concerning which sail route to take. It was her call.

"It comes down to this: I want to explore as much of the Caribbean as possible. This time of year, weather permitting, we have two main routes. Island-hop southeast through the Bahamas and Turks and Caicos, head down to the Dominican Republic and Puerto Rico on the east side and then go east to the Virgin Islands. Or we can—"

"Permission to speak, Captain," said Paddy.

Shannon nodded.

"What's your thinking on that first option?"

"It seems the safer route, closer to landmasses and easier to get provisions," said Shannon. "We'd wait for each weather opening to punch through some heavy seas and easterly trade winds below latitude twenty-five degrees." She traced the route on the chart. "Then pick our way through rocky islands with tricky on-shore winds."

"Good, you've done the homework. What else?"

"If we had a smaller vessel and more time, we'd probably take that route."

"What's the rush?"

"You have a wedding date, and I'm to get you there on time, remember?"

"We could shorten the itinerary," he said.

"Hmm. I like a second option: We take the skipper's delivery route through the Bahamas for blue water sailing. The *Second Wind* can easily handle it. It will be six hundred and fifty or so miles of beating east, mostly under power, until we take the southeast turn at longitude 065 west. Then we sail four hundred miles to the Virgin Islands. With no delays, we make it in ten days."

Paddy folded his arms. "What about being out in the middle of nowhere, possibly short on fuel and water, or needing medical attention?"

"This will be my true test of seamanship." Shannon put her hands on her hips. "The *Second Wind* is sixty-five feet strong, well equipped, and a seaworthy brigantine. Her powerful diesel engine propels a mil-spec generator for electric, and a belt-drive RO desalinization system for fresh water. This sail will be a human endurance test—and I am determined."

"Determination is the critical factor for that route," he said.

"And I can count on you, my expert first mate. We leave today. Weather radar shows we miss a norther by the time we put out of Miami."

Paddy took in a deep breath and grinned. "Yes, Captain."

The sail back to Miami was now familiar to Shannon, and Paddy was true to his word. As first mate, he followed her lead, and as teacher he asked and answered questions. Every day was immersion learning, and he created professional distance more than once with the refrain "You'll figure it out, Captain."

Caesar had passed Shannon a duplicate edition of Ernest Hemingway's *The Old Man and the Sea* as a book cipher, to convert their words into numbers corresponding to page, line, and word.

He had also set up private alias email accounts for them to keep in touch via SailMail, a popular email service for yacht owners with marine SSB radios and modems hooked up to laptops or tablets. She would wait to receive Caesar's first message before admitting the matter to Paddy.

She rolled her neck and shook out her hair. Passion and elation mixed with jumbled thoughts—the last time she had felt this kind of hot crush was at sixteen. She tried to clear her mind, thinking about the treasure and journey ahead.

Paddy and Shannon made smart work of their business in Miami. The treasure hoard from the Marco storage locker was now secure in two private, high-security storage vaults.

Shannon had selected three large rough emeralds from the trove. Paddy arranged for a gem cutter to team with a jeweler and fashion an emerald pendant set with earrings, jeweled rings and other items. Daniella's law office would arrange with a Miami attorney to oversee the process and ship the package to her office in Kingston to hold for the wedding.

After provisioning the *Second Wind,* lashing extra water and fuel containers on deck, and completing last-minute checks, Shannon filed the float plan.

She had briefed Paddy on daily routines and watch schedules. Part of each day would be devoted to gaining mastery of shipboard instruments, communications gear, sail rigs, and interpreting weather patterns visually and by radar and marine forecasts. They agreed on training maneuvers. Paddy's belief in Shannon would help her build her own confidence.

On the third day of their headwind voyage, as they encountered moderate wave action, Shannon attempted her first trial of the essential sailing skill—heaving to.

She directed her uncle from the exterior helm station. "Trim the mainsail and the jib tight."

"Aye, Cap."

"Cutting power and tacking across wind."

The jib filled to push the bow away from the wind and Shannon wheeled the rudder to keep the vessel back to it. The mainsail and the jib balanced out at sixty degrees off the wind.

"She does heave to, and in a fine slow drift, Captain," shouted Paddy.

Shannon steered in small adjustments as she returned the thumbs-up from Paddy. "What a rush," she said.

After forty minutes of calm seas, she ordered Paddy to dog down the lines, hatches, and equipment. "It's getting gusty."

Heavy waves formed and she worked the helm to stay in the troughs. *Feel is as important as technique,* she thought. Paddy worked on deck, and her mind wandered to how young she felt when she was with Caesar. The combination of ship, waves, and reverie was hypnotic.

From the corner of her eye, she spotted a large wave approaching, and the *Second Wind* began to climb.

"Hold on," she yelled.

Shannon had not sufficiently luffed off to meet the rogue wave head-on, but instinctively tried to bore off before striking the wave top. Seawater smashed onto the deck as *Second Wind* rose up and slid through the next roller. Paddy lost his footing and fell hard. His head slammed on the gunwale. Her heart sank to see him that way, but she had to stay put and fight the crashing white horses.

She regained control of the vessel with the rudder, powered up the engine, and headed directly into rising waves and wind. Shannon took a risk to reset the autopilot, and crab-walked over to Paddy. He was out cold, but his vitals were okay. She struggled to pull him to the helm station, to no avail. She laid a blanket on him as the swells nearly toppled her over.

"Can you hear me, Paddy?" she repeated three times close to his face. He did not respond, but Shannon was relieved to hear his breath. She stayed low to hold his head. Torrents of bow spray drenched them. Thankfully, the *Second Wind* plowed steadily to the east.

The gusts and whitecaps abated. Shannon adjusted Paddy's head onto her thigh and shouted his name three times. His jaw began to move and his eyelids twitched, but his head rolled sideways and then lay still. She bunched some of the blanket under his neck and then raced to get the first aid kit, ripped open a box of smelling salts, and broke an ampoule of ammonia inhalant to put under his nose. It worked.

Paddy's head turned. "What? . . . Ugh . . . Jesus . . ." He put his hand to his eye and temple.

"Don't move," she said.

Shannon checked the swelling bruise around his eye socket, asked him questions, and had him track her finger with his eyes. She felt his neck and moved his head in slow movements with her hands.

"I'm all right," he mumbled. The bruise next to his right eye spelled otherwise.

"Sorry. This is my fault. Let's get you upright, but slow."

"My neck's okay, but my head's pounding," he said.

Shannon knew head and neck injuries were hard to diagnose. She cleaned and dressed his wound, applied a cold compress, then helped him down to the galley. She set him up in a reclined position on the galley sofa.

Paddy rotated his right wrist, rubbed the edge of his hand, and winced. "You did good, Shannon. I haven't been so steady lately."

"You're holding that hand strangely," she said.

"Sprained it trying to break the fall," Paddy said, and manipulated the edge of his palm with his left thumb and forefinger. "Sonofabitch, a fractured fifth metacarpal."

"How can you possibly know that?"

"Mileage, Shannon. Not the first time—a classic brawler's injury. Need to make a cuff and tape it."

Shannon gave him a cold gel pack from the fridge. She helped him rise slowly and test a few steps before easing him back onto the galley sofa.

Maybe his hip is injured and he's downplaying it, she thought. Paddy seemed his true age for the first time. She tamped down overwhelming concern for her uncle. *A captain must keep a level head.*

Paddy rolled his wrist and looked back at her. "I can use the fingers for light duty—just can't lift much with my right for a while."

"This was my fault," Shannon said as tears spilled down her cheeks.

"No big deal," he said. "But now you have a one-handed mate with a headache. Next thing you know, I'll have a hook, a peg leg, and wear an eye patch."

Shannon smiled but knew she would have to pace herself. Long night watches and checking on his condition were in store. *It could have been worse*, she thought, and chastised herself for allowing amateur distraction before hitting that rogue wave.

Washburn's warning haunted her. She whispered, "Always be a little afraid out here." Her complacency was the bitter lesson, but self-loathing would simmer. Captain Walbridge's complacency may have undone the *Bounty*. Captain Jonathan Haraden was ever vigilant.

She prepared a hot mug of tomato soup and a ham and cheese sandwich for Paddy.

"Thanks for the comfort food, Shannon. I'll help with watches tonight."

She stood over him like a hospital nurse and handed him two ibuprofen with a cup of water. "Get some rest here in the galley." Shannon looped a walkie-talkie onto his left wrist. "We'll communicate in bursts with these as I navigate. I set a timer in my pocket to alarm every ten minutes so I can keep check on any vessels in these open waters with time to maneuver out of the way."

"At least let me get set up in the interior helm station."

"Stay down here for now," she replied, stepped up to the interior helm station, and piloted into darkening skies. *The seas are not ominous*, she thought. Regardless of her positive self-talk, her heart pounded.

VIGILANCE

Eight days later, Shannon and Paddy entered Road Bay Port in
Anguilla, tired but relieved.

"Land, ho!" Paddy cried out in a hoarse voice.

"A thousand miles, ho," said Shannon. "This is the frontier of my
dreams."

Paddy set out a small vintage brass salute cannon with a gunwale mount,
loaded it with a blank 12-gauge shotgun shell, and gestured for Shannon to
pull the firing mechanism.

The cannon's roar echoed back from the island.

As the smoke cleared, Shannon held her hands high. "We did it, mate."

"You single-handed in blue water, Captain," he said with pride. "I was
a useless couch potato."

"More like a squawking *coach* potato, but highly informative." She
laughed.

"I'm glad you weren't tempted to stop in the Virgin Islands."

"That can wait. You're getting checked by a doctor as soon as possible."

Paddy shook his head. "I'm healing up fine."

The immigration office was at the police station by the dinghy dock
in Sandy Ground. After that, it was straight to the nearest medical facility.
Good thing, because the doctor had to reset Paddy's metacarpal and put a
hard cast on his hand. Everything but his pride was intact.

As they were leaving the clinic, a woman in her fifties seated at the reception counter stood and gave a long smile at Paddy. She held up a felt-tipped marker, winked at him, and removed the pen top.

Shannon stepped to her, swiped the marker, and wagged her head at the woman. She gave Paddy an adoring hug, pretending to be a girlfriend, and spoke aloud while writing on his cast. *To my hero. Love, S.*

Shannon addressed the woman with a wink. "He's quite the catch. Would you like to write something, too? The purple looks good on white plaster, don't you think?"

The woman's face flushed. She sighed and looked down at her desk.

On the way out the door, Shannon paused. "And Patrick, you'll make a fine cook, cabin boy and deckhand. Don't worry, when the cast comes off in five weeks, you'll be the luck of the brotherhood."

"Deckhand? Arrgh." He played along with the charade.

"Steersman, then. Give way, I'm the captain here." She pitched a dramatic voice. "And ye be my charge now, too."

"Bah, flatterer," he said.

"It's not so bad. You'll be the pretty one by your wedding day," Shannon said and glanced back at the receptionist. The woman regained her friendly composure and waved to them with a chuckle.

Paddy and Shannon sat at the long crescent beach at Sandy Ground with their legs in the water.

"The doc said your eye will be fine, but what about the balance issues?"

"He had me perform simple tests and suggested I get treated for an idiosyncratic condition known as Meniere's, affecting my inner ear. I've had bouts of this before."

Shannon knew this had to be hard for him to admit, so she just let it go.

They walked along the beach, admiring its brilliant white sand and gazing over the calm sea and back to the upscale villas hugging the coast.

After Shannon took a dip in the water, they went to a beach bar that offered tastes of Pyrat rum from the islands, produced in a two-century-old rum factory that had recently closed.

"Anguilla is a nice British territory. A bit tony for me," she said, "but a few miles northeast, the deep-sea fishing for wahoo, sailfish, and tuna is supposed to be very good. That goes on my bucket list."

"Where do you want to go now, Shannon?"

"I want to cruise and explore the best of these Leeward and Windward Islands."

"Each Caribbean island, nation, or territory is unique," Paddy said. "They range in size, wealth, culture, language, and geography. What will you value most?"

Shannon did not hesitate. "Places of natural beauty where locals and travelers take pride in it."

Paddy smiled.

"Travelers aren't all rich," she said. "But this posh island, loaded with yachts and a few remote hotels, is more appealing than overbuilt places with cruise lines, busloads of vacationers, and getting hustled everywhere you turn."

"So, you're a working-class girl with refined taste?"

"As like as not, mate."

Paddy chuckled and pretended to hold up a glass for a toast. "To a fair wind and days filled with enchanting beauty and turquoise waters." He scanned the horizon. "Most of the islands are volcanic or formed by large coral beds."

Shannon wondered how many future generations would be able to appreciate it like this, and worried about how fragile the ecosystems of the coral reefs really were. "I want to see as much as I can in the time we have left."

Paddy said, "There is always next year."

She rubbed her face. "I'd like to split the next four weeks, cruise the Leeward Islands from here to Dominica; then the Windward Islands, from Martinique to the Grenadines."

"You'll feel torn from each place. Just allow enough time to get the

Second Wind dry-docked in Trinidad for annual inspection and depot maintenance, from rigging to hull paint, before we sail back to Jamaica."

"How long will that take?" she asked.

"I'm estimating nine to ten days for the maintenance. I'll schedule that now and we can explore Trinidad and Tobago in a charter while the *Second Wind* is in repair."

"Between now and then I want to see the natural gems of Guadeloupe, Martinique, Dominica, and Bequia."

"Those are among my favorites, Shannon. We can take a small plane and rent a boat for that. By the way, the locals pronounce it *Beck-wei*. The name in ancient Arawak meant 'island of the clouds.'"

Shannon learned the intricacies and protocols for customs in each port of entry. But without Spanish or French, she was at a disadvantage in several situations. With two language dictionaries provided by her uncle, her goal was to learn 400 words and key phrases from each. *That was a stretch goal, for sure,* she thought.

More than once, Paddy sat back with a grin and folded his arms as she struggled to communicate with islanders and customs officials. To help her learn, he spoke with her in French or Spanish, and occasionally Dutch, for everyday conversation.

She accepted the professional distance of their daytime work roles. In the evenings, they carried on with relaxed banter as family. After dinner, she would study Coast Guard manuals in her cabin.

Every few days she marked up pages of her copy of *The Old Man and the Sea* and exchanged delayed coded messages with Caesar. When she came into each port of call, she connected with Daniella to further plans for Paddy and Jenny's wedding. Day by day, Shannon's confidence grew seaworthy, and she came to know the *Second Wind* as a friend.

One afternoon, no land in sight, she gazed up at a heap of friendly cumulus clouds. A dog shape chased another, and a chariot shape rode over the top. The clouds began to cluster and transform into projections of Anne Bonny and Captain Jonathan Haraden.

Anne's long locks floated in the wind, and Jonathan Haraden's serene face, with glinting hawk eyes, turned to Shannon.

Anne spoke in a strong, funneled voice. "Fear has no place on a vessel."

Haraden thundered in echo, "Hold vigilance, not fear."

They just drifted in like that: Anne, fierce as fire, and Captain Haraden, cool as ice.

Shannon took a deep breath. She thought of Caesar and wondered how she would, could, or should control her impetuous heart.

Shannon and Paddy sailed south from Dominica in calm waters. It was midafternoon and they would hail Martinique by daybreak.

"Beyond here be monsters," said Shannon. "Like your tattoo of sea serpents on this eastern edge of the Caribbean Plate."

"Mostly monsters of low-pressure systems from West Africa slugging huge waves, wind, and dust that shape hurricanes here."

"Who knows what beasts may surface from the trench," Shannon said. She gazed astern for a while. "You were right, Paddy."

"About?"

"You said I'd feel torn from each island. After Guadeloupe and Dominica, we're less than twenty miles south and I want to go back and never leave the Leeward Islands."

"Dominica deserves its reputation as the nature island of the Caribbean," said Paddy.

"I'll never find another place with more bird and plant species," she said. Her mind flashed with memories and moods of lush rainforests, rivers, gushing waterfalls, unspoiled habitats and beaches.

Shannon thought of the fishing she did not get to do, and of the bonefish, tarpon, snook, and other fish she did not get to catch. But it was time to let go and move forward—time to get back to business.

Studying the skies for the weather pattern, she turned on the ship's radio. Paddy and Shannon listened to repeated and inconclusive remarks about cold fronts to the north, swells, and intertropical convergence in the area.

"Those swells don't usually make the Windwards," said Paddy. "But we have forty miles of open seas to get there."

"What is this convergence?"

"Not much to worry about. We'll probably get some rain squalls or cloudy weather. If they said tropical disturbance, we could be in for more intense squalls. When they say a tropical depression, expect more intense winds to thirty-five knots."

"Good, you're not concerned."

"When a tropical storm with forty-to-sixty-knot winds or, worse, a hurricane approaches, then I'll be concerned. But we have to pay attention. You can usually see squalls in time to avoid them. The radar can indicate a squall line hundreds of miles away."

That evening, Shannon took down the fisherman topsail amidships, the large square course and the smaller square foretop. Then she double-reefed the gaff mainsail and raised the headsail for balance.

Paddy took over, leaving Shannon to the midnight watch. She put the safety harness on him and went below to her bunk to read and rest, but she soon fell into a deep sleep.

Her digital timer woke her; she prepared hot peppermint tea with a heavy dose of raw honey, and joined Paddy at 11:45 p.m.

"Nice air, moonlight and visibility," he said. "I saw a shearwater bird angle close to the water with its long straight wings. They are fun to watch."

"Nocturnal. That's interesting," Shannon said. She sipped from a thermal travel cup. "I actually slept for a change." She took a longer sip of the fragrant brew. "Mmm. Peppermint tea gives me an energy boost without caffeine."

She eyed Paddy, who seemed hyper-alert, which could happen on night watches, and tapped him on the shoulder. "There's still hot water in the thermos bungeed next to the range, with chamomile tea packets to ease you to sleep."

"Thanks, Shannon. Let's sit together awhile."

"I get you, Paddy."

"What do you mean?"

"Drawn by a seafaring life, but I wonder if it gets lonely."

"Not for me, Shannon. The natural world engulfs and enriches, as does joy to be with family and friends. I have interesting characters for crewmates, and you'll meet two of them at the wedding."

Shannon pondered in silence while keeping her eyes on the sky.

Paddy grunted and spoke again. "But eventually you tighten the circle and head to homeport." He stood. "I'm going below now. See you in three hours, Captain."

She selected a classical playlist on her media player, slipped on headphones, and stood at the exterior helm. The moon glided through stratus clouds accompanied by Wagner's "Ride of the Valkyries."

About 2:30 a.m., she felt cooler air and noticed the prevailing northeasterly breezes turn from the east. She pulled off her headphones. A towering dark cloud ahead covered the stars like a curtain. The moonlight allowed her to see its raggedy edges with black wisps of rain angled under it to the right. She judged the squall to be ten miles away and first in a line. She set the autopilot, rechecked the sails, put another reef on the main, and tacked left.

Shannon took slow breaths as she increased engine speed, recorded the *Second Wind*'s position in the log, and blasted the portable signal horn to roust her uncle.

"Hey, mate, we got weather. Secure items below."

She checked the VHF radio, then donned raingear and a personal flotation device.

Paddy yelled up to her, "Clip your harness onto the jack line."

"Done," she said.

A scaly black seabird took cover under the visor of the helm station, shook out its wings, and stared with Shannon through the windshield. Sheets of rain doused the cabin.

Paddy came halfway up the companionway. "All secure," he said. "What's your plan, Cap?"

Shannon pointed to the blotted sky. "Get far east of the nose of that squall line."

"Good," he said. "Let's have some fun." Paddy assessed conditions and sail rigging, and then spoke with his hand to her ear. "Nice work, Captain. We'll be fine. That bird's a good sign."

She made a mental note to ask her uncle why later. Now, she needed to focus. "Get your gear on," she said. "I need you at the interior helm so I can work the sails."

"Aye, Captain." Paddy stepped below, secured the passageway door open, slipped on his raingear, and sat in the pilot chair below.

Shannon felt the mass of moving air turn chaotic. The dark cloud came close as a neighbor's house. Rain pounded in spray, then with punches of blinding artillery.

A blast of cold air pressed down upon them, flattening the water. Gusts of high winds followed. Shannon fought to bring the *Second Wind* behind the cloud. The vessel's smooth performance was a relief.

She found a break in the stir. Poking the adamant brigantine through boisterous waves, she crossed the squall line. Heavy cold winds veered with spray in all directions. Rain stung her skin in the total chaos. Then a patch of sunshine came with a lull before the big brother to the first squall raced away with a trail of little ones.

That's what a tropical disturbance with intense winds feels like, she thought. It was a first for her to navigate a squall line. Shannon found it strange to be so satisfied with something yet in no hurry to do it again.

Paddy patted Shannon's back. "Congratulations, Captain. Well done."

"Your nonchalance really bugged me."

"I wasn't worried. I wanted you to put me in my place and think for yourself. Which you did."

Shannon spoke in her gravelly pirate voice, "So there's an end to it, matey." She chuckled and punched his shoulder. "What did you mean about the bird being a good sign?"

"That was a young, smart, sooty tern that judged the situation correctly. He had choices. Not a big storm cell, could have veered off, but took easy protection."

"Heh, birds don't think like that."

"Call it instinct if you must, but that was skill. Millions of his ancestors have been doing it longer than us." Paddy looked up at the clear skies. "Someday that juvenile will grow to be a foot long with a three-foot wingspread. He'll be quite handsome in black, with a white head and underparts, and he'll spend decades at sea."

"Sounds like you, mate. I should call you 'Seabird.'"

"You've always been a seabird, Shannon. Now you got your big wings."

BRIGGY

Shannon and Paddy watched the *Second Wind* hoist from the slipway at the large yacht service facility in Chaguaramas, Trinidad. The underwater inspection of the vessel went well. Paddy kept his gaze over the dripping hull of his vessel as he spoke.

"It's important you know each step of this process, Shannon."

"She looks huge out of the water," she said.

Paddy seemed in a trance, nodding as droplets rolled down the side of the keel, jittered and fell to the watery shadows of the *Second Wind*.

After a long pause, he asked, "Remember the boat survey checklist?"

Her mind raced through possible repairs and service of electronics, rigging, canvas work, hull repair, sandblasting, welding, mechanicals, subsystems, upholstery, woodwork, paint application, polishing and buffing.

She took in a big breath. "Of course. Do I need to know all that?"

His tone became urgent. "You need to know much more than that."

Shannon wondered what he was getting at. She'd never managed a project of this scale.

"They do let you do some of the work yourself right here, but you also have to manage all the subcontractors as well as the work yard to get it right." Paddy pulled out an airline ticket. "The Grenadines will have to wait for you, Shannon. The schedule has changed. I'm flying to Jamaica for a few days to organize a honeymoon and evaluate a business investment."

"You're entrusting me to oversee the work?"

"Yup, but there's something I haven't told you."

Shannon bit her lip.

Paddy reached out to hold both of Shannon's hands. "I've been tough on you. But for a reason."

Shannon noticed Paddy's lips quiver, and his eyes got watery.

"As a captain, you have attained level four. Others take years to do it."

Her brows knitted. "I should be excited to hear that from you, but you don't look happy."

Paddy hugged her and gestured for them to sit on a bench near the slipway. "Happy tears, Shannon. Everything in your life and mine has led to this moment." He took a bandanna from his pocket and wiped his eyes. "I'm going to do something that's best for both of us."

Shannon had not seen her unflappable uncle so emotional. "Whatever you want, Paddy."

He turned to her. "When I come back from Jamaica, you will be the owner and captain of the *Second Wind*."

Shannon was speechless as the corners of her mouth turned down hard. *Is he serious?* She felt a warm glow. Her eyes and face tightened, and then she sobbed, "You have done so much for me. This is too much."

They sat for a while, arm in arm. Paddy kissed the top of her head.

"Shannon, you are helping me make a big transition in my life, and I in yours. You deserve this inheritance. All of us—Jenny, Daniella and I—want this for you, if you want it."

Shannon realized that she was helping him, too, and sat up straight. "You know it."

"There is only one condition."

"Anything."

"As long as you own the *Second Wind*, you'll visit and cruise patches of this part of the world with us."

"That's a no-brainer."

"Then it's settled. Daniella will fly here with my two Jamaican crewmembers to join you for a few days. You and Danny can complete the final wedding plans for Jenny and me. You get to know Trinidad and everything about maintaining a cruising vessel. When you approve the work, my men sail the *Second Wind* to Jamaica."

Shannon counted off her fingers. "So I fly to Kingston around March 25th."

"Exactly."

"How do you suggest I get the *Second Wind* back to Gloucester?"

"Jenny and I will be on honeymoon in Ireland. My crew can go back with you to Gloucester Harbor. They are excited to do it, and can take the time. You can make it by early May."

"What's that route like?"

"Make your plan with Lonnie and Duncan. Consult with sailors who have done it. You want to own this adventure."

"You're right—becoming more proficient is to plan and work a plan."

"That's a fine sea change, me hearty," said Paddy. "And plenty of seasoning years to become a master mariner."

"It's plain beyond disputing," said Shannon in pirate-speak.

"You have Haraden blood, so no doubt," he retorted.

In full drama mode, she said, "Methinks yer seasoning and critiques best taken on tropical winter waters, Patrick." Shannon shut off her mobile phone. "I've kept a secret, too, Paddy, and hope you'll approve," she said softly.

"Shoot."

"Caesar and I have been communicating over SailMail with a book cipher. He can come to the wedding—if you agree."

Paddy laughed. "Young love is right up there with old love. I agree. You sure dog-eared that copy of Hemingway's best. But don't worry, I didn't snoop."

Paddy and Shannon drove a rental car twenty miles from the haul-out facility to Piarco Airport in Port of Spain to pick up Daniella and Paddy's crewmembers, Lonnie and Duncan. Paddy had only mentioned they were good Jamaican sailors in their early forties.

Shannon swiped through photographs on her mobile phone as they waited together in the terminal. "I'll make a photo journal of our voyage."

"Jenny and I will love it. What do you say about our hike on the Trail of the Jesuits in Martinique?"

She traced her fingers in the air. "Majestic. Who wouldn't love the ridge views, rainforest, and Mt. Pelée?" She closed her eyes and sat back. "I now understand how the French painter Gauguin was inspired by the tropical flowered landscapes. I can't thank you enough," Shannon said, then focused on another photo. "I snorkeled along coral reefs with legions of painted fish." She pushed her hair back. "The afternoon wreck dive with a water scooter by Saint-Pierre, unforgettable." Shannon put her hand over Paddy's cast. "Sorry you had to sit that one out."

Paddy gave her a serious look. "You have a choice before we prepare paperwork for the *Second Wind.* Do you want to change the hull paint to white, or rededicate the vessel with a new name? Now is the time to do it."

"I like her just way she is, and will never forget what she stands for. But I do have a nickname for her."

"A diminutive girly one, is it?" he asked.

Shannon put her hands on her hips in defiance. "You knot-head, it's 'Briggy.'"

He clamped his lips together, gave her a big nod with high brows, and smiled. "Briggy . . . I fancy it."

"Harr."

Daniella's flight was on time. Wearing a dark power suit, Daniella strode through the glass security doorway holding an attaché case. Two Jamaican men followed, wearing tracksuits and dark sunglasses, toting luggage. One, lanky with long dreadlocks, moved in a smooth rhythm. The other, stocky with a braided Mohawk hairstyle, poked his head forward with hip-hop steps.

Daniella broke into a trot on high heels when she saw her father and Shannon. She set down the briefcase and swung her arms wide around them. They held close without words before she spoke.

"Love you both so much. I came right from my office. Sorry, but I'll need this suit for a few appointments here."

"You look sharp," said Shannon.

"Patrick," the men said as they greeted Paddy.

Paddy exchanged handshakes and hugs with the two men. "Shannon, meet my mates, Lonnie and Duncan. Among other things—navigator and cook."

Lanky Lonnie and Duck Duncan, she thought, committing names to memory. She reached out both hands in greeting. "My pleasure. My uncle said you're good sailors but gave no details."

Lonnie winked at Shannon. "St. Patrick here, the humble and courageous diviner of mysteries, with jolts of wisdom."

Daniella and Shannon nodded.

Duncan piped in. "Didn't say we are good sailors, did he? But he can be agreeable at mealtimes."

Lonnie turned to Duncan. "You buy his praise with culinary art on board."

"And you with mere poetry and philosophy," said Duncan.

Lonnie retorted, "As you both sleep safe, I navigate by the stars."

"And you two, grumpy as hungry kings," said Duncan.

"*Basta, andiamo,*" said Paddy.

"Now with Italian," Daniella said. "A butcher of languages."

"I understand St. Patrick was part Italian," Shannon said.

They checked into the hotel at the haul-out facility complex. Daniella and Paddy went to their respective rooms. Shannon invited Lonnie and Duncan for a drink at the lounge.

"Do you two know Mae West?" she asked them.

"Personal Flotation Device," said Lonnie.

"Required safety equipment for men," Duncan agreed.

She let that pass. "I mean the actress they were named for."

"Mae West. We watch old movies," said Lonnie. "Bashy lady."

"In any dimensions you want to put on it," said Duncan.

Shannon got serious. "Get out your résumés, boys.'"

Lonnie and Duncan looked at each other.

"Let's start with your skills and how you know my uncle."

Lonnie looked back at Duncan and spoke first. "She wants to know about Tata, shrink heads, and if our cereal was hot or cold when we were kids."

"Donno, mon, if we should talk about Tata," said Duncan.

Shannon screwed up her face. "Tata?"

"We call him Tata because he was," they said in unison.

Shannon called for another round of drinks. "Try me."

"We were rescue dogs for him. Two of his projects from the slums, like he run da *Island of Dr. Moreau*. Shapin' us up, anyone he choose be ship-shape," said Lonnie.

"I loved that movie," Shannon said.

Three drinks later, Shannon had their stories. She liked the two singer-songwriter musicians. Lonnie played rhythm and bass guitar, and Duncan was a percussionist with congas and just about anything else.

Shannon admired the way Paddy had apprehended and guided the wayward nineteen-year-olds that stole boats.

They told her how Paddy had changed their lives. Instead of turning them over to police for taking equipment from his Nauticat 38 pilothouse ketch, Paddy bound and interrogated them on the vessel, then returned them to their distraught mothers. He offered the boys work and taught them how to be sailors.

Paddy ensured they had marketable skills and paid for their trade school educations. Duncan became a cook and Lonnie studied electronics. Together, they crewed for yacht owners and on yacht-repositioning charters. They teamed up like brothers to learn how to shoot and edit video for arts, music, and social events.

Jenny had grown fond of them after her initial protestations of bringing the no-goods into her and Paddy's life. Jenny was a booking agent for Jamaican creative talent and advanced the boys' music careers. Duncan was now married with two kids, and Lonnie was a single dad.

Shannon terminated the interview and sat back. "Okay, when we all get to Jamaica, I want to hear your live music, see your digital videos, and experience your seamanship on the *Second Wind*. And how you can help with Paddy's wedding."

"Anything for Tata," they said.

"Good. You can do something for me in Kingston. Get me on the best deep-sea fishing boat to hunt for blue marlin, wahoo, mahi-mahi, tuna, or sailfish."

"No problem—I buy direct from the best boat captains," said Duncan.

"Do you two fish?"

"No," they said. "Never did."

"You're coming with me, and we'll see if you're cut out for it."

PORT ROYAL WEDDING

Two unlikely vessels, the white trawler *Salacia* and black-hulled brigantine *Second Wind*, rested at anchor by the shore of Port Royal. Shannon awoke to the ring of *Salacia*'s bell. She untangled her arms from Caesar's body and rolled onto her back. She daydreamed of that balmy-turned-stormy sail with Paddy south of Dominica when a sooty tern took cover under the visor of the helm station. He said those birds spent decades at sea but returned to the same Gulf Coast island near Texas to rejoin their mates as seasonal monogamists.

"Breakfast is ready," said one of Caesar's crewmen with a quick knock on the door. Glassware clinked and the sound of footsteps fell away.

Shannon had thought she would never feel so sexually alive or romantic again, yet in three nights with Captain Caesar, she felt half her age. She peered around the cabin, her eyes adjusting to the morning light provided by a tiny porthole as she focused on a framed picture of herself.

Shannon slipped into Caesar's robe, cracked open the cabin door and retrieved the breakfast tray of coffee, two stemmed glasses of orange juice, and small plates of ackee fruit, cherries, salt fish, and fried dumplings. A small bottle of champagne was set in an ice bucket.

Setting the tray on the nightstand and lying back down, Shannon fondled her sleeping Mediterranean man. He murmured with pleasure and tried to kiss her.

"Relax, Caesar. I don't want to wear you out—just wake you," Shannon said with a teasing smile. "Let's have a toast."

"Ahh, mimosas," Caesar said. "I think my crew must be helping us celebrate Paddy's wedding today with my stash of champagne. Or congratulating me on my beautiful conquest."

"Your conquest?" said Shannon. "Hmmm. Who really conquered whom? Although, with a name like Caesar, I guess you've had your fair share of conquests."

They raised their glasses and toasted the wedding of Paddy and Jenny. It wasn't long before the champagne tickled and aroused Shannon's senses, including her sense of adventure.

"Tell me, Caesar, in ancient Rome did slave girls really feed fruit to men of power?" she asked as she dangled a cherry near his lips.

"Only the most beautiful slave girls," he said.

"Well, my emperor, we are not in ancient Rome. We are in Jamaica," said Shannon as she took the cherry away from Caesar's mouth before he could capture it. She stood, slipped off her robe, and pulled him to a sitting position on the side of the bed.

Caesar tried to pull her back toward him.

"Wait," she said, and took a sip of the champagne straight from the bottle. She kneeled and took Caesar in her mouth as he moaned, fully alert from the chill and the bubbles. Before he finished, Shannon pushed him back down on the bed and got on top of him.

"Shannon, you are so beautiful, so different from anyone I know," Caesar said looking at her face. He positioned himself to enter her. "I think . . . I—"

"Quiet, my Caesar," said Shannon as she leaned forward and her red hair fell around them. "Tell me again, who is conquering whom?"

Shannon showered and primped in Caesar's cabin bathroom. She took her time to rake her tangled hair and partially dry it. She studied her face in the mirror. *Smile and frown lines are achievements,* she thought. *When was the last time I used makeup to make up for the years?*

As Paddy's best man, Shannon chose a swashbuckler style for the groomsmen. Today, she, Lonnie and Duncan would wear white, non-pleated tuxedo shirts with open lay-down collars, black studs, vests, pants, and side-buckle shoes. Shannon had purchased gold neck and wrist chains in Kingston for the boys.

"Caesar, I need your help in here."

He slid into the small bathroom, put his arms around Shannon and nibbled her ear. They stared at their smiling reflections in the mirror.

"I want to remember this day forever," she said.

"For sure, and tonight we will dance like never before."

Shannon removed her pirate necklace from a wood jewelry box. "Please clasp this for me."

Caesar hefted the heavy necklace, weighing and admiring the large gold chain and doubloon pendant in his hands. "*Cristo,* where in God's name did you get this?"

"A family heirloom is all I can say. After today, it stays on my neck till my last wretched breath."

Caesar kissed the pendant, secured the chain around her neck, and fixed the onyx studs in the buttonholes of her tuxedo shirt. "I like the way the pendant nestles there."

Shannon added a stud just above the pendant and straightened the open collar. Only the sides of the thick gold chain would show. "We should get going."

They stepped onto the deck of the *Salacia.* Shannon took a picture of Caesar in his light-tan casual linen suit with white open-collar shirt and loafers with no socks. *So Mediterranean.*

Caesar pushed back his long black hair with his fingers, pulled her close, and kissed her. She liked his stubble against her cheek.

He looked at his diver wristwatch and smiled at her. "We're still on schedule."

Shannon huffed. "It took you all of eight minutes to look like a movie star."

He combed his long fingers through her red waves. "Why does Paddy sometimes call you 'pirate'?"

"Too many questions," she said, then bounded to the sparkling clean dive boat suspended by the *Salacia*'s dual crane arms. Before allowing Caesar's crew to lower the tender, she insisted they take a picture of her and Caesar as it descended.

Caesar and Shannon shuttled the tender beside the *Second Wind*. Shannon clambered up the rope ladder to inspect the readiness of groom and mates. Paddy, Lonnie and Duncan sat ready at the aft deck table playing poker.

Shannon gestured for them to rise. "Let's have each of you turn around."

They obliged for five minutes of her adjustments and instructions. "Not a serious face here," she said.

"It's a wedding, mon," said Duncan. "Be happy."

Shannon looked at them with a stony expression.

"Everything irie," said Lonnie.

Paddy had a big grin. "Chill, Shannon, we ship-shape."

"Enough with the laid-back-dude crap," she said. "You all look fantastic. Let's watch for Daniella's signal."

They stood quietly to observe movements by two white tents on the narrow beach a 150 yards away.

Shannon led Paddy amidships and admired the fit and look of his white tropical-weight tuxedo dress suit, black bow tie, and pants. She adjusted his tie. "You look fabulous, Seabird."

"Thanks for not making me wear a monkey suit."

"You are the leading man of intrigue."

Paddy straightened up and beamed. "I can't wait to see my bride. She's a beauty, like our Daniella."

Shannon smoothed over Paddy's shirt and felt the shape of his gold doubloon pendant through the fabric. "How does it feel to wear it?" she asked.

"Potent and roguish at seventy-two," he said. "It also evokes strong connections—to you, history, and Calico Jack's family."

"The doubloons are throwbacks, like us," said Shannon. "The rough imprint of the cross of the crusades, the lion, and castle make me think of times even before the buccaneers."

"I like that," Paddy said.

"Paddy, I have a plan to discover the lost history of Jack Rackham and Anne Bonny from Anne's cellar vault in Charleston."

Paddy tightened his lips, squinted at her and then relaxed his face. "Heigh-ho, a plan, she says."

"No worries, Uncle. It's a patient plan, and strictly legal. "

He smiled, looked over at his mates and back at Shannon. Then he whispered in her ear, "I love those boys like sons, but you really are my best man."

Shannon and Paddy strode back to Lonnie and Duncan. She took a pair of binoculars from Lonnie and scanned the shoreline. Wedding guests and a clergyman entered the main tent. Daniella and a man with photography equipment scurried the twenty-yard space between the side flaps of the two tents. The fortress of Fort Charles loomed above the tents and framed the sky beyond.

Shannon handed the binoculars back to Lonnie to keep watch and called down to Caesar on the tender. "Come up, I need you to take some pictures."

She went to her quarters, retrieved three black bandannas and her Anne Bonny short sword, which she secured to her hip with a black garrison belt. Shannon then tied a black bandanna across her forehead and back to dangle with her long red locks, and came up on deck to hand bandannas to Lonnie and Duncan, who studied her wordlessly.

"Put these on," she said. "It's just for pictures here."

Paddy watched them adjust their outfits. "What a handsome crew. I will always remember this."

Lonnie shifted during the photo shoot to keep an eye on the beach with the binoculars. "They are ready," he said. "A man next to Daniella just waved the green flag."

Shannon called out, "Fire the signal cannon, Duncan."

"Aye, Captain."

The cannon's roar marked the commencement with echoes sounding from the stone walls of Fort Charles.

Shannon collected the bandannas and secured the sword below deck as Caesar ushered Paddy and the groomsmen into his dive boat. Shannon boarded last. Caesar motored as if in a no-wake zone, and glided to the dock nearest the tented beach. Shannon took Paddy's arm to lead Lonnie and Duncan, two by two, in measured steps to the large white tent. The professional photographer craned to shoot every possible angle as they passed.

It felt a timeless moment for Shannon. Paddy's was a happy face. She looked up to the fort and envisioned the likes of Lord Horatio Nelson, Captain Henry Morgan, privateer-turned-pirate Henry Jennings and pirate Charles Vane there. Vane and Jack Rackham were executed at Gallows Point.

She looked across the water to Rackham's Cay where Calico Jack's dead body was tarred and hung in a gibbet for all passing ships to see. Anne Bonny and Mary Read were spared that end by pleading their pregnant bellies at the pirate trial in nearby Spanish Town.

Forty more pirates hanged on that cay within two years of Jack's demise. *How ironic,* she thought. *I would not be here today if British law did not provide a reprieve for pregnant felons.* She smiled. *Anne's hellcat spirit lives, as I do now.*

From the entrance of the large tent, Shannon gazed at the small gathering of guests. She was pleased to see what looked like Lonnie and Duncan's mothers in attendance to enjoy the festivities.

Shannon nodded to the distinguished female minister, from Kingston's North Street United Church, who received them. Shannon liked her instantly at the rehearsal, and understood why Jenny was so passionate in volunteering in the church youth outreach programs.

Paddy, Shannon, and the groomsmen lined up by the portable altar and pulpit. Paddy faced Shannon. "Jenny and I wanted an intimate wedding here and an open crazy-good Jamaican reception in Kingston later. We will allow for party naps at the house this afternoon."

"A fine idea," said Shannon.

A man approached to greet the lineup of well-dressed rogues and introduced himself as Lance, and then apologized for missing the rehearsal as he was away on business.

That one is dashing and confident, thought Shannon. *Daniella has a good eye. Lance is the real estate lawyer, entrepreneur, and weekend sailor she mentioned back in Miami.* She watched him with her family. *I see Paddy approves, but I guess Jenny is not sure yet. Once Lance finds his way into Jenny's heart, though, he will feel like family.*

Shannon's heart leapt when Jenny, Daniella, and bridesmaids appeared at the entrance to the tent. Jenny looked like a radiant Caribbean queen with braided hair in a rainbow of fabric head wraps. She held a stunning bouquet of pink orchids against her white dress. Daniella had a euphoric glow. The gold and emerald pirate jewelry she and her mother wore was fit for royalty.

Shannon searched her cousin Daniella's face: it seemed to be masking a grin, and was fuller with color and sheen. *Her eyes are wide and glowing. Could it be?* Shannon laughed aloud. Daniella was either overjoyed for her mother and father, pregnant, or both. *Now, that would make Paddy very happy.*

"What's so funny, Shannon?" asked Paddy.

"Nothing at all. Isn't this grand?"

After the ceremony, Daniella stood with the minister to invite everyone to a private showing of a new exhibit at the Fort Charles Museum. Shannon knew Daniella would execute every detail of the Port Royal wedding just as they had planned in texts, calls, and emails, and the two days they spent together in Trinidad.

The fortress is a perfect backdrop for dramatic wedding photography, Shannon thought. She looked around at the high archways, lookouts, wrought iron gates, and dungeons with fetters and chains. They posed on the stone ramps and in the courtyards. The Royal Artillery store and views of Kingston Harbor delighted Shannon.

The Port Royal Museum entrance was a gated battlement with large black cannons in arched brick portals. Daniella and the curator addressed the wedding guests gathered before them.

Daniella spoke first. "Recently, an anonymous donor made a remarkable gift to this museum through my law office. I believe the items will attract people from all over the world to Port Royal, Kingston, and Jamaica. I do hope you will enjoy the first-ever preview."

"Thank you, Miss Clarke," the museum curator said. "What Daniella did not say is that she waived her fee for negotiating with the donor and Jamaican National Archives for this location. Her hard work and commitment to this project allowed us the first viewing. The official opening will be three months from now. Many items and exhibits have yet to be readied."

He led the way into a stone exhibit room with lit display cases. Eight-foot illustrated storyboards of Port Royal's historic figures hung from opposing walls. The wedding guests fanned out to satisfy their initial curiosities.

Shannon appreciated the illustrated boards with images and notations of Anne Bonny, Mary Read, Jack Rackham, and Charles Vane among the rogues' gallery on one side, and other historic figures like Oliver Cromwell, King Charles II, and Jamaican royal governors on the other.

A dramatic painted mural on the back wall depicted Port Royal scenes and Jamaican plantations with West African and Irish slaves working in fields under their masters. British soldiers unloaded goods and people in the harbor.

The curator stood with Daniella under a large, blank canvas on the front wall. "Please, gather around." He waited for everyone to quiet.

"As many of you know, Port Royal was once the epicenter of pirate activity in the Caribbean, known for its wickedness and great wealth," he said. "Four hundred years ago, a massive earthquake sunk most of the city around us. The city was rebuilt on higher land, where pirates continued to thrive until their way of life was no longer tolerated. A great fire and more earthquakes followed—today, this is a humble fishing village.

"Most items recovered by archaeologists from sunken sections nearby are everyday living implements of the late 1600s kept in other locations of the National Archives. Today, you will see the history of the people here and items that turn pirate lore into fact."

He turned to Shannon's cousin. "Daniella, you have a comment."

Daniella cleared her throat. "Many of us have tried to get World Heritage status for the Port Royal archaeological site for years, but progress has been disappointing. The designation would be a boost for our challenged economy. The artifacts recently gifted to this small museum can make it all possible."

The curator flipped on spotlights to illuminate the square canvas, and then released the rope. The canvas fell to reveal a black pirate flag with a white smiling skull and crossed swords.

"This is the Jolly Roger flag of pirate Jack 'Calico' Rackham. Before today, only sketches based on descriptions were available."

The room fell silent.

Shannon and Caesar stood in the back. "They are stricken," she whispered to him. "You'd think they were in the Louvre staring at Leonardo's *Mona Lisa*."

"The design is flamboyant and wicked all at once," said Caesar.

"That was Rackham's personality."

The curator continued with juicy details about pirates and buccaneers. Several of the guests kept turning to look at Shannon and back to the image of Anne Bonny on the wall. "This fort was built after the British conquest of Jamaica, and named Fort Cromwell." He pointed to the poster of Oliver Cromwell. "Cromwell was a Puritan dictator who led the brutal enslavement of Irish people, punished them for their Catholic and economic rebellion, shipped them to Barbados, and distributed them to Jamaica and other islands to work sugar plantations of the Caribbean." He paused. "Many of you look surprised."

He continued. "After Cromwell died, the English people wanted religious tolerance and restored Charles II as king. This fort was renamed in his honor." He pointed to the panel about Charles II.

"Please, all stand 'round," said Daniella.

The curator put on examination gloves and held up the dueling pistols of privateer Henry Jennings. He told them of Jennings's exploits against the Spanish with Charles Vane, and his later role as a pirate king of New Providence in Nassau.

"After today, these pistols will be displayed under glass. I will allow three of you to hold them." The curator asked for the shortest, the oldest, and the person who had traveled the farthest to volunteer.

The rapt attendees looked around and spoke among themselves. Some shook their heads, and others raised their hands. A young girl, a grandfather, and a Jamaican woman from a distant village stepped forward. The curator gave them exam gloves so they could handle the pistols.

He spoke to the photographer. "You may only take pictures of the exhibit with a film-based camera, and must turn the film over to attorney Daniella Clarke for the anonymous donor's personal use."

The visit concluded with a tour of display cases with artifacts from the Golden Age of Piracy, including a few gold and silver coins, jewelry, nautical instruments, spyglass, weapons, handcuffs, and tools.

"The reverend and I have discussed a theme to give healing context for the history of this place. Reverend, please explain," the curator said.

The minister smiled warmly and looked at each person in the room before she finally spoke. "At the reception tonight, we will continue our celebration of the union of Patrick and Jennifer Clarke at the Bob Marley Museum. We will also celebrate Jennifer's ministry of helping our church youth over the years."

Shannon beamed with pride for *Aunt* Jenny. She held Caesar's hand.

The minister held her arms wide to all in a gesture of embrace. They gathered closer as her voice rose. "Tonight, we embrace an inclusive community of friends, relatives, neighbors, parishioners and strangers that will gather in wonderful Jamaican wedding custom."

The minister paused. "I believe this exhibit should put history in the context of unity. What, you may ask, does a message of unity have to do with artifacts from a brutal age?"

Shannon exchanged a quizzical look with Caesar.

"I offer this," said the minister. "When reminded of man's inhumanity to man, we must embrace our humanity, and unite to win the day."

She continued with uplifting messages of proper observance to achieve unity. She said that oppression knows no one face and no one race, and no one gender, or age, or disability, or station in life.

Shannon thought of the pattern of abuse passed down from her Portuguese grandfather and mother.

"The history of Port Royal and Fort Charles is the struggle of humankind," said the minister, now standing amid the group. "The whole point of history is to learn from our mistakes, not to dwell on them. Perhaps we all have an inner pirate to manage. Oppression has no one face."

This speaks to me for sure, thought Shannon. *I've had an inner pirate to manage my whole life.*

The minister closed the homily. "Let us experience Bob Marley's message of 'One Love' and Christ's message to love thy neighbor. Let us embrace the African word *harambe*—'working together.' Now, I would like you to hug the neighbors around you in the spirit of *abrazo.*"

After hugs all around, Shannon and Caesar embraced. "*Abbraccio,*" Caesar whispered to her in Italian.

"Thank you very much, Reverend," said the curator. "Over time, this exhibit will examine the history of Jamaica, British rule, tyranny, privateers and pirates. A travel exhibit will provide fresh insight of the enslavement of Africans and Irish by British planters. Do you have anything you would like to add, Daniella?"

"I do," she said. "My mother, Jenny, and I are descendants of African and Irish slaves, but we do not see ourselves as victims. Today, Jamaica is a rich cultural fabric to be celebrated. I agree with our reverend. History has shown we can unite and work in peaceful ways to stop oppression."

Shannon and Caesar lingered in the exhibit hall after people shuffled out. He looked at the panel of Charles II. "You like sassy poems. Read this."

Shannon chuckled. "I like it. A quote from the second Earl of Rochester, whoever that was." She read:

"We have a pretty witty king,
"Whose word no man relies on,
"He never said a foolish thing,
"And never did a wise one."

Caesar put his hand on the small of her back. "No wonder they called him the Merry King." He embraced Shannon. "You look like pirate Anne Bonny on that poster, like you did this morning when we took pictures with bandannas and you with the sword. But I know nothing of her."

Shannon smiled. "You don't know much about me either."

"Your pendant necklace and sword look like museum pieces to me. Am I to believe you bought them over the internet?"

She laughed. "Among other things, I'm an actress. Do a search for galleon gold replicas or pirate coin jewelry, or theatrical costumes. No problem."

Caesar whispered in her ear. "I don't need to know your secrets."

"Good, I'm excellent at keeping them."

క

A limo took Paddy, Jenny, Daniella, Shannon, and Caesar back to the Clarke family home. Paddy and Jenny took a siesta, as did Daniella. Shannon and Caesar sat on the back porch.

"I have something I need to tell you," said Caesar.

"Okay."

"Agent Roberto Costa knows I am here and asked me to tell you Franco will appeal his case and might get out of jail in a few years. Franco is negotiating with information he claims to have on the Latin American organization. He still has friends in that network."

Shannon sat for a minute and stared out at Paddy's martial arts training area with its wood-plank targets and structures.

"Let's go out back," said Shannon. "With a maze of federal agencies, plus you and me as lines of defense, I'm not too worried about Franco."

"He is blood-crazy and we should both be concerned."

"We just need to be vigilant, and we have a superior advantage, Caesar. Franco has a war to play on three sides—the courts, the feds, and the cartel. If he gets by all that, he will have to deal with us."

"You're right, Shannon—vigilance. In Italian it is pronounced *vee gee lay*."

She nodded and went into a storage shed and removed a sack of items.

Shannon pulled out two tomahawks, three large throwing knives, a heavy-duty staple hammer, and three small paper plates.

Caesar rubbed his jaw and grinned at Shannon.

"Staple these on that vertical plank structure," she said. "Put two plates over one at chest height."

Caesar tacked the plates up and came back to her side. Shannon took the three knives in her left hand, walked to the target board and leaned back on it. She paced off ten steps, turned around, marked a line with her foot, and set up to throw the first knife with her right hand.

"Stand behind me," she said.

"Yes, my Captain," said Caesar with a grin. He took two steps back.

Shannon held the knife blade between her index finger and thumb. She positioned her elbow forward to the target, rocked back and flipped her hand and forearm to release the knife straight from her shoulder.

The knife rotated and *thunked* through the upper right plate into the wood structure. On the second throw, she used the same motion and the knife struck the upper left plate but fell to the ground. On the third throw, the knife landed hard into the center of the lower plate.

"Arrgh," she said.

"You are fierce. What do you mean, this 'Arrgh'? Franco dies from the first throw and bleeds out his stomach on the third."

"It's a fun word that can mean anything, depending on how you say it," Shannon said. "I must have a murderous expression when I do this, but am I a murderess, Caesar?"

"No, or you would have killed already, Shannon. I see no wrong in battle instinct or self-defense. Your throws are impressive."

"Franco will be too interested in humiliating me, Caesar. I'll be ready, and I do have a pistol permit."

"We will know when he gets out of jail, Shannon. And I will hunt him like a dog before the feds find him or he comes near to you." Caesar pulled a stiletto from his pocket. "Italian craftsmen still make the best and most valued stilettos." He fired the knife open. "My dad gave me this for my eighteenth birthday. It is good for close work. Please teach me how to do your throwers."

"*Vee gee lay*," said Shannon. "Now I know where the word 'vigilante' came from."

Daniella and Shannon took a walk to the blue volcanic mountain behind the family home before they departed for the wedding reception at the Bob Marley Museum.

"Paddy may have mentioned he was looking at some property, Shannon. Here is the story. I am a partner with him and Jenny to build a restaurant-bar in Port Royal adjacent to a marina that will be commercially developed."

"That sounds awesome," Shannon said. "Every Irishman's dream."

"After they return from Ireland on their honeymoon, we will complete the planning process. We already have the land. The name of the bar will be 'Rackham's Revenge.'"

Shannon laughed. "Perfect."

"Paddy will be general manager and barkeeper to get it going. Jenny will manage the dance hall, book the entertainment, and handle promotion. What do you think?"

"What a hoot. Paddy always has a plan."

Daniella chuckled. "He's so excited that I acquired the right parcel. He keeps running around the house saying, 'It's a gold mine.'"

Shannon laughed. "With investment going into Port Royal, I believe it." She put her arm around Daniella's shoulder as they walked back to the house.

Daniella said, "There's more. When it is time to reveal this down the road, we will ask Lonnie, Duncan, and their bandmates to be a regular act. If things go well, we may hire Duncan as the chef."

"He would love that. You know, I still haven't had a chance to hear them play or sing together."

"You will tonight. There will be some over-the-top dance hall music."

"Caesar and I will love that."

"I didn't say much about the food. As you know, Duncan arranged the whole buffet and made a lot of dishes you haven't tried yet."

"I can only imagine. The things he makes in a small ship's galley are mind-blowing."

"I didn't mention that you and Caesar will enjoy a Jamaican wedding tradition," Daniella said. "Married women from the neighborhood bring homemade fruit-and-rum cakes covered in lace and white cloth for the reception. Jenny will not have seen the cakes until tonight. The minister will receive the first piece and then Jenny and Paddy. Leftovers will be offered to those who could not make the wedding."

"I love folk traditions," said Shannon. "But I feel that I didn't do enough to help you prepare for the wedding—or the festivities."

"Don't be silly. Your ideas were great; you took care of the men and kept Paddy out of it for us."

"What else can I expect tonight?"

"A party that lasts till tomorrow, with a lot of people we do not know. You will meet our friends, members of our church, some of my clients and colleagues. Others will show up from the neighborhoods. Rita Marley might say a few words along with our minister, who can be very funny, and we will dance like maniacs."

"What about Lance?" Shannon asked.

Daniella smiled. "He will be there. How is it going with Caesar? Do we really need details?"

"Yes," said Shannon. "You and I are like sisters now."

They both laughed and promised to communicate in every possible way after Shannon, Lonnie, and Duncan sailed the *Second Wind* to Gloucester.

HOMEPORT

Shannon and the Jamaican mates had planned each day with great expectations. They agreed to sail from Jamaica to Norfolk, Virginia, go up parts of the ICW ditch, make passage via Cape May, Sandy Hook into New York Harbor, East River past City Island, to Newport, and Cape Cod Canal across Massachusetts Bay. Captain Shannon had demurred about stopping in Boston Harbor—she was bursting to get home.

It was a new world for Lonnie and Duncan to see the expanse of North America's eastern coastline. It was new for Shannon in a different way. She was seeing her America from the helm of a cruising vessel, filled with the adrenaline of responsibility.

Barring minor navigational errors, and with good fortune for weather, the trip was pure joy. Her heart pounded as they crossed Massachusetts Bay.

Lonnie sped the *Second Wind* to Boston's North Shore past Marblehead, Salem, and Beverly. Shannon relieved him at the helm and headed east of Manchester. He had kept on course with the GPS. Shannon grinned and patted Lonnie on the back. "Just your eyes now." She checked messages on her mobile, left six unread, and made an entry in the logbook—*Manchester, Saturday May 4, 11:20 AM. Clear, sixty-two degrees, WSW 12.2 knot winds.*

Her Gloucester friends expected her arrival by sail around noon; they only knew she had spent the past five months in the Caribbean with her worldly uncle, with few reports. *Details can wait,* she thought, *with private matters and secrets kept.* They would be surprised to meet Briggy and her new Jamaican friends.

Shannon considered her achievements proudly, yet her ego also craved a dramatic entrance. *A captain's humility should extinguish such a silly indulgence,* she thought. *But a little suspense and style may be okay. Thanks to your example, Paddy.*

Shannon sighted home port, and winds gusted to sixteen knots. She tacked by the westernmost point of Gloucester's outer harbor with full sails like giant wings raging at race speed.

"Lonnie, Duncan, use the binoculars. There." She pointed port to a rocky reef. "Norman's Woe of Longfellow's fabled poem, 'The Wreck of the Hesperus.'"

Lonnie's mouth gaped. "Tap a di tap, Longfellow."

"What's that on the shore behind it?" asked Duncan.

"Hammond Castle. I'll tell you later."

"What's the low moaning sound?" asked Duncan.

Shannon squinted ahead to the empty harbor as her right hand shook out toward Eastern Point Lighthouse and the Dog Bar Breakwater that protected the harbor.

"I hear it, too," said Lonnie.

She turned her head in line with her outstretched arm pointed back at a large red whistle buoy. "That's 'The Groaner,' with safe water around it, for moonless nights and thick fog. T.S. Eliot wrote it as 'a heaving groaner among voices of the sea.' It sucks air in when the water swells, and groans out through a hundred-fifty pound cylinder when it falls."

"Jah. Da Grona," said Lonnie. "T.S. Eliot, 'The Dry Salvages,' and love da 'Hollow Men.'"

Shannon chuckled to hear her Glosta-speak in Lonnie's patois. But her smile faded as the *Second Wind* bounded with parting spray to a quiet Gloucester Harbor. *It's May already,* she thought, *and a weekend.* She recalled the gloominess of the previous spring with fewer boats fishing and fewer fishing days. Now they did not go out much before June because of the catch-share system. *Not even a friggin' recreational boat out here.*

Duncan scanned the shoreline with the binoculars. "Pretty island lighthouse there. Like a postcard."

Shannon raised her voice in the wind. "That's Ten Pound Island, and Gloucester's inner working harbor behind it."

Duncan put his hands on his hips, threw his shoulders back, and sniffed a deep breath of briny air. "Creative forces here."

"Big up creatergy," said Lonnie, who stood next to him at the bow.

"Good one, dups," Duncan said. "Salty-ruggedy."

"Reduce sail," Shannon commanded, and they got busy.

Shannon looked from right to left across Gloucester's Pavilion Beach to the drawbridge at the granite cut to the Annisquam River. Two dozen people stood along the boulevard near the rising decks of the bridge.

The bridge hatched up, and she recognized Gael's boat emerge into the chop of the harbor, followed by a trail of vessels with blasting air horns.

Shannon feathered and drifted with the rudder to slow the vessel. "We will be dropping anchor, Lonnie." *No need for a stupid accident,* she thought. *They might be drinking already. I'll let them approach.*

She turned her attention to the right. The city launch boat approached from the inner harbor with two dozen passengers and the harbormaster, Jack, at the wheel.

Shannon jumped with her arms in the air. She lowered them open to the awed faces of friends. Fish boat captains angled up to behold *Second Wind* and its Jamaican crew.

"Permission for one to board," announced Jack.

"Yes, sir, my gracious." She recognized every face on the launch and hailed them by name.

Duncan lowered the ladder.

The harbormaster tapped the shoulder of a man next to him, who faced away wearing a dark classic wool pea coat and beanie cap. The high collar obscured his identity.

The man turned about and stood. It was Brooks Washburn, who bellowed, "Welcome home, Shannon. I'm coming up." Washburn slowly pulled up the shaky ladder with his right hand, and had a large pineapple tucked under his left arm like a football. Lonnie helped the eighty-three-year-old on board.

"You must be Lonnie," Washburn said. "And Duncan; what's cookin'?"

"Yes, Washburn, sir," they chimed and hugged him like a grandfather.

"You know them?" asked Shannon.

Washburn handed the pineapple to Duncan, embraced Shannon, and whispered, "Congratulations, young lady. You did it. I haven't been to Kingston to see these boys in years, and your brigantine looks just like the day Paddy took ownership."

Tears rolled over Shannon's cheeks as she held Brooks close. "Paddy never let you tell me a thing, did he?" she whispered.

"Nope," he said. "Paddy wanted you to find your own way. If you weren't cut out to be his successor, you wouldn't have known you had the chance."

"Thanks for your years of encouragement, Brooks. In a month, I'll be the shortest captain in Gloucester, with a license to charter this beauty and a boatload of paying customers."

She waved and blew kisses to neighbors and boat captains, who cheered her from the launch boat. "Thanks so much for coming. So good to be home."

"Proud of you, Shan," Brooks said. "There's the gang."

Gael's honking armada slowed to approach. Gael, Marcy, and Allegra stood.

"Wow, a brigantine," said Gael, loud enough to carry.

"Way to go, Shan," mouthed Marcy, with thumbs up.

"Let's party," said Allegra as she danced in place.

"Where's Paddy?" Marcy asked.

"On honeymoon," Shannon said, pleased to know Washburn had told them nothing.

Lonnie and Duncan waved to the people on the boats that now crowded by the *Second Wind* and laughed heartily. Lonnie broadcast his words. "Funky Glosta—greetings from Jamaica."

A round of cheers went up, honking air horns droned and fizzled out.

Gael yelled to Shannon and over to the harbormaster, "Take us for a lap by the boulevard then head for the terminal. We'll follow."

The harbormaster waved agreement.

"Pull up the ladder, Duncan," Shannon said. "Weigh anchor, Lonnie."

"Yes, Captain."

Washburn stood next to Shannon as they paraded *Second Wind* by onlookers and friends along Stacy Boulevard, motored to the inner harbor, and eased past the Gloucester Marine Terminal.

Shannon piloted neatly in the narrow head of the harbor and took berth at the terminal facing the open sea. More friends and townies streamed out from the lounge to look at the brigantine, while other vessels docked nearby.

A reception party awaited them in the terminal. Many a drink passed to Shannon before she was to deliver a speech.

Soon enough, someone thrust a microphone into her hands. Shannon faced the crowd for a long moment to acknowledge the familiar faces—a community of waterfront families, small business owners, tradesmen, artists, fishermen, sailors, merchants, retirees, and kids. She thought of the neighborhoods they were from: Riverdale, Bayview, Lanesville, Annisquam, Magnolia, downtown, West and East Gloucester. This was her extended family.

She gestured for Lonnie and Duncan to stand with her. She sipped water and cleared her throat.

"We are fortunate to toast my uncle Patrick today. Some of you, like Washburn, may remember him before he left Gloucester High School for the Navy at eighteen. My father, John, saved Patrick from drowning in a riptide off Good Harbor Beach when they were boys. Some of you knew my dad, who lost his boat to a nor'easter and faced hard times.

"Patrick served in Vietnam and spent many a year at sea," continued Shannon. "He taught me to sail in blue water. In Jamaica, he helped raise my new friends here, Lonnie and Duncan, who are accomplished sailors and musicians. Lonnie is a poet and Duncan an outstanding cook. Please welcome them for the next several days and show them around."

The crowd cheered.

"We are all on a journey, full of surprise," she said. "Uncle Paddy just married his longtime soulmate, and I have a family in Jamaica I never knew I had. Paddy gifted me his brigantine dream. I nicknamed her Briggy, and she is my second wind."

Shannon choked up at that point, took a glass of wine from Duncan's hand and downed it by half. The room fell silent. Shannon wiped tears with her sleeve, snorted with a puckered mouth, and wiped her face again. "I'm a blobfish."

The crowd laughed with her. She wondered if 'Blobfish' would stick as a nickname, and then finished her address.

"Thank you for a warm welcome home. The *Second Wind* is a historic charter vessel. I promise you all free tours at some point, and discount afternoon sails. Patrick gives you his best, and I will do my best to grow the measure of captain as he. Let's raise a glass to all of Gloucester's finest."

After many toasts at the microphone, with jokes and stories told at Shannon's expense, Captain Bill Davis of the schooner *Vega* stepped to the microphone, and faced the audience.

"Heads up, everyone. I just spoke with members of the Schooner Race Committee here." He turned to Shannon. "Will you consider entering the *Second Wind* as the official flagship vessel for the Schooner Festival and starter for the Mayor's Race?"

Shannon squinted at Captain Davis and the sea of faces. She began to speak, shook her head, and smiled. "Just when I think the ribbing and kidding is over, he says this."

"I'm dead serious," thundered Captain Davis.

"I'm already branded the kayak she-pirate from last year in the *Gloucester Times* story." Knowing chuckles flitted through the crowd.

"No, Shannon, we want you to do it. Please."

She noticed members of the race committee among the crowd nodding support for her, and she savored his word, *please*, with a slow sip of pinot grigio.

"Of course. What an honor. Thank you."

Shannon held her arms up to six-foot-plus Captain Davis and pursed her lips for a kiss. He bent down a bit to share a hug and kissed her on the cheek.

With her hand outstretched with a glass of wine, Shannon said, "Thanks for that, too."

Laughter echoed in the room and settled.

"It is fitting," she said, and winked at Davis. "The brigantines came before schooners. It makes *HIS*-torical sense for a brigantine to welcome, observe, and signal for the schooner race."

Shannon sauntered over to her pals.

Gael said to her privately, "Don't blow it, girl."

"Just slurring around," Shannon said with a giddy laugh.

After the party, Captain Davis approached Shannon. "What's with the tone about schooners and brigantines—or is it something else?"

"I'm sorry. I'm tipsy, and you weren't supposed to get that."

"Maybe I'm not the only one who did."

"Please, Bill, it's nothing."

He put his hands on her shoulders. "Say what's on your mind. I want you to do this anyway. It will be great for you."

"I'll say it. In schooner weather, they are fast. But a brigantine, rigged right, can be more agile. Square-rigged seamanship is tricky and died out, but it has a place too."

"You want to race? You think because the captains are men that we give a damn if a woman enters?"

Shannon took another gulp of wine. "Yeah, I'd like to race but was only jesting about the *his*-torical bit. I know you guys don't feel that way." She plopped on a chair and reeled her head. "Maybe I had to eat my pride for too many years. That doesn't give me an excuse to be an asshole now."

"Shannon, it's natural to protect our vulnerabilities. Sometimes we bury shame with pride. You have earned every reason to be proud. People love and respect you. Give yourself and us a break."

"You're letting me off the hook, Bill. You are so damned handsome

". . . and so married." She pressed her hand to his lips. "Oops."

"Thank you for the compliment, but I have an idea," he said. "Let's race the *Vega* and the *Second Wind* in a private race on Thursday, just before Labor Day weekend. It will be fun and good for my crew to train for the Mayor's Cup on Sunday. We'll race from the Groaner to Half-Way Rock by Marblehead, and back to the tip of the breakwater by Eastern Point."

"Mmmhmm . . . and?"

"The race result is confidential. Only you, I, and our crews will know."

"You're on," she said, and they shook hands.

"I'll try to get you a good berth in the harbor for your charter business. Your brigantine will be quite the attraction."

"Wow. Thanks."

"This year, be the flagship for the Schooner Festival weekend. Next year, I can take up with the committee if a brigantine with a hermaphrodite brig-schooner rig like the *Second Wind* would qualify for the schooner race. I could argue that she is a close vintage predecessor, not a post-schooner sailboat. But we only race wood schooners now."

"You're too good, Bill. Thanks for helping me understand. I may be tipsy, but the message sticks. I'm moving forward."

"*In vino, veritas*," he said. "Go home."

In the following days, Marcy, Allegra, and Gael hosted Lonnie and Duncan. They toured Cape Ann as a troupe. Shannon's pals enjoyed Duncan's cooking and Lonnie's poetry. Local musicians embraced the Jamaicans to sit in with instruments for bluesy, funk and reggae sets at three of Gloucester's restaurant-bars.

Lonnie and Duncan refused payment from Shannon for serving as her crew and said they would do it again. Gloucester was "real folk, a big up real place," and they wanted to return for a visit. That would make her annual return easier, and she could look forward to family gatherings in Gloucester and Kingston.

Lanky Lonnie and Duck Duncan had acquired a passion for fishing from Shannon in Jamaica. Now they were addicted to catching striped bass off Cape Ann before their flight home to Kingston.

Three weeks later, Shannon passed her captain's license exam.

DOGTOWN

Another Cape Ann summer yielded to cool nights in late August. Shannon spent most every day on the water. She sat at her small oak desk in the family cottage with a predawn morning coffee. She mused how her chronic sleep issues had abated. Pure excitement stirred her, for it was Thursday, August 29, heading into Gloucester's annual Labor Day Schooner Festival and race.

A lifetime of images compressed in her mind. Only a year ago she fought depression. Now she relished Caesar's sea stories of the *Salacia*. Internet video calls kept their relationship astir. *We both love the sea*, she thought. *He holds part of himself away, as I do. That's exciting in a lover but doesn't work so well in a marriage. It's not realistic to think my relationship with Caesar is perfect. We were to get together during the summer but were just too damned busy, and miss each other. Truth be told, I may be more comfortable with love at a distance, for now.*

Shannon's kids, their dad, Eric, and Grandbaby Paula had come for Fiesta. They would be back again this Labor Day weekend. She reflected on how so many of her views of life and family had changed. She particularly mused that most families were dysfunctional in their own special way.

In seven hours, it would be Team Briggy versus Team *Vega* in a private and friendly grudge match. She considered the highs and lows of her experience since last year's Schooner Festival, and the sailing skills she had acquired. Racing was another matter.

Captain Bill Davis had picked their private race route, and if he believed that advantageous for his *Vega*, he may have figured wrong. Knowing *Vega's* average speed from its race history, her optimism grew during her team's practice runs. *The twenty-four-mile route is six times longer than the schooner race on Sunday,* she thought, *so Briggy could have plenty of time to run downwind.* She and her crew devised race Plan A and Plan B.

Shannon reloaded her coffee cup, pushed papers and receipts around, and reconciled numbers for the accountant. The charter enterprise was a joy, but the business end was not. Still, the joint marketing and business plan she and Gael conceived resulted in a profitable enterprise, even after start-up costs. *Second Wind* had more than earned her keep with lighthouse sails, evening sails, historically themed sails, and longer romantic sails for couples.

Shannon and Gael referred clients to each other and promoted the charters of Captain Davis and two other schooner captains, who in turn supported theirs. Gael's sport fishing charters provided well enough for her father to hire a replacement dockmaster at his marina. Shannon and Gael became closer as friends and shared their love of the sea, spending most summer days doing charters or fishing.

By far, the most popular of all day-sails from Gloucester Harbor that summer were Saturday pirate-themed sails on the *Second Wind*. Shannon researched, wrote, directed, and produced professional-grade skits. Shannon, Gael, Marcy and Allegra made period costumes to play female pirates Anne Bonny, Grace O'Malley, Mary Read and Rachel Wall, respectively. Internet videos and chatter became positively viral.

Shannon opened a letter addressed with a young person's handwriting. She laughed and called Gael on her mobile.

"I just got a love letter from an eleven-year-old boy. You remember 'Wobby'—that's him. He saw an article about our pirate tours and is coming up this weekend with his mother. Of course, we're not doing a charter Sunday, but I'll invite them to join us as we flagship for the schooner race."

Shannon was proud that her team became a tight sailing crew, handling the *Second Wind* like an extension of coordinated minds and limbs. She established solid professional discipline, from scheduling to entertaining sail productions.

She reviewed the slush pile of letters, bills, and documents in the cubbies next her desk. The uncontested divorce with Eric was final. They would keep the cottage for the family in both their names. Other than him covering ongoing repairs, taxes and upkeep on the place, she only wanted to keep his friendship and the family close.

After she completed and prioritized paperwork, she decided to visit her mother's grave for the first and last time since the funeral seven years ago. She hoped to pay respect, forgive again, and finally let go of ill feeling.

With hiking boots, gaiters to protect her from deer ticks, and a small pack, she skirted the downtown area up a steep road. She took this to a short footpath, which led to Gloucester's industrial park. Across a parking lot, she tromped down an overgrown trail through a wooded gully and across train tracks. She usually loved hiking in these woods, but not for today's destination.

After passing the Babson Reservoir, the trail was steeper where the boulders, known as glacial erratics, grew to the size of cars and buses. Soon, she stood in Dogtown Common, a thatch field surrounded by stone-lined pits, once foundations for humble homes. Many were built by women who had escaped the Salem witch trials. It had been a community of hardscrabble lives, away from the booming economic waterfront or any decent arable land. No wonder it had fallen into oblivion. After the last inhabitants were gone, wild dogs wandered.

With a sense of eerie spirit presence, Shannon remembered her hikes and mountain biking with her son through the trails there. She knew the locations of the granite boulders with words carved by unemployed stonecutters hired by Roger Babson during the Great Depression. Roger was from a tenth-generation Gloucester family, attended MIT, and became an investor, entrepreneur, and contrarian financial theorist. He predicted the stock market crash of 1929 and remained a wealthy man and philanthropist.

Shannon passed the naturally shaped monuments, reading the chiseled phrases—*Spiritual Power, Stay out of Debt, Work Hard,* and one that simply screamed *MOTHER*.

The rest of the trail widened and she soon exited the storied and strange interior of the island's Dogtown. She walked along a row of Gloucester's idiosyncratic housing styles, angled to view sunsets over the Annisquam River.

The world's architects could not classify Gloucester's character-diverse constructions. Maybe Gloucester-utilitarian, she decided because of the many reused materials integrated by rough or finish carpenters in the family.

That is why everyone everywhere likes the place, she thought: *because it has a sense of place in everyplace.* Lonnie and Duncan divined it best as "Funky Glosta."

At Seaside Cemetery, Shannon now looked at another stone monument, much smaller than the massive boulders of Dogtown, with cold geometry, hard, bumpy edges, two polished sides, and *Regina* on it.

She took a tiny notebook from her pack and let her pen do the talking.

> *I wait for the thing*
> *To provoke*
> *Thoughts and feelings*
> *To tumble at will*
> *What be this heartless stone?*
> *Never loved nor could*
> *Raped from the earth*
> *Butchered at birth*
> *Beaten, Cut, Crated,*
> *Alienated*
> *In a graveyard*
> *Of hope.*

Shannon put the notebook away and tapped the pen on the back of her hand.

"I did not come here for you, Regina. I came here for me, and my family, to let go of your abuse and express gratitude for opportunities provided to me.

"I now understand you never had a chance. You carried great ancestry but suffered abuse by your father. That corrupted your childhood. Mother power is a force for good, but yours was ruined before your firstborn.

"You were a corrupt mother but smart enough to marry a kind man, though no man could have extinguished your pain. You gave me a loving father who brought kindness. This made you hate yourself more.

"Because of you, I struggled to be a good mother, for lack of example. I protected my unborn, and my children.

"Because of your wickedness, I wanted to be a good wife.

"I learned to become my own best friend.

"Because of you, I learned not to trust in anything, but hope for everything good in the world.

"As the youngest of your beaten, unwanted children, I could not expect or plan a thing.

"I know the pain of abandonment.

"I braved the world with a happy face and taste for approval. But I learned to tame it.

"You provided me the horrible chance to run away, and become the mother I never had.

"This chance allowed me choices. A choice to be more than a victim. A choice I have made to be captain of my own life. Beyond forgiveness, to compassion.

"Now I have compassion for you as I have had for others. I believe you did the best you could, when you didn't know what the best you could do was."

Shannon put her hand on the gravestone. The sun's rays had warmed it. Her fingers slid to the base of the stone and she began to clear away some leaves and weeds.

"I'm sorry for the hardships you endured, but the cycle stops with me. I took care of you when you took sick, and I have no guilt. Goodbye, Regina. May you rest in peace."

HALFWAY ROCK

On the Thursday before the annual Labor Day weekend schooner festival, *Second Wind* lined up helm to helm with the *Vega* by the "groaner" whistle buoy just outside the Dog Bar Breakwater. Shannon and Captain Davis made eye contact, mobile phones pressed to their ears. Their first mates held timers. Each team faced windward with their backs to Gloucester. It was a schooner weather afternoon, and Shannon knew the *Vega* would soon steal her wind.

Davis spoke into his mobile phone.

"Shannon, as agreed, I give the first air horn blast to cut the engines, and a second for the start. If a false start, we repeat."

"Roger that," Shannon said.

Both vessels worked engines and rudder, jostling in both the wind and current to ready for the start. Shannon knew this process could take a quarter hour's time. It seemed an eternity for her, as she and Captain Davis gunned and reversed to stay in line with the red groaner buoy.

Shannon patted the sheathed, jeweled Anne Bonny sword on her hip. Glancing at her sturdy and able mates in their bold, authentic-looking pirate garb, she smiled to think of the appropriate casting of Gael, Marcy, and Allegra as Grace O'Malley, Mary Read, and Rachel Wall. She delighted in the way they used witty pirate calls and retorts in response to the gross taunts and indistinguishable rebukes of their opponents.

The *Vega* team made another thrust back to the starting line.

One of their men called out, "You effin' pansies gonna loo-ooze."

Gael stood as Grace O'Malley, the Gaelic chieftain, in a bodice and woolen cloak draped over her shoulders. She spoke into the bullhorn. "Damn you, villains, and from whence you came."

"You panty-waists face early defeat," bulled a crewman from the *Vega*.

Marcy, as Mary Read, stepped next to Gael to take the bullhorn. She pushed back a large cloth hat trimmed in leather and fur. Her metal-buttoned waistcoat and puffed shirt were distinguished by a diagonal satin-and-leather sash with a brace of pistols. A cutlass swung from her hip along her breeches down to buckled ankle boots. "I warn ye," she said. "This is no hen frigate. We're lady adventurers and living legends here to set the record straight."

"Skanky-panties going to lose," a *Vega* man retorted.

"Spanky-wankers—not men yet," said Allegra through the bullhorn as the alluring temptress Rachel Wall. "See you bloodsuckers in hell."

"Anytime, blondie" was a reply from the *Vega*.

Shannon laughed. If the men sailed as poorly as their wisecracks, the race should be a breeze. She took the bullhorn with Anne Bonny in mind. "What fools have broken adrift here? Do not give us that bilge, boys. We're here to race."

Davis sounded the first blast. Engines quieted. The vessels aligned, and the second blast of the horn sounded for the start. Straight to the wind, the *Vega* defied inertia to take an early lead. By the time they reached Beverly, the lead was substantial.

Shannon was pleased nonetheless to have *Second Wind* in proper trim for the half journey from Gloucester to Boston and back. They headed to what old mariners coined "Halfway Rock." She expected to be second to reach the monolith, which rose thirty feet above sea level and descended nearly one hundred twenty feet below sea at the base.

The race will depend on what happens by that rock, three miles from Marblehead's shores, thought Shannon. Her goal right now was to stay as tight to windward as a schooner.

She considered the geometry of each vessel. Compared with the *Second Wind*, the *Vega* was sleeker in length by eight feet and narrower at the beam by a hand, with 10 percent less displacement. The *Vega* had a foot and a half more in draft. *It can lie hard in a turn, but we will see how wide and long that takes.*

Shannon figured her vessel had the advantage with certain changes in wind conditions. *It also has a higher topmast by two and a half feet*, she told herself, *and a generous thirty-two hundred square feet of sail area.* Her large rudder, hull design, and rigging would all come into play. *Us 'girlies' will paste our square-rigged seamanship in their face by the end of the race.*

Her confidence held up, beating to the headwinds, even as the *Vega* increased its lead past Beverly. The *Second Wind* seemed to have little chance to overtake the *Vega*, which bounded ahead by nearly a mile in approach to the sixty-foot-wide domed monolith.

Allegra stood fast at the bow with binoculars trained on the *Vega*. She soon made a circular sweep of her hand over her head and turned to warn Shannon. "They're making the turn at Halfway."

Shannon eyed the stopwatch, GPS, and radar. "Get back to your stations." Halfway Rock seemed to grow from the Atlantic waves as she penned numbers and notes on a scratch pad, rocking forward and back in excitement.

Her hand found comfort on the handle of her jeweled pirate sword. She pulled it up from the steel scabbard a few inches and shoved it back down with a savage metallic sound. Anne Bonny had slain many with it.

Four and a half minutes later, she prayed that her mates would execute "the pivot" as practiced to perfection. "Now!" she screamed at the top of her lungs.

Gael and Allegra lowered the large square course and adjusted fore and aft sails. Shannon turned the large rudder hard and *Second Wind* responded with a tight radius around the towering rock. The *Vega* had swept further east from its turn but still had a comfortable lead. Now Shannon wasn't so sure of victory. Muttering to herself, she said, "We must prevail." But a quarter hour passed and *Vega* kept its lead. Her mates' anxious looks fed Shannon's doubt and she stroked her jeweled sword one more time.

A puff of wind blew Shannon's hair forward. She looked at her watch and relaxed. Soon trade-like winds filled the Dacron sails as she had hoped. The brigantine ran downwind to Gloucester, yard by yard, and nautical mile by nautical mile, to close the gap. Being in the game was triumph enough for Shannon now.

They overtook the *Vega* near Manchester-by-the-Sea. Marcy and Allegra blew sexy kisses to the schooner boys from the stern of *Second Wind*. It would be fair to say Captain Davis and his mates had an obscured view of Gloucester behind the brigantine's expansive array of sails.

Second Wind's lead grew like a runaway touchdown toward the watery goal by Eastern Point. Shannon called out to her mates with a big grin, "We're going with Plan B."

What happened next had to be unexpected for the men on the *Vega*. Only fifty yards short of the finish by the breakwater at Eastern Point, the sails of the brigantine luffed, slowed, turned forty-five degrees starboard, and drifted out of the race path.

Shannon called Captain Davis on her mobile. "It's a bitch, Bill. We have a malfunction and have to forfeit the race."

"What malfunction? You okay?"

"We're fine. You finish. We will motor in. See you for drinks shortly." She turned off the phone, donned a red velvet pirate hat with a red feather, and clambered up the side of the pilothouse.

Vega's puzzled crew broke into smiles and laughter at the antics of *Second Wind*'s pirate crew: Allegra bared her chest as pirate Rachel Wall. Gael and Marcy shook their hips and danced and waved as their male rivals passed amidships.

Shannon belly-laughed from the pilothouse roof, adjusted the boarding axe and pistol on her sash, and raised her Anne Bonny sword to Captain Davis and his crew. "My mate Allegra had a wardrobe malfunction. Fair winds to you men on Sunday."

Gael threw her voice across the wind. "Hark'ee whey-faced laddies, we bid you sweet dreams."

Captain Davis shook his head and tipped his cap. *That's all he can do,* Shannon thought. It was a fair fight, and he did not know the plan. It was her Plan B all along—beat them silly and let them finish first. No need to rub it in.

The wind whipped Shannon's hair as she piloted into her beloved homeport, Gloucester. She had many plans and tomorrows in mind. She would give back to the community that raised her, particularly organizations that provided support for disadvantaged children of Cape Ann. Her next voyage could unveil Anne Bonny's true place in history and the untold story of short-lived Calico Jack Rackham. She owed that to Uncle Paddy—and more.

BOOK DISCUSSION GUIDE

SETTINGS

Beyond Beauport introduces us to a place of simpler times. What places like this remain? Do you hold an imagined Arcady to cure the blues or salve for the human condition? Where have you found it in literature or travel?

What places, real or imagined, do you yearn for? What places would you like to visit, explore or return to?

If you have not visited Gloucester or Cape Ann (one hour north of Boston), how do you now picture it in your mind? How would you describe its physical and cultural attributes? If you have visited Gloucester/Cape Ann, how do you feel *Beyond Beauport* immerses you in setting and in the characters of Shannon Clarke and her friends? What makes Shannon a compelling lead character and a product of her environment?

What symbolism does the sea provide in the story? What imagery and emotion does it provide?

Which story locations did you enjoy most? Gloucester, Charleston, Barfield Bay, Lovers Key, Key West, Jamaica, Eastern Caribbean? Sailing in deep blue water?

Key Characters

Shannon

Shannon, at 46, suffers deepening depression as she battles past traumas and recent abandonment from her grown children and a straying husband. She questions her life just as her uncle Paddy arrives and their nautical quest begins.

How do you react to the term 'midlife crisis'? Is it a cynical reaction? Is this what Shannon is experiencing? How does one take a positive or negative turn in midlife? See it as an opportunity?

What types of barriers or choices prevented Shannon from achieving her childhood dream to become a sailing captain?

Shannon's childhood trauma left deep emotional scars. What strategies did she use to mask and cope with her traumatic past? How does this play out in the story?

What parts of Shannon's character resonate with you?

Paddy

Paddy is a seafaring man in his early seventies who may be ready for a change in his life. First, he must complete what might be his last adventure at sea as he teams up with Shannon to discover the truth about their family's past, and possibly find authentic pirate gold.

How do Paddy and Shannon facilitate each other's life transitions?

Do Paddy's three Ls—living, loving and learning—comprise a cogent philosophy and meaning for human life/existence?

Paddy brings a wealth of wisdom and knowledge from his life's experiences and his own reading/research. Shannon is evolved, with practical knowledge gained mostly from experience. In your life, have others surprised you with their depth of knowledge and understanding, despite limited formal education? What does that say for schooling in general?

Anne Bonny

Anne was an Irish-born pirate, born circa 1698. She sailed the West Indies and, although historical accounts differ, she was said to have avoided execution in 1720 and assumed a new identity as a wife and mother in South Carolina.

What did you already know about female pirates of the past? What was your impression of a woman like Anne Bonny living as both a pirate and then a wife and mother?

Do you have dreams of a more adventurous nonconventional life, or have an inner pirate that you need to manage?

What are the parallels between the lives and temperaments of Anne Bonny and Shannon, other than physical characteristics?

More Character Questions

The brigantine *Second Wind* is a central image and character in the story. What does it symbolize for you?

What are the similarities of Caesar and Paddy; Shannon and Jenny?

Daniella and Shannon are quite different but form a bond. How does Daniella stand out from the rest? Have you formed friendships with others different than you? What makes friendship precious for you?

ANCESTRY AND ANCESTRAL MEMORY

Does ancestry matter? Explore that in your group.

Shannon and Paddy search to understand their distant relatives, who are famous and infamous historical figures. In what ways do they search for identity, family and purpose?

Beyond Beauport employs Paddy's notion of ancestral memories as a literary device with magical realism, particularly in Shannon's lucid dreams of Anne Bonny and Privateer Captain Jonathan Haraden. Have you experienced vivid or lucid dreams? Have you ever dreamt you were someone else, living in a different time period?

How do you feel influenced by any of your ancestors' experiences? Has anyone ever told you that you have the same personality traits or temperament as a parent, aunt, uncle, grandparent or great-grandparent?

CHALLENGES AT SEA

When Shannon and Paddy are hijacked at sea by villainous Franco Torre, they faced death and physical abuse. How does Shannon survive it and rebound?

Shannon is appalled to learn that that her evil tormentor, Franco, is Caesar's half-brother. She tells Caesar that "a family is like a hand; each finger is different." How does this resonate in your own experience?

How did the pirate and privateer history in the novel support the story and offer a new understanding of the Age of Sail vs. Hollywood pirate movies and romance-focused pirate novels?

Is the hunt for authentic pirate gold primary or secondary for Shannon or Paddy? How do you imagine they would handle newfound wealth? What would you do with recovered pirate gold on public land?

How does the thought or experience of treacherous or balmy seas make you feel fully alive?

RELATIONSHIPS AND ROMANCE

When Shannon and her husband, Eric, finally talk about being depressed with an empty nest and emptiness in their marriage, Shannon says, "Infidelity begins at home but changes everything." What did she mean?

Shannon's budding romance with younger Caesar is kept in suspense. What is going through Shannon's mind and heart at this stage of her life?

Is it fear, common sense, or other goals that predominate?

Marriage and family is raised as a philosophical and practical question for Shannon, her friends, Daniella, Paddy, Jenny, Anne Bonny, and Caesar. Is a realistic view of modern marriage presented in the story?

OTHER QUESTIONS

Beyond Beauport is an example of cross-genre fiction, mixing elements of drama, nautical adventure, historical fact and fiction with a touch of romance. What scenes or aspects of the book resonated most with you?

Examine the meaning of the statement made by Captain Bill Davis of the schooner *Vega*: "It is natural to protect our vulnerabilities. Sometimes we bury shame with pride." What does this mean to you?

How did themes resolve in the final two chapters, Dogtown and Halfway Rock? What was left to ponder? How do you feel about Shannon's graveside "talk" with her mother, Regina?

At the conclusion of *Beyond Beauport,* did Shannon's choice not to complete the race against the schooner boys show a change in her? In what ways has Shannon changed or stayed the same? How does Shannon's character shape her destiny?

Which parts of the story evoked the strongest emotions in you?

ACKNOWLEDGEMENTS

I'd like to thank the following:

The talented team at Koehler books. Joe Coccaro, the executive editor, taught me how to be a better writer. My early drafts benefitted from editing and critique, thanks to Lisa Wroble, Ann McArdle, Christopher Anderson, and Terry Weber Mangos.

Joe Snowden for his detailed insights on story and character arc from the very beginning.

Ron Gilson and Joe Garland, who inspired me with knowledge and historical perspectives of Gloucester and Cape Ann.

My advanced readers who provided suggestions and critique: Sandy Bravo, Brian Conway, Jacqueline Ganim-DeFalco, Tina Greel, Captain Terry Greel, M. Kristine Fisher, Marc Ginsburg, Cynthia Hendrickson, Sharon Killeen, Ned Polan, Lee Ormerod, Linda Vermillion, Ingrid Whyte, and Heidi Zimmerman.

Stephanie Buck at Cape Ann Museum, and the archivists at Gloucester Lyceum, Sawyer Free Library, Gloucester City Hall, and Peabody Essex Museum.

The late Norma Rogers Andrews, former owner of the Haraden House, who meticulously researched the genealogy of the Haraden family dating back to 1657, and to Nancy Polan, a descendant of Nathaniel Haraden (sailing master of USS *Constitution*) and Nancy's husband, Ned, who shared genealogical research on the Haraden family.

Gloucester skippers, residents, and waterfront personalities who provided interviews with historical and cultural insight.

The dedicated leaders, presenters, and members of the Gloucester Writers Center, Eastern Point Lit House, GrubStreet Boston, Sanibel Island Writers, and Boston's Muse and the Marketplace.

The fine organizations that celebrate and preserve the cultural and maritime history of Gloucester: Cape Ann Museum, Gloucester Fishermen's Wives Association, International Dory Racing Committee, *Gloucester Adventure, Inc.,* and Maritime Gloucester.

My brother Eugene and my son, Jason, for their encouragement and suggestions.

Judi, my lovely inscrutable wife and epic purveyor of stories, who took time away from her own creative pursuits to share this novelistic journey of places, times and lives of pirates, privateers and Gloucester sea captains. Her encouragement, insights, and contrarian ideas kept me going.

AUTHOR'S NOTE

The idea for this contemporary nautical adventure with a historical toggle switch was a journey in itself. As an ordinary boy who enjoyed beach and fishing trips to Gloucester, Massachusetts, I knew someday I would live there. It became my home port in 1981, and the whole of Cape Ann continues to enchant.

Gloucester and its surrounds of natural wonders offer a bounteous culture, with a strong sense of history, place, and community. After long immersion in all things Gloucester, with many close ties and a burgeoning collection of Gloucester and Cape Ann history books, I was determined to pinpoint elusive qualities of local experience.

A specific hypothesis emerged: Gloucester-born-and-bred folks associated with the waterfront economy are special, particularly the women. The questions of how and why they are special inspired my research for *Beyond Beauport*.

To paint a broad brush over any group of people is folly, but there was something to this idea. I needed a new lens and investigated primary, secondary and anecdotal sources beyond my friends.

Here is what I learned:

Gloucester women in midlife best described the changes in the community since the 1960s, and are able to relate past to present, with an outlook to the future. I was particularly taken by those who grew up in working-class families. Their good humor and rugged independence are refreshing. They are natural storytellers deeply connected to family, nature, and the sea. They are inquisitive and favor straight talk. They demonstrate pragmatism and resourcefulness. Generous, frugal and irrepressible, many compete with men as sport and some have dangerous occupations of their own. They are worldly-wise and insanely local.

Gloucester's women played a key role in four centuries of maritime culture marinated in the resourceful island community of Cape Ann and greater Essex County. The region played on a world stage of discovery and trade, long before the United States of America became a country. The way today's Gloucester women evolved from this had been elusive—while outward manifestations and evidence of seafaring people and enterprises receded, a strong maritime culture survives within them.

The natural charms of the place play a big factor. Fishermen came for the abundant catch; artists for the unique lavender light; clergy for the natural spiritual power of the place; and stonecutters to work the best granite on the planet. Others came to escape intolerance, oppression, witch trials, or to find a cure for existential doubt. To know the seafaring families and women of Gloucester is to know their hearty sensibilities through joyful, proud, and tragic stories.

Cape Ann must account for the role of its women in holding families and community together in the wake of thousands of men lost at sea and to war. Gloucester's past narrative is rich with stories of its men of the sea, told by men. This is changing.

The iconic *Man at the Wheel* statue by the outer harbor now stands with the recently dedicated Fishermen's Wives monument across "the cut" drawbridge that connects the Annisquam River to Gloucester's deepwater harbor. While the *Man at the Wheel* has faced all manner of vessels in the harbor for decades, the two monuments now share a view to a bright future.

A female protagonist emerged for this contemporary/maritime history adventure novel with a genealogical twist and parallels to new and old-world pirates and seafarers.

A lead fictional character began to talk to me. I asked what she suffered as a young girl and what her dreams were. She wanted to be a sea captain but never had the chance.

We needed to come up with a good reason. I suggested she was a troubled runaway from a broken family. She laughed and asked me how I knew that.

She wasn't pleased when I told her she would have to be older. It was a midlife adventure. We quarreled about her age. Then I suggested she'd be a juvenescent grandmother. She wasn't pleased but got used to the idea.

I suggested her ancestors were famous ship captains and women seafarers. She really liked that but did not know any. I found some and asked if she would like to go on a seafaring journey to follow the travels of Irish pirate Anne Bonny in the Caribbean in the 1720s, and solve a legend.

That is when we both got excited and added a hunt for authentic pirate gold. She agreed to let me decide on the other characters and the problems I would throw at them. She insisted the other characters be interesting to hang out with, and it would not be an adventure if I told her too much in advance. She wanted to drive a lot of the action.

When we settled on her Irish name, my historical research and writing work really began. She provided her voice and I had to find my own.

I hope you enjoy Shannon Clarke and my tribute to all of Gloucester's finest.

LEARN MORE

To contact the author with questions or comments,
visit www.jamesmasciarelli.com

CPSIA information can be obtained
at www.ICGtesting.com
Printed in the USA
FFOW02n1227170618
47139276-49697FF